TWO
WORLDS
APART

LENORA CADE

Editing by paulaproofreader.wixsite.com/home

Bosnian translations by Dragana J (@jadepeaches on Fiverr)

Book cover by Lenora Cade

First Edition 2025

FOREWORD

This is just the beginning of the Concrete Hearts series.

Be sure to sign up for my newsletter to receive the most up to date info regarding upcoming releases, bonus materials, sneak peeks, and freebies.

Author's Note

For a list of sensitive topics and themes that occur in this book, please visit my website at www.lenoracade.com.

To my family, who have been my cheerleaders even when my stories were truly terrible.

Thank you for letting me torture you so I could get here... eventually.

Contents

CHAPTER ONE

No one, ever, had heard of Blackthorn, Arizona.

Well, no one who didn't live there, that was.

It wasn't to be found on a map in school, save for the one hung in my fourth-grade history class—the teacher had written it in himself and circled it with a red, felt-tipped pen. To the outside world, we didn't exist. Blank stares greeted me when outsiders heard its name, despite its proximity to Tucson.

When I'd ventured to share my background with a few of my new classmates at university there, they'd all worn matching expressions—confusion.

"Where?" one had asked.

I'd feebly explained, but who was I kidding? They didn't care. *I* didn't care.

It's in some little pocket universe, a less-cute Mayberry from the *Andy Griffith Show*, a thing of fiction. Nothing bad happened here because, well, nothing *ever* happened.

"Which account did you want it transferred to, Mallory?" Deidra's eyes flicked away from her computer for a nanosecond.

There you go, case closed. This was the highest level of security you were going to get in Blackthorn.

I offered a tight-lipped smile. "My mom's checking, please." Even though the entire town used this one bank, the teller didn't bother asking for any more details. She knew exactly who every single inhabitant was by name and face.

"All right, hon, you're all set," she said, printing out a receipt. "Anything else?" She handed me the slip of paper.

I held back a shudder. I didn't need to look at it. I knew the amounts there—low. It would only spike my anxiety about spending even the barest minimum I was about to on this trip.

Breathe. Change was on the way. I—we—could manage until then.

"Thanks," I said, stuffing the paper into the deepest, darkest corner of my purse.

Transitioning from the air-conditioned interior out onto the blazing sidewalk along Main Street was always a shock to the system. It didn't matter if you had been born and died here; we all experienced that same mix of shivers across our skin that preluded the sweats. I shook it off, pulling out my phone and opening up my to-do list.

Check in for my flights.

Check.

Paper copies of emergency and travel documents printed.

Check.

Transfer money.

Check.

I sighed, wishing that measly amount was more to hold my mother over while I was gone. But my stupid little job at the corner shop on weekends barely paid for my expenses, even while living at home and commuting to school. Still, my mom's waitressing job in a town with zero tourism only let us scrape by growing up. At least she didn't have Sydney, my older sister, to worry about financially anymore. Secretly, I suspected Sydney might be making her own contributions to our mom's scant funds. Two and two never quite added up with what my mom could afford, even if they were simple basics.

But I'd never asked, and she'd never said. Sydney wasn't what you'd call the warm and fuzzy, sharing-over-cocoa type. Or any kind of talking, for that matter.

I wandered through town toward the grocery store. The last remaining things on my list were items for dinner. The few faces I passed were ones I'd seen every day of my life. Predictable. Expected. Normal in every way.

A rush of excitement hurried my steps. In less than twenty-four hours, that would no longer be the case.

The squeaky wheel of my grocery cart announced my arrival down each aisle. I was met with curious looks, and the odd well-wish for a pleasant trip. Maybe they thought I didn't notice their looks of bafflement or the shake of a head just before they turned out of sight.

I shook my own. Small-town life. Everyone's business was somehow all of ours. It was stifling, close-minded. I yearned for freedom, adventure, escape. I used to wish I fit in, that I could be a country bumpkin that just enjoyed gardening or sitting in a corner reading while the rest of the world swirled by out of reach. But for the first time ever, I was going to be part of it, not observing from the outside.

"When are you leaving?"

I jerked out of my daydream. The steady *beep beep beep* of items being scanned like an apathetic heartbeat infiltrated my much more appealing alternate reality.

Janice, my middle school's notorious head mean girl, who had never quite grown out of it, shoved the last items down the counter to the bagging area. Great. As if I needed yet another reminder of why I craved a change of scenery.

"Tomorrow." I tucked a piece of my dirty-dishwater-colored hair behind one ear after handing her cash.

She puffed out a bored sigh, stabbed at her register screen, and handed back my change. "Have a great time." Her tone wished me the opposite.

"Thanks," I said too-sweetly with a simpering smile.

As I drove home toward the outskirts of town, I took my time, drinking in every last detail I had already memorized over a lifetime. On the right was the corner where Sydney had taught me to ride a bike after school while my mom worked her double shift and my dad was who knows where. I'd ended up with a lot of scraped knees from the pot-holed asphalt. The tiny school around the corner served kindergarten through high school on the same small lot, divided by two prisonlike buildings. Mr. Billings sat on his usual bench along the main street feeding the birds. Mrs. Clark herded her six-child brood to McTier's, the second-hand store.

Gravel crunched beneath my tires as I pulled into the dusty parking lot of the weathered apartment complex my mom and I called home. I scowled at our dinky balcony and the busted eave hovering limply above it. It had slumped during a particularly violent dust storm. Frank, our drunken landlord, said he'd get to it on Tuesday—a month ago.

The bags of groceries teetered in my arms as I carried them up to the second level. I banged on the door with the toe of my shoe. The patter of muffled feet approached, then my mom was swinging open the door.

Her eyes, the same shade of steel-blue as mine, filled with reproach as they homed in on the bags. "I could have come down to help," she fussed.

"It's fine." I set them down on the counter, and she immediately began helping me put things away.

After dinner, we watched TV until finally, my mom fell asleep on the couch. I clicked the TV off and touched her shoulder.

"Mom, go to bed."

She mumbled a vague protest.

"Get some sleep. You're going to have a late drive back tomorrow."

At that, her eyes flew open and found mine. Panic flashed behind them. The sight sent a hand clenching around my heart. My poor mom, ever the mother hen.

"I'll be fine." It was perhaps the hundredth time I'd said it since I'd announced my trip. Before the ink on my diploma had even dried, I'd sent out my resume and signed up with a traveling nurse agency. Little had I expected my first assignment to be for a five-month stint at the esteemed Haven Oak Medical Center in Houston, Texas, starting in the fall. Could I have chosen others that started sooner? Yes. But a light had clicked on.

Europe.

It was now or never before I focused on my career. In the brief summer weeks before starting my dream job, I was going to accomplish another. A dream I'd been planning on the world map poked and prodded to within an inch of its life on my bedroom wall. I blamed cable. Once we'd moved closer to town after my parent's divorce and our rabbit-eared antenna gave us access to the myriad of travel programs, there was no going back. Before I settled into the routine of life, I was going to experience the life the little girl in me had dreamed of. I could give her that.

Even at the expense of my mother's insecurity of letting me out of her sight for more than a day. Or a time zone. On the other side of the world.

But to her credit, in this moment, she bit her lip and simply nodded, rising from the couch and going to her room in silence.

Guilt churned in my stomach along with butterflies as I readied for bed, each toothbrush stroke stoking an argument and counterargument through my head.

You shouldn't leave her. What could happen while you're gone?

She's a grown woman. She'll be fine, and Sydney is only a phone call away.

You're leaving her in a bind financially.

That will be a nonissue soon.

Yeah, but now?

Shut up. It's now or never and it will *never* be never.

I set my toothbrush back into the holder with a decisive thunk.

As hyped-up as I was, I was also exhausted from the packing, the planning, and the emotional load. I dozed off as soon as I closed my eyes.

But when my alarm screamed at me only hours later, I was instantly awake. Not a shred of sleepiness survived the influx of adrenaline that propelled me through my remaining packing.

It was time.

Time to see the world.

Time to see what kind of stuff I was made of.

_____

Two hours in the car with my mom and one tearful goodbye later, I was on the plane. My mother had held me so tightly outside security, I worried she would never let go. Her fear of being completely alone for the first time was palpable. Her life had led from her parents straight to my father, and, even when he'd finally gone on his merry way, she'd still had me and Sydney. Until now.

I'd tried to be reassuring as she panicked, using every excuse in the book to convince me to stay. *Don't leave me*, had been the real plea hidden behind them all.

"This is a bad idea."

"Do you *really* need to be gone for so long?"

"I won't get to celebrate your birthday with you."

"Don't fall in love."

When I'd opened my mouth in protest at the last one, she'd cut me off.

"Things happen. It's when you're not looking that it's the most dangerous."

"Dangerous?" I knew in her case it had been true with my dad. He had shown his true colors after the initial love whirlwind had settled right back into what it really was...dirt. Gambler, addict, abuser—take your pick. But I wasn't my mother, and what she was saying was ludicrous, so I'd kept it light. "Okay, I'll let you know if I meet some devastating vampire hunk in Transylvania."

She'd frozen. "You're going to Transylvania?"

I'd rolled my eyes. "Mom."

Her hand had waved, dismissing the tangent. "Promise me."

"I promise that I'll be so absorbed by beautiful sights, drool-worthy food, and taking crazy risks, that I won't be able to fit in falling in love, all right?"

One chastising "Mallory!" and another hug later, I was through security and running for the plane. I'd nearly missed it.

My flight to the United Kingdom took just about twelve hours. The initial novelty of looking down at the world from so high above wore thin quickly, but my excitement to get there and start the journey grew with each minute. Daydreams and pins on a map were all that constituted my so-called "vacation planning." Although, I had set a reservation in Venice as a guide to aim for mid-trip, and in London before my flight back home. The general path was etched into my brain: France, Italy, Croatia, Austria, Germany, the UK. But the gaps between and smaller, unknown details enticed me just as much as the large boxes I'd checked off. Because this was it. It was finally happening. I was finally going.

My hands shook a little in my lap.

"Is London your final stop or just the first jump across the pond?"

I looked toward the friendly face on my left. She was a white-haired woman in her mid-seventies, the laugh lines around her eyes warming her curious expression. Her British accent was posh, which made me smile.

"A jump," I responded. "I've got a connecting flight to Paris from Heathrow, but I'll be spending a few days in London before I fly back home again."

"Ah." This seemed to please her. "It's a beautiful city, if I do say so myself. Have you been before?"

I shook my head. "This is my first time anywhere."

"Phoenix is lovely." Her eyes twinkled. "Home is hardly nowhere."

I laughed. "Phoenix, yes. But have you been to Blackthorn?"

Her lips pursed. "No, I can't say I have."

"Then let me know what you think after you've visited," I said dryly.

She chuckled. "It's a deal."

"What brought you to Arizona?"

Her face dimmed. "A funeral, I'm afraid."

"Oh, I'm so sorry," I whispered.

She shrugged. "It was a fine gathering, seeing old friends and family. That's the good that comes out of such things."

"I suppose." Luckily, grief was something I hadn't had to experience yet.

"So, who are you meeting up with on this adventure of yours?"

I shook my head. "No one. Just me and my backpack." I considered for a moment. "I think I'll call her Bertha." Big blue Bertha. It had a nice ring to it.

"Oh?" There was only the slightest trace of worry in her voice, but she schooled her expression well.

"I wanted to go alone," I explained before she could ask. It was always the inevitable next question.

"Why?" Her lips pulled up into a gentle smile.

"Because I can," I said honestly. "I don't want anyone else to control this experience. It's mine. Where I go, what I do, who I meet. If I get lost, I get lost. If I want to go out, I'll go out."

"Does it worry you at all?" No judgment, just curiosity.

I paused. It wasn't that I hadn't thought of the risks—or been reminded of them by my mom every chance she got. I could handle getting lost, being in countries whose language I didn't share, being alone. Darkness didn't wait around every corner.

"I know the concerns," I said. "But it's also part of the excitement."

She nodded slowly and, for the first time, I realized I was talking to someone who actually got it. With a small smile and a look something akin to pride lighting her eyes, she asked, "Where are you going?"

I breathed deeply, the excitement bubbling again. "Paris, to start. Venice at one point. I generally know which direction I'll head next, but it's all flexible otherwise."

"I like that," she agreed. "Do you have Croatia on your list, by chance?"

I grinned. "Yes. It looks amazing."

"It is. The inland countries are nice as well, though some are a little drier and desert-ish. But I suppose you're used to that." She gave me a knowing wink. "Bosnia, Montenegro, up into Slovenia as well."

I pulled out my phone, opening up a note-taking app. "Bosnia, Montenegro, Slovenia," I repeated back as I typed. "Great, thanks for the advice. So have you traveled a lot, then?"

She blinked. "Yes, once upon a time." She looked away, and I had the sense that she was fighting back tears.

I bit my lip. "Sorry, I didn't mean to upset you."

A small sniff, then she twisted back toward me. "Dear, when you get to my age, you'll realize that the good times and the bad are all intertwined. You can't be reminded of one without the other. It's just life."

I didn't know what to say to that, so I settled with a simple nod and a soft smile.

We were silent until after drinks and food had been passed out, the trash collected.

"What are you most excited about?"

I didn't even hesitate. "I'm excited to explore beautiful places and meet new people, to see how they live and what they love. I want to sort of test myself, too." I looked up at her, wondering if that sounded strange.

The woman stilled, her eyes seeming to bore into my very soul. She didn't blink, which was somewhat unnerving, but I met her gaze evenly.

She grinned. "Yes, what will you discover, I wonder?"

When the pilot finally announced our approach to Heathrow Airport, I stared eagerly out the window, straining for my first views of England. It came in fits of pasture lands spotted through misty clouds and, eventually, of skyscrapers in the distance before touchdown. Several people clapped after the bounce of the wheels on the tarmac. My stomach fluttered as I realized I was on foreign ground for the first time in my life. I couldn't hold back my grin.

The seatbelt sign dinged, and passengers leapt to their feet. I made to do the same, but narrow fingers pressed gently over mine, and I paused. The other hand held out a napkin.

"You're under no obligation, of course," the woman said, "but should you need help or want to share your adventure with an old woman, I would be happy to hear from you along the way."

I took it. Her name was Gail, and the address she listed on the back was in London, along with a strange-looking phone number.

"Thank you," I said sincerely. "That would be wonderful." I flipped my hand so I was holding hers. "My name is Mallory. Mallory Roth."

"Sounds like a name from a fairy tale." She leaned in, inches from my ear. "I hope you discover yours." She pulled back and gave me a wink.

"Me, too." I smiled, sharing a special secret with this stranger. But she didn't feel like a stranger. It felt like I was looking into a mirror, recognizing some peculiar kinship with this woman that was unmistakable and, at the same time, indefinable.

She squeezed my hand before letting go and stood to swing a simple cross-body purse over her head.

"Can I help you with your bags?" I offered, rising uncomfortably into a partial crouch to avoid banging my head on the luggage compartment.

She waved me off. "No need. I travel light these days." Her hands smoothed down her shirt as she stepped into the aisle to join the queue pushing toward the front of the plane. "Have a wonderful time, Mallory. I look forward to hearing from you."

I couldn't help but laugh a little as I watched her disappear into the crowd. What a cool lady. What adventures had she been on in her life? Perhaps I'd ask her when I had something to share.

The idea brought the swoop of excitement back, and I glanced around. The plane was almost empty now. I rushed to the open aisle to grab my tall, bright blue pack—the newly anointed Bertha. She settled with a weighty thump high between my shoulders, and my brows pinched. Perhaps I should have edited my wardrobe a bit more.

After running from one end of Heathrow to the other, I just made my connecting flight. Jet lag caught up to me as we flew over the English Channel. A spectacular sunset cast the curve of the earth in a peachy hue that could only be described as a dictionary definition of sunset-orange. My window speckled with ice as we zoomed over first sea, then land. I settled back in my seat once more as the purple of night cascaded across the shores of France.

CHAPTER TWO

THE BUSTLE OF CHARLES de Gaulle had a different tenor than that of Heathrow. I walked past people casually sipping their coffees. No one was dashing through the terminal, desperate to make their flight. It was a lazier, more relaxed vibe.

I smiled, for the first time feeling as though I was in someplace *other*.

When I emerged from the final metro station, it was to a lively street glimmering with neon lights and the steady heartbeat of club music. Car horns honked aggressively. Couples walked by hand in hand. To my joy, the windmill of the Moulin Rouge turned in a languid circle ahead.

My hotel was just around the corner, and I found it easily. I breezed through check-in and collapsed onto my bed. It squeaked in protest. If it hadn't been for Bertha's weight crushing me from above, I would've refused to move. Instead, I went through the absolute essentials of my bedtime routine: shower, teeth brushed, pajamas on. I crawled beneath the covers, the sounds of the nighttime crowd living their best lives tapping on the windowpane behind the old-fashioned curtains.

After a quick internet search the next morning, I boarded the train and landed on the opposite side of the Seine. My target was a café I'd spotted on Instagram, a place so quaint it was practically a cliché, as were the picture-perfect pastries I eagerly devoured there. I only wanted to spend three days in Paris, so I'd divided up my to-do list as evenly as possible. Today was Notre Dame, getting lost in the streets of the 6th arrondissement, and eventually making my way to the Eiffel Tower by dusk. I'd tossed a coin between visiting by day or night. Night had won. Everything I had read said Paris at night glittered.

I lost myself in the gorgeous neighborhoods. Without meaning to, the day trickled through my grasp. Upon leaving Notre Dame, the sun was already closer to the horizon than I would have expected. I crossed the Seine, zigzagging through streets where little boutique shops displayed stylish clothes, rare books, and more. I stopped in a few to browse, the shopkeepers giving me a terse nod or automatic "Bonjour," before returning to their work. It felt odd compared to the overtly friendly sales associates in American stores. At least these people didn't follow you like puppies.

After a few hours of exploring, night began its takeover of the city. Ahead, the Eiffel Tower radiated amber before it was suddenly set ablaze with glittering lights, its spotlight reaching across all of Paris. My footsteps slowed as I took in the show before it returned to its normal glow, the backdrop of a dusky blue sky its perfect complement.

Once in the tower, I ascended each platform, pausing to take in the views. By the time I reached the top, it was fully dark, the barest hint of horizon delineating where the sky and streets began and ended. I pushed against the railing, mesmerized as I stared down.

I strolled along the viewing platform, snapping pictures from each angle, before claiming my spot and gazing out at the Seine, trying to commit it to memory. The grand arch of the Arc de Triomphe stood out on my right. Past it toward the horizon, the domed church I knew to be Sacré Coeur stood bathed in spotlights. I tried to get my bearings, turned around in this large city set into a grid of spirals.

Movement at the corner of the platform caught my eye, and I watched an older couple, perhaps in their late fifties or early sixties, exchange a kiss. She stood pressed to the railing with his arms wrapped around her. She nestled deeper against him, her neck curved so her head rested on his shoulder. His head drooped to the side with his cheek against her forehead as they both took in the sight. There was something about them that was intoxicating to watch. Her elegant faux-fur coat billowed in the breeze, her sleek gray hair cropped bluntly at the jaw. His brown suede hat was pushed back on his head so it wouldn't impede her view. They just looked so comfortable, so at peace, so right. Two people cut from the same swath of fabric and stitched back together with a bond that wouldn't break even when they eventually moved apart. I turned to avoid staring, only to find that another couple was making out passionately on the opposite end. My head jerked forward.

Something hollow pitted deep inside me. I could feel it, as if it'd been sitting there, waiting for me to notice. I frowned. This was the city of love. I shouldn't be surprised that I was one person among many couples. The idea of traveling alone truly hadn't bothered me. Heaven knows I'd been asked about it often enough. So why were my insides squirming?

I pushed the feelings down where they belonged as I began my descent, taking one last stroll at each level. The general thrum of voices surrounded me, various dialects melding from the mass of tourists. Walking along the first level, I watched people scurry about like ants far below through a transparent pane in the floor. I crouched, drawing patterns across the glass, imagining a building here and another there, creating my own cityscape for them to explore.

A silky voice called out in French from my right.

My head whipped around, and I spotted a young man. His expression was a mix of wonder and horror as he stared straight at me, meanwhile standing as far away from the tower's center as he could manage. I glanced over my shoulder to make sure he was speaking to me before responding. "Sorry, I don't speak French."

The tightness between his brows relaxed a fraction as he said in English, "How are you doing that?"

"Doing what?"

"Looking down like it's nothing?" His thick accent rounded his words beautifully.

I realized the problem and stood, stepping onto the glass where I'd just been doodling, and performed a spin. "Oh, this?" I quipped innocently with a flourish.

His Adam's apple bobbed.

I shook my head as I walked toward him, my fingertips skimming across the clear barrier surrounding the chasm. "Why are you up here if you're afraid of heights?"

He pointed overhead. "My friends are there. They wanted to do it. I couldn't go any further, so I wait."

I stopped next to him, solid floor once again beneath my feet. "There are easier ways to impress a girl," I said with a wink, trying to distract him from his discomfort.

He turned to face the city and closed his eyes. "I think I may be sick."

"I'm going down," I offered sympathetically. "Want to come?"

Even in the darkness, his pallor was a pale green as he gave a tight nod.

We squished into the back of the elevator. A loudly crying child pierced our eardrums the entire claustrophobic ride. By the time the doors slid open, my ears were ringing.

"Safe and sound," I announced.

His eyes flew open, and he took a deep breath as he stepped out.

"Never again." His long strides propelled him beneath the belly of the tower. He craned his neck skyward. "Idiots."

"Are you all right?" I asked, inching away.

"Yes, thank you." He followed me a few steps.

"Um, I'm going that way," I said, gesturing vaguely toward the river.

"Oh." He hesitated before pointing up at the tower. "Would you like to join us? Once they come down, I'm taking them to visit a few clubs. I could show you the real side of Paris." As he spoke, he pulled out a pouch of tobacco and began rolling a cigarette. It was mesmerizing. He

15

did it so effortlessly, barely looking down before he finished and pinched it between his full lips. The spark of flame from the lighter highlighted his dark eyes as he peered at me.

A flutter tickled my insides. He was cute, I had to admit, though a few years younger than me. But hadn't I just been feeling left out being alone?

"Sure, that sounds great," I said, grinning.

He returned it as he puffed out a tendril of smoke. "I'm Alexandre."

"Mallory."

We sat and chatted, looking out over the giant lawn until his friends joined us. From there, our group crawled from dark, underground rooms packed with people, the first paying homage to Paris's golden age while the next sizzled with laser lights. The music was a mishmash of eclectic French songs and oldies I recognized from my mom's collection at home. Whenever one came on that I knew, I belted out the lyrics, tone-deafness be damned.

As the evening wore on, the music changed, sultry house beats taking over. People ground together on the dance floor, the mood in the club morphing with the new sounds. Alexandre and I swayed, bodies close, his hand running gently along the back of my neck. It was pleasant, the warmth of drink sweeping through my body, the pulse of music a heartbeat through my skin. Reluctantly, I twisted Alexandre's hand to check his watch.

I tapped its glass face with my nail. "Time for me to go."

"It's still early." His fingers brushed away a sweaty strand of hair stuck to my nose.

"Maybe for you," I scoffed lightly, pulling out of his arms. One of my hands was still clasped in his. He didn't let go at first, but when I didn't falter, he brought it to his lips for a quick kiss, a pat, and let it drop.

"How long are you in Paris?"

"A few days," I said. "Thank you for tonight. I had fun. You're a good tour guide."

He made a flashy bow, his hand waving him down as his eyes glittered mischievously. "Happy to be of service, mademoiselle."

We wove through the dancers back to our group, where I bade his friends farewell. Alexandre escorted me outside.

"Do you know your way?"

"I think so." I punched directions to the hotel into my phone. "Yep, not too far."

"Good." He took my phone and added his number to my contacts. "In case you are ever in Paris again," he explained, handing it back to me.

"Thanks," I chuckled warmly. "I'll take you up on that." I held out my hand, and he shook it, but also pulled me in to kiss me on either cheek. "Au revoir."

He stifled a laugh at my horrible accent. "Bonne nuit."

Then he turned, disappearing back into the club with a swoosh of his charcoal overcoat. I matched it, sad to see him go even as my feet moved forward, carrying me through the magical streets of Paris.

———

The next day, I shifted my notepad awkwardly to my other knee, finishing off my first note to my new friend Gail as my bus sat in traffic, heading to the seaside town of Marseille.

The architecture, even the entrances to the metro stations, were amazing! I won't say how many croissants I ate (it was a lot, okay?). I think I pissed off a few Parisians with my terrible French, but I tried my best. It's a strange feeling, just the difference between how people behave or their demeanor or something. I can't quite put my finger on it. Alexandre and his friends were nice at least (and he was cute, I'll admit it). He texted me a few local Paris spots to check out and messaged again this morning wishing me a nice trip, so I've already made another friend! :) Between you and Alexandre, I think I'm off to a good start.

Anyway, that's all for now. I hope you made it home safely, and I will write again soon.

Your friend,
Mallory

I'd bought cheap postcards on a whim at the Paris bus station. The first one I wrote was to my mom as I waited to depart. It was heavily redacted, just the basics about my days in the city. In this second one to Gail, I blathered about every detail, including the juicy ones about Alexandre. It was true, though, I mused as I reread it for spelling errors. There was an unmistakable difference between the people here and what I was used to back home. And that was okay. I had been expecting differences—hoping for them, in fact.

But this?

The culture shock upon arriving in Marseille was on an entirely different level.

I wove through the concrete station, startled when a pair of assault rifles turned the corner ahead of me, their owners dressed in military garb. They passed me, chatting away, and I couldn't help but turn as I walked, watching them. They weren't running toward trouble, no alarms sounding, no mad mob on their tail.

I shook it off, pulling Bertha's straps tighter around my shoulders like a hug. As I moved through the crowd, I took my phone out of my pocket, hopped onto the station Wi-Fi, and punched in directions to the apartment's address. Twisting in the right direction, I headed outside, crossing a busy intersection and winding through sun-soaked sidewalks, the wind whipping harshly at my face through the narrow streets. Finally, these opened up to a broad square.

Buskers played in a cacophony of contradictory sounds against the background lap of waves, which licked the hulls of boats docked in the harbor. The toot of a small train, similar to an amusement park kiddie ride, drew my attention as it slithered away from the curb, chock-full of tourists. I watched as it weaved through the streets, heading up a hill to where an enormous church sat sentinel above the town.

Following its path to my left, the sparkle of the sea dazzled me even as the stronger wind drew tears from my eyes. I put on my sunglasses and it helped a little as I studied my map. I was close, but the tiny side streets were unlabeled as far as I could tell. I tried one street, then another, but each time ended up back at the harbor, my apartment remaining hidden. I pulled up the booking app, thankful for the slow spot of data my phone discovered, and messaged the property.

Surprisingly quickly, I received a text back.

Where are you? it read.

I searched in vain for a street sign, instead typing in the name of the restaurant across from me.

I'll come get you.

I didn't wait long. A tanned man, perhaps in his early thirties, was making directly for me with sure steps. Did I have a sign blaring FOR-EIGNER strapped around my neck or something?

"Hello," he said. "Are you looking for Appartement Magnifique?"

"Yes," I replied, recognizing the name from my booking.

"Welcome to Marseille," he said with a grin.

"Thank you." I returned his smile with my own and offered a hand. He took it and promptly brought it to his mouth. I flushed.

"You were nearly there. It's just this way."

I followed him to the first street I'd tried, but he turned to the right down a dark alley, dim even in the bright, late-day sun. A whitewashed building with twisted staircases led up to my room on the third floor. He opened the door to my room, and I walked in. It was a studio, complete with a wide futon, kitchen, and balcony overlooking a U-shaped court-yard.

"There's tea and coffee in here," he said, moving about the kitchen and opening a cupboard. "Help yourself. And at the end of your stay, just put the key back in the mailbox. There's a false bottom inside." He held up an old-fashioned brass key with a bright orange chain, then set it on the kitchen table.

"Thank you. This is lovely."

He smiled again, looking me over as he tucked a lock of his shoulder-length chestnut hair behind one ear. "Where are you from?"

"America."

He laughed. "Well, yes, I gathered. But where?"

"Oh," I chuckled. "A small town in the middle of Nowhere, USA."

His brows raised in question, so I explained.

"Is this your first time in Marseille?"

"It is."

"Ah." He shuffled toward the door. "Do you want a tour today?"

"Really? Sure, that would be great. Could I clean up first, though?" I laughed. "I've been on a bus for a few hours, and I wouldn't want to subject you to that."

He smiled, then checked his watch. "Seven?"

"Perfect."

"I'll meet you at home."

"Your home?"

"No, yours." He raised an eyebrow at me as he left. "I know where you live." The door closed softly behind him.

CHAPTER THREE

I TOOK THE MOST heavenly shower, despite the lackluster water pressure in the apartment. Something just gets through your clothes during travel, a tangible sheen across your skin. I dried, fluffed my hair, and added a touch of makeup.

Sudden bursts of the sea breeze kissed my body as I stood out on the balcony. Below me, the fire escape rattled, joining the sounds of life as the surrounding apartments filled at the close of day. Music wafted through open doors, the chatter of a TV here and there, while families came together for the evening hours.

A knock at the door had me spinning to open it, but it was already swinging wide.

"Hello," I said with surprise as he let himself in.

"Bonne soir." He was dressed in jeans and a simple button-down shirt. "Ready?"

I nodded, grabbing my purse. He held the door for me and locked it before I followed him downstairs.

First, he led me to a park overlooking the mouth of the port. The sun dipped toward the horizon, bathing the buildings in that magical, golden-hour glow. Ships breezed by on silent winds, which had calmed significantly since my arrival. Near the shaded point, we sat on a bench in silence for a while, admiring the view.

I was about to ask him something when, suddenly, I realized I didn't know his name.

"Damian," he answered when I asked.

"I'm Mallory." But he probably already knew that from the reservation.

"That is a beautiful name. It's actually not an uncommon one here. Are you sure you're not French?"

I sniggered. "Not at all. Can't you tell?"

He grinned lazily, pulling a strand of my dark blonde hair between his fingers and rolling it. "I suppose." He pressed in close, and I tensed a fraction at his touch.

He released my hair, turned back to stare at Vieux Port, and began telling me about Marseille. He pointed out various buildings and mentioned the prison island off the coast, which was famous now for the book *The Count of Monte Cristo*.

"It is a popular spot to visit," he continued as we walked around the perimeter of the park. "But on days like today, it's difficult to go out on the sea for small boats or tourists. Very choppy. There is a place along the shore that most tourists do not visit, high cliffs you can paddle along in kayaks." He looked at me. "You should come with me in the morning."

"You aren't busy?"

"I do not work tomorrow, so I will sleep in, but we can go later."

I lifted a shoulder. "It sounds nice."

We'd reached the park entrance once more. It was almost eight o'clock, and I hadn't eaten yet, which was made apparent as my stomach gave a loud grumble.

Damian smiled. "Can you stand waiting another twenty minutes or so? I'm going to take you to the beach. It has...what do you call them? Grandes roues." He raised a hand overhead, indicating something tall, then spun his finger in a wide circle.

I scrunched my lips, trying to guess.

"You ride them," he prompted.

"Oh! Ferris wheels?"

He smiled. "Yes."

"Sure, I can wait."

We boarded a bus on the main street, and I watched the city go by. It was getting busier the longer the night grew. It seemed our destination was popular, as the bus became more and more cramped. He stood at my back, the distance between us nonexistent by the time the bus crawled to a stop, and he said into my ear that we needed to disembark.

I was grateful for the cool air as we stepped outside in front of a corner shop lit with brilliant lights. He pointed to it, and I followed him inside, where he gathered together bread, cheese, meats, a bottle of wine, and an opener. I pulled out my wallet, gathering enough Euros, and paid the man behind the counter for the entire haul. I figured it was the least I could do to return the favor for him taking time out of his life to show around a tourist like me. Damian didn't protest, but carried the bag out as we scurried across the street to the parade of lights along the entrance to the beach.

The beach stretched into a great W, a rocky divider breaking up the two curves of perfect white sand. The junk food booths, along with the children's rides, reminded me of photos I'd seen of the Santa Cruz boardwalk in California, which I'd only dreamed of after adding it to my must-visit list. My head craned skyward as he led me past the giant turning wheel toward the ocean. The unmistakable tang of salty brine hit my nose as gentle waves lapped the shore.

We found a wide patch of vacant real estate and set out our dinner spread. I looked toward the inky black water, the horizon lit by the last of the dying sun. The muffled chatter of people above near the street filtered down to us. Everyone seemed far away. Couples and families down on the beach secluded themselves in their bubbles, everyone minding their own business.

"What do you think?"

"It's beautiful," I answered, piling a slice of bread high with fixings and digging in. I was starving and downed it in two bites. I was in the middle of building another when he offered me a plastic cup.

"Wine?"

"Thanks." I took it, about to take a sip, when he suddenly threw an arm around my shoulders. My muscles tensed. I looked down at the cup, then peered at him out of the corner of my eye. His other arm was slung over his bent knee, his hand dangling and relaxed as he gazed out at the ocean. He must have felt me staring at him, because he met my gaze with a smile. I returned it nervously before peering into my wine.

My college years weren't so far behind me that I'd forgotten the golden rule of partying. Mind your own drink at all times. I'd been busy eating when he'd poured it. Better safe than sorry. I took a breath and put the cup to my lips, pretending to drink before setting it back down in the sand on the other side of me.

"How long are you traveling?" he asked, taking a drink from his cup.

"Almost a month," I said, welcoming the easy topic.

"Where to next?"

"I'm not sure. I have a general trajectory in mind. Any tips?"

"Nice is nice," he quipped, clearly playing with the name of the seaside town I'd spotted on a map not far from here.

I waited, but apparently wasn't getting anything more. "And you? Tell me about your life here."

He shrugged. "I'm not that interesting."

"Don't say that," I objected. "I'm sure—"

He cut me off in one swift motion. His arm tightened around me, drawing me in to his chest. His insistent mouth found mine, his tongue forcing my lips open. The surprise of it made me gasp, giving him exactly what he wanted. I supposed I'd never, in the true name of it, been properly French kissed. It was uncomfortable and messy. Maybe he was just bad at it. Or perhaps it was just because this was what I'd feared when he handed me that cup. The shock finally dulled enough for my body to take action.

Protest grumbled in my throat, and my hands snaked up to press forcefully against his chest. He finally broke away, a lazy smile on his face.

I frowned. "What are you doing?"

His head tilted to the side. "What do you mean?'

"I mean, why are you kissing me?"

He gestured around him. "Why wouldn't I? You're beautiful. We're here on this beach eating and drinking while watching the sunset."

I guess I could see his point. If I'd led him on, I hadn't meant to. Was I just overreacting?

"Sorry," I offered, "but I'm not interested in that."

He smiled like he didn't believe me and leaned in again. I tilted back to match his distance, and his eyebrows raised.

"Just kissing," he said. "Have you ever been French kissed before?"

"Not like that." I tried to keep my voice from revealing how unpleasant it had been.

"Did you like it?"

Ugh.

"We do it differently where I'm from." That sounded diplomatic enough. Why was I being so nice about this?

"Really? So show me." He leaned in again but stopped just shy of touching, his eyes meeting mine.

I hesitated. New horizons, right? What harm could a simple make-out session do? Some women probably traveled to France just for this kind of experience. After all, French men were supposed to be legendary lovers. If that were true, either I hadn't given this enough of a chance out of shock, or I'd netted a dud.

I held out my hand, my palm facing flat toward him. "Just kissing."

He didn't answer, but closed the distance.

I was no prude. I didn't live in a closet. But something here felt different. I was on edge, only half aware of his lips moving against mine.

My ears searched for any sign of approaching footsteps in case I needed help. They noticed the crowd quieting as families with children packed it in for the night. Every sense was heightened, so when his hand started crawling up my ribs beneath my shirt, my breathing quickened.

I tried to push it down with my elbow, hoping he would take the hint, but his hand was at my bra, my shirt pulled nearly above it, and his hand dipped inside.

"Hey!" I broke the kiss.

"Shh," he murmured, his mouth pecking down my neck as his other hand joined in.

"Get off!" I insisted, pushing against him with all my might. His hands exited my shirt to grab each of my wrists, rolling me onto my back and pinning me from above. Panic seared through my chest, my head rolling wildly from side to side as I searched the empty beach helplessly.

What a fool. Tears streamed down my face.

"Shh," he whispered again against my collarbone. Goosebumps prickled across my arms and legs, raising the hair on the crown of my head.

"Relax." He continued to speak in that calming voice, like a lover. Bile rose in my mouth, my mind racing. I was all alone. I had no one to depend on but me, so how was I going to get myself out of this?

I made my body to go limp, dead. My eyes closed as I took a few deep breaths through my nose. I felt the grip on my wrists loosen a fraction. Hating myself for what I was about to do, I opened my eyes and met his gaze. I prayed my expression was neutral, at the very least.

My eye contact seemed to do the trick in this dim light. He smiled lazily again and bent to kiss me. I forced myself to play along, deepening the kiss as every fiber of my being screamed against it. Finally, he released my arms, his hands wandering once more across my skin. His fingers skimmed my lower belly down to the button of my shorts. My heart beat double time, but I used the fact that he was off balance in this position to twist. He was on his side, then beneath me. His breath huffed out in surprise at the sudden shift, but his slack grin said he didn't mind. His hands gripped my hips and dug into my flesh as he pressed into me. I fought the urge to shove him away, waiting for his hands to loosen.

It was when his fingers trailed up my back, looking to spring my bra free, that I made my move. My toes were already firmly digging into the sand. I rocked forward onto the balls of my feet and pushed up, my left leg swinging over him. But I didn't do it fast enough. Out of reflex, his arm shot out, just catching the top of my foot. I spun in the air, landing face-down in the sand, the air whooshing from my lungs.

As I gasped for breath, I scrambled, fingernails tearing through the sand. I could hear him moving behind me and blindly kicked out with one leg. A grunt told me I might have caught him in the stomach, but I wasn't about to waste precious seconds looking back.

I was on my feet, but the soft sand made me run in slow motion. The concrete staircase was mere feet ahead of me. When its cool metal railing was beneath my hand, pure relief sang through my body. I bounded up the steps and burst into the bathed glow of the carnivalesque atmosphere. It felt so wrong, like wandering through a fun house. Colorful, cheerful, and utterly creepy.

I scanned the street wildly, spotting a bus pulling up to the stop across the way. Whether it would take me back to the apartment or not, I had no clue. But it was heading in the right direction at this moment, and that was good enough for me. I bolted through the street, earning angry honks from oncoming traffic. Just as I stepped onto the curb, I heard the telltale hiss of the doors closing.

"Hey!" I yelped, waving my arms. I made it just as the wheels inched forward and banged on the plastic. The driver scowled, but I nearly hugged him when he opened the door.

"Merci," I panted as I handed over the fare.

Once I'd sat in one of the many vacant seats, I finally searched outside through the windows. Damian stood at the top of the stairs, his head on a swivel. I scooted lower, trying to hide in the dull, yellow light. It was only when the bus was on the move did his eyes home in on me. My heart crashed in my chest as I watched his lip curl over his teeth, but we were already moving too fast for me to see what he did next.

As it turned out, my nightmare of an evening wasn't completely without luck. The bus was the right one to have taken. I checked the time. I had twenty-five minutes to decide what to do next.

Should I go to the cops? What would I say?

Excuse me, officer, but a boy kissed me. No, he didn't threaten me. No, he didn't rape me. No, he didn't kidnap me. I went with him willingly.

I shook my head. I'd made my feelings perfectly clear to Damian. Maybe he would just leave me alone if I did the same with him. But pieces clicked as the night swirled by outside. His total disregard for my boundaries made it obvious he didn't care if I wanted him or not. He knew where I would be, and he'd let himself in earlier, so he had a spare key.

My blood ran cold.

I grabbed my purse as the bus rounded the corner. The familiar port glowed ahead, and I recognized the park we'd visited earlier on my left, now shrouded in darkness. I launched out of the bus, running toward the apartment. I didn't know how frequently the buses ran or how much time I had before he might reach me if he'd gotten a cab.

If he was coming.

Confusion muddled my brain, twisting between blaming myself for being so naive, him for forcing himself on me, excusing his actions if I'd misled him, and wondering if I was giving myself too much credit that he'd bother coming after me at all.

I jogged up the steps, holding on to the paint-flecked railing to avoid doing another faceplant. The keys shook in my hands as I tried and failed to get them into the hole. Finally, the deadbolt slid open, and I ducked inside, my back flush against the cool barrier between me and the outside world.

I pushed away from the door, my skin crawling, mind flying. Pack.

Police. No police. Bus. Plane. Boat. Run. Where?

Bertha sat open in front of me on the bed, my toothbrush and makeup bag in either of my hands. When had I grabbed them?

I shoved them in, cinching the pack closed and hauling it on. One trip to the bathroom, then a glance around the kitchen and closet, my eyes unseeing as I checked for anything left behind. I made for the door to drop the keys in the box outside, but hesitated. How long had it been since I'd arrived? I would guess seconds, but knew it had been longer. On tiptoe, I crept to the door and peered through the peephole. A dark blob obscured the view, but as I watched, it withdrew. My hands clamped over my mouth to hold back the scream building there.

I wasted no time, scrambling backward in my socks. Numb fingers dropped the keys on the bed as I passed by it to the outside. I tipped my shoes over the balcony and climbed down the rickety fire escape. When I was close to the ground, a door slammed above me. I jumped the last few rungs, landing in a crouch as I collected my shoes, a slight shock pinging through one ankle. I braved a look up. His silhouette looked right back. I turned and bolted around the edge of the U-shaped building, ignoring my protesting ankle.

Noise from the main street beckoned, but here in the narrow alleys, there was hardly anyone around. I ambled up the cobbled footpath toward the road. There, finally, traffic.

I scanned up and down until I spotted a cab and hurried to it.

The driver switched on the meter as he mumbled a greeting.

"Airport," I said, skipping the niceties.

The trip was over in less than twenty minutes. Twenty minutes in a sanctuary that smelled of cigarettes and sweat. My heart slowed a little, the panic held at bay. My freak-out would have to wait until later. When we stopped at the curb, I handed him a wad of bills and hobbled to the entrance.

Inside, the blinding overhead lights illuminated every corner of the waiting ticket desks, the large glass wall panels trapping the night outside.

I released a tense breath, calm seeping in. I'd feel a lot better once I was through security.

Signs pointed left to the Bureau D'Information. I limped past a family with a little girl bawling her eyes out and a few solo travelers, but otherwise the airport was relatively quiet.

My sneakers slapped an uneven rhythm against the floor, causing the bored-looking customer service agent to look up as I approached, assessing me in an instant.

"Hello," she said, going straight to English as her eyes raked over my backpack and practical clothes. "How can I help?"

"Where's the soonest flight with availability heading?"

The woman was well-trained. She turned to her computer without question, typing quickly and scrolling even faster.

"The first you'd be able to make is an 11:26 p.m. flight to Moscow."

I could already see it. *The Tale of A Dumb American Girl Traveling Solo in Russia* would be the title of my posthumous memoir.

"Next."

She sighed, shaking her head. "Unfortunately, the next flight with available seats isn't until 6:12 a.m. tomorrow."

I checked the time on my phone. I sure as hell wasn't about to sleep, so I could sit in the terminal for that long.

"Where is that one going?"

"Sarajevo. It arrives at 2:39 p.m."

Sarajevo. I knew it had once hosted the Olympics, and that was about it. But then Gail's voice echoed in my head. She'd mentioned Bosnia, hadn't she? I had planned on Italy after France, but it was too close. Plus, with Venice booked, it at least put me in the right general direction to hit Croatia, then move up the coast toward Italy. And right now, I needed distance from France.

"Yes, Sarajevo." My voice trembled. "That one."

Her cool demeanor softened as she pulled out a pad of paper and wrote down the information. When she handed it over, her wish for me to have a pleasant flight sounded genuinely sincere.

I returned to the ticket machines, braved security, and moved through the terminal. People sprawled across the floor with jackets under their heads or over their eyes. Others nibbled at late-night meals or sipped at drinks. A few wandered through the glaring shops, but their body language gave them away—aimless, bored.

At first, I sat down on one of the long, stiff benches and waited. My skin felt dirty, but I knew even a long shower wouldn't purge me of that sensation. Instead, I shoved in my earbuds, which blocked out the ever-present buzz of the terminal. I focused on the muffled feel of my heart and the loudness of my breathing, trying to get them both to fall into a steady sync.

Images I didn't want to see crept along the periphery of my mind's eye. I threw up a barrier, blocking them out, focusing on something mundane. Where was that family across from me headed? What should I get from the vending machine? Anything at all to distract me.

Time slowed to a crawl as I kept firmly inside my bubble. When my gaze finally landed back on my phone, I had spent forty-five minutes of my wait already.

I want to go home.

The thought floated up through me like a ghost, vanishing in an instant, but the lingering feeling remained. I couldn't remember the last time I'd thought that, if ever.

I took a moment, fighting the prickle of tears until they were no longer a threat. I needed to move around, do something. My knees creaked in protest as I stood and stretched. The last thing I wanted was to hoist Bertha back into place, but even with the nearly empty airport, it wasn't worth the risk.

The coffee and scone I bought from a zoned-out worker brought me back to life as I roamed the few open shops, tossing the wrappings into a bin outside a bookshop as I made my way to their travel section. There, I perused books, first on Croatia, and then Bosnia and Herzegovina, flipping through the history of the war-torn countries, their cultures, and noted cities. In one there was a long entry on Sarajevo, the capital, but another caught my eye. Beneath the heading of MOSTAR, even in black and white, the picture of an elegant bridge spanning high over a rushing river was beautiful. *Stari Most*, it read in the caption beneath, *was destroyed during the Croat–Bosniak War, lasting from 1992–1995. Reconstruction of the bridge was completed in 2004, and it is now a UN-ESCO World Heritage site.*

Sarajevo was big and modern, I would imagine, in both build and culture. Mostar seemed remote, small, safe.

I closed the book with a decisive snap.

The rest of my airport stay was spent planning and booking while pressing a bag of ice that I'd scrounged from the bored coffee shop worker to my angry ankle. From Sarajevo I was to take a two-and-a-half-hour bus to Mostar, leaving me time to get dinner and explore. Movement was good. Keep moving until you drop.

I sat in a daze on the tiny plane as we waited for takeoff, the only person in my row. My hands trembled as I buckled my seat belt, my eagerness to fly away so thick it should've been palpable to my fellow fliers. Across the aisle, I watched two burly men, heads shaved, wearing wife beaters and heavy gold chains around their necks. They sat back in their seats as we rolled out onto the runway. The engines whined as they spun faster and faster. I stared at the men again as we gained speed. Just before the wheels left the ground, in unison, they made the sign of the cross.

With a bubble of laughter and the hope that I'd left every worry on the tarmac, I twisted back to the window, the streets and buildings already far below us. I couldn't tell where Marseille began and ended. The ocean lapped in fine lines against the pure sand, growing to a steel-blue farther out from shore, white-capped waves battering the tiny prison island Damian had told me about.

I shivered.

Clouds raced to overtake the plane, and soon they engulfed us in their pearly blanket. I sat with my palms pressing into my thighs, a sort of heady high leaving me on cloud nine.

My head fell back against the seat, my eyes drifting closed.

I was free, I told myself, fighting against the lump still in my throat, choking me. *I was safe.*

CHAPTER FOUR

MORE THAN ONCE, IT felt as though I were hurtling toward my open grave.

After touching down in Sarajevo, I boarded the bus bound for Mostar. "Bus" was generous. Rather, it was a cramped shuttle van in desperate need of repair. I squeezed into a seat near the rear, my stomach rolling through white-knuckle sharp turns and the occasional slam of brakes as sheep blocked the road on blind curves. Steep ravines stretched below, not a safety rail in sight as the van rocked in high winds. As if my anxiety needed any more of a boost.

At one point, two passengers made their way to the front and began arguing animatedly with the driver. Worn down, he shrugged, spun the bus in the opposite direction, and headed on to what I guessed was an unscheduled and possibly bribed stop.

I glimpsed road signs for Mostar through chaotic flashes of headlights in the pitch-blackness. We were beyond late for our scheduled arrival, and my stress skyrocketed every time I dared to check the time. Upon entering the city limits, we wove through narrow streets spotted with graffiti before pulling up to a deserted bus stop. At least the extended time off my feet meant my ankle had gone from puffy down to a fairly normal size.

That being said, my legs were like I'd been aboard a ship, wobbling beneath me as I disembarked from the godforsaken bus. My eagerness to be rid of it evaporated at the sight of the station, the ticket window dark, a lonely yellowed light covered in cobwebs the sole beacon of hope. It flickered miserably. I searched around me, but my fellow riders had vanished into the night.

This couldn't be right.

I swiped open my phone, switching on roaming. The bars flashed, searching for a few moments, before giving up.

"No." My heartbeat ratcheted up a notch.

So much for saving my data. When I needed it, it didn't even matter. I shoved the useless thing into a pocket and hauled Bertha onto my tight shoulders. I made my way toward the dark alleys, choosing one with the smallest hint of life.

I passed by shuttered windows and heavy wooden doors, a lone cat roaming the street my only companion. At last, up ahead, I sighed in relief as the cold, sharp light of a grocery store seared my retinas. I hung outside, wondering if anyone might speak English. The solo teller chatted with a woman as she paid, and I waited until they finished to approach.

I caught his eye immediately. "Hello," I said. "English?"

He shook his head as he helped another shopper.

I bit my lip and brought the screenshot of the map showing my hotel up, then pitifully held out my phone toward him. I pointed at it as he glanced at me again from his register. Feeling like a complete fool, I raised my hands in a universal sign for "clueless" and offered a sheepish grin.

He held back a chuckle as the next customer stepped forward. He let out a thoughtful "Hmm," before motioning for my phone again. Then he brought his current customer, a man perhaps in his early thirties, if I had to guess, into the conversation. They spoke quickly, taking it in turns to zoom in on my map.

I waited patiently, embarrassment churning my stomach. After a few moments, the teller gave a nod and turned to me. He motioned toward the man he'd been conferring with, then to me, before laying one hand flat and walking two fingers across it, then pointing out the door.

The message was clear enough. I nodded fervently, my mimed gratitude completely overdone.

I waited for the man to pay, then he gestured for me to go ahead. He watched me with curious hazel eyes and pushed a shock of dark, curly hair from his forehead. Nervously, I shot a shy smile back as I followed him out of the store, doing my best to avoid limping despite my still tender ankle. He moved right, and I adjusted course, mirroring his steps across a small, black square with a gnarled tree sprouting from cobbled stone. On the other side lay a very dark, very narrow alley.

My feet froze.

He'd reached the entrance before noticing I wasn't by his side and turned to find me. The crease between his brows deepened before he once more gestured down the alley.

Blood pounded in my ears.

Stupid. Imbecile. Death trap. Suicide.

I couldn't pick. They all seemed equally applicable.

How the hell had I gotten myself into this position *again*?

At first, he waited stoically. Finally, he gave a resigned little shrug, then took a few steps into the mouth of the alley, hesitating to check if I was following him.

I weighed my options at supersonic speed. The risks were obvious, but what was my alternative? To roam, lost, through countless other streets and never find my way? At least I knew someone was waiting in the shadows and was prepared for it. Plus, I'd sought out this someone, not the other way around. My heart banged wildly in my chest. Feeling on the verge of a panic attack, somehow my feet moved forward in a pathetic shuffle.

The man seemed satisfied, though his eyes tightened as he appeared to notice my uneven gait. His gaze dropped, and he turned his back on me, keeping a slow and steady pace ahead. The walls surrounded me like a tomb, muffling out all sounds of life...

No, don't think about it, just keep moving.

Forward. Forward was the way out. And at least all this stone would carry a good, healthy scream if necessary.

He walked farther in the gloom as he peeked over his shoulder. I'd caught up close enough to him as to not be impolite. Still out of arm's reach, but near enough to make out the concerned lines framing his mouth, which was twisted into a frown.

Of course. Because he wasn't some monster in the dark. He was a human being helping me.

Get a grip, Mallory!

I gave what I hoped was a normal smile. His eyes warmed before he faced forward, crossing the last few strides to the end of the alley.

He stepped into the warm glow first. I practically lurched into it, so eager to exit the claustrophobia. I sucked in a breath as I looked around and nearly laughed with relief.

This street was packed with people. Soft music whined from an old radio perched next to a group of men. They clustered together on stairs leading to an open door, a welcoming, soft light bathing them from inside. From there, I scanned up the stone path.

Every single stoop and step were similarly occupied with people enjoying their evening—chatting, playing cards, or being ushered in for dinner. The rattle of doors locking as stores closed for the night melded with the steady rush of the river I knew ran in front of us, but was too dark and low to see. To my left, the arched Stari Most bridge hung elegantly over the cavern, a perfect replica of the photograph from the guidebook that had first introduced me to this place.

Everything emanated calm, peace, and comfort. I spun back to the man, who stood watching me take it all in before he tilted his head, indicating for me to follow him. I was walking closer now and accidentally ran into him when he stopped without warning to join one of the countless doorstep groups.

"Sorry!" I said, pushing away from his muscular torso.

Understanding lit his features before he said in heavily accented English, "It's fine." He pointed ahead once again and added, "Just a few more blocks, then on your left. It's a tall, yellow building."

"Thank you," I breathed. "I really appreciate it. Good night." I looked at his friends. All of them were biting back shit-eating grins while smirking at my guide. When their gaze darted to me, I felt my ears redden.

"You're welcome," he said, drawing my attention to him once more. I gave a little curtsy out of embarrassment, which only made me feel even more ridiculous, and shook my head as I hurried off.

It wasn't long before I heard boisterous laughter and the slap of hands, and I spied the group discreetly over my shoulder. The man was pushing his friends away as they whooped and patted him on the back, obviously giving him a hard time. He ducked to hide his shy smile.

My heart gave a small flutter as I turned with a smile of my own.

But I was alone again and, though this friendly street was not the same as those I'd fled through in Marseille, they were not dissimilar, either. My eyes pierced through the gloom, searching the unlit house numbers.

Finally, there! Just as the man had said, it was tall and yellow, a stark, utilitarian building with a set of metal staircases winding up the center. I wandered up the walkway, noticing a young man with a pleasant face sitting on the steps leading to the entrance.

I retrieved the screenshot of my reservation before approaching him.

"Are you Ivan?"

He rose, smiling. "Yes."

"I'm so sorry I'm late," I apologized. "I got lost coming from the station."

"Ah, not to worry!" he said with a wave of his hand. "I'm glad you found us. This way."

He led me upstairs to the fourth floor, and I couldn't help keeping half a staircase between us. When he led me inside, it was to a simple room—modest, clean, and comfortable. A narrow bed against the wall was adorned with a cheerful floral duvet. Beyond a glass door was a concrete deck overlooking the city below.

"I'll just need you to sign these," Ivan said, shuffling through his papers to the correct page. After I did, he straightened them. "I'll be right back."

"All right." My gaze darted about the room until I heard his returning steps.

"A little something to welcome you to Mostar," he said, holding up a massive slice of fluffy white cake.

"Oh, how sweet of you, thank you!" My stomach rumbled its appreciation as well. It seemed like days since I'd last eaten.

"I also brought you a map of the city and circled a few of the most popular spots, as well as a few I'd recommend. Did you have any questions?"

I hesitated. What was there to ask? I had nothing to go on, no agenda.

"No, this is all wonderful. Thank you so much. And sorry again about being so late."

He waved his hand once more. "Not at all. Thank you for staying with us. Please let me know if I can help and have a good night."

He shut the door quietly, and I slid the dead bolt before flopping onto the bed with a grateful sigh. My body was dead weight, drained from the break-neck journey at every turn and lack of sleep. And then there were the other worries, the memories I'd been trying to quarantine to the background all the while.

I sat up, my head pounding from the sudden movement. For a while, I perused the map, my finger following the path of the Neretva River to Stari Most bridge, which Ivan had circled. My mind wandered aimlessly, and I gave up on the map, succumbing to the soft mattress instead. I hadn't noticed the time when Ivan had gone, so when I did roll over to look at my phone, I was surprised by how late it was. The noises from the people surrounding the apartment building had barely dulled.

The bed creaked as I pushed off it, turning the doorknob to go out onto the balcony. Wind blasted me, grit catching in my eyelashes. I closed the door behind me, tears streaming to clear my vision as the gusts died for a moment. I leaned against the chilled railing, breathing deeply as I spotted the Big Dipper peeking out between spots of clouds. The moon shone down across the undulating waters on my left. The peaceful setting sent a stream of calm through me, and my body finally relaxed.

Sleep eventually found me, but it was fitful and restless. It felt as though I'd been asleep for a nanosecond when I bolted upright. Hair stuck to my skin. The room was stifling, even after having propped the balcony door open. But that wasn't what had woken me.

The last image from my nightmare was of two shadowy eyes watching me through the night. They reflected back at me still, like the flash of a bulb in the darkness. I blinked them away, remembering where I was, the rest of my senses slowly returning to reality.

Music wafted in from somewhere outside. No, not merely music, a haunting voice. As I listened, I remembered the photographs from the travel book at the airport, including images of the pointed tips of the mosques that bordered the river. My pulse slowed as I took several deep breaths. As I lay down listening to the call to prayer, I squinted at the clock.

It was 3:23 a.m.

I sighed, willing myself to go back to sleep. But the call resonated through my bones, the man's soulful voice echoing through the small canyon carved by the river. I was almost sad when he grew quiet, but his soothing tones lulled me into a deeper, dreamless sleep.

When I awoke once more with the sunlight glowing through the curtains, it was as if I'd never slept. I felt drained, my eyes burning and scratchy. My body protested sluggishly at the prospect of leaving the comfort and safety of bed.

Still, the promise of a new day dawned. Either I could lie here like a lump or go make something of it.

I flopped an arm over my face and groaned.

CHAPTER FIVE

I STROLLED THROUGH THE same streets as last night, but the clear, golden morning sunlight transformed them. Gone was any air of foreboding, replaced with calm. The cobblestones were already warm underfoot as I bent over the low wall to peer down at the pristine river. I shifted my weight, pleased that my ankle seemed to have recouped well overnight with rest and a healthy dose of painkillers. A cool breeze billowed the baby hairs around my face as I gazed out over the canyon, and I closed my eyes, listening to the growing babble of noise.

The river water brushing the rocks clean.

Sounds of a mother and child hidden away above me somewhere making breakfast.

The tinkling of stalls as stores worked to put their wares out on display.

The smell of coffee.

I sniffed the air appreciatively and chased the scent to a small café. I gorged myself on burek, a flaky pastry filled with rich cheese and meat, and finished with a decadent coffee and baklava drizzled with honey and nuts to satisfy my sweet tooth. I'd be returning for a top-off of the latter every hour, I vowed.

As I left the café, I explored the narrow streets with Ivan's map beneath my nose. Next to the circled bridge were his other recommendations, including a museum about Stari Most. Since I knew nothing about the town, it seemed as good a place to start as any.

I wandered to the tower holding the museum, which sat to one side of the bridge's graceful arch. I bought my ticket and followed the path through the entrance. It was unlike anything I'd ever visited. First, I dove into the tower's underground where glass showcased the original foundations, before heading upstairs to the historical displays. There, photographs documented the war and the rebuilding of the bridge, images which painted a grim picture threaded with hope.

I moved through the exhibits, growing more and more invested in this extraordinary town's history the higher I climbed. The eastern and western sides were literally and symbolically connected by the bridge, which I looked down upon through the windows in a new light. Even the shattered glass and pockmarked buildings were reshaped from a disquieting, crumbling sight to one of strength and perseverance.

War seemed such a distant thing of the past back home, but here, the fresh scars were still healing. The river had been a physical divide between the two sides battling within their same town, now linked once more by a rebuilt Stari Most and its neighboring bridges. How far did that symbolism stretch these days? How deep had those wounds cut between the people who called this place home?

Dust motes danced in the sunlight through the windows rimmed by stone. I watched a crowd gathering atop the peak of Stari Most, two young men in nothing but swim trunks bantering away. One seemed to be the principal speaker, his sun-kissed hair tickling his wide shoulders, which screamed "swim team" along with his near-zero body fat. Even from this distance, his smile was charming, and I could easily see how his magnetic aura drew people in. He received a big laugh from the group, as well as a few coins accepted into a hat by his companion. I wondered what their skit was about to have drawn such a mob, but the rest of the story inside the museum was calling my name, and I gave in.

When I finally exited, I wandered down the cobbled streets with a profound sense of ease. I hadn't felt this relaxed since I'd left home, which seemed odd given everything else. But each pair of eyes that met mine as I walked past followed with a friendly smile or a simple, "Zdravo," which I'd gathered meant "Hello" in Bosnian.

One shop's glittering metal display caught my attention, and I wandered in. Inside, it was dark except for the strip of light shining through the doors. It hit like a spotlight on a hunched figure at the back. Thin white hair rose in soft tufts around his head. Narrow shoulders bent toward the wood table, on top of which sat a bronze disk. *Tap, tap, tap,* went his hammer against a thin tool as he embossed a pattern I could not see. My shadow cast across him, and he raised just his eyes for a moment, gave a nod, and immediately returned to his work.

Rows upon rows of shelves held his immaculate creations—bowls, figurines, coffee sets, jewelry boxes, and more. One shelf, though, gave me pause. There, bullet shell casings lined up side by side, soldiers standing at attention. Each had decorative, inlaid designs and *MOSTAR* stamped across the bottom. I picked one up and flipped it on its end where the number fifty was engraved.

"Curious?"

I jumped at the voice, not having heard anyone approach. I tried to laugh off the scare as I turned, and my jaw dropped.

It was him, the man from last night. His eyebrows rose over those gorgeous hazel eyes, reshaping his teasing expression into one of pleasant surprise. He pushed back that same stubborn cascade of dark curls from his forehead as his head tilted down at me. "Hello again."

"Zdravo," I tried, certainly butchering it. If I did, he was generous with me.

"Very good," he complimented me without a hint of mockery. "I see you've learned a lot in just a few hours."

I blushed, my brief stint as a mime the other night in the store a memory I'd rather not relive. "Yes, I do try not to make a fool of myself, generally speaking." It came out in a rush, one word tripping over the next. Whether it was my lack of diction or that he didn't understand enough English, he simply nodded, then pointed toward the casing still in my hand.

"It must seem odd."

"A little," I admitted with an apologetic smile.

He closed the small distance between us, picking a different one from the shelf. "We call it trench art. The idea is, you take a thing meant for ugliness and turn it into something beautiful." He set his back down among the rest, but I twisted mine between my fingers. Dark dots and slashes formed a decorative frame around the casing in sections, their centers bearing either a diamond or a fleur-de-lis.

It was strange—wrong, wicked—holding a thing in my hand that had possibly taken a life. But then someone else had come along, picked it up, and touched it with love. Now, it was a blend of both worlds, not forgetting what it had done, but accepting it and moving toward a better and brighter future. It was like a grave dotted with bright flowers.

"That's incredible," I whispered.

He nodded at the old man. "Amin lived through it. Lost both his sons to the war, but he stays. He works."

I shook my head. "I can't imagine. I think I'd want to crawl into a hole and forget."

The man's brow furrowed curiously. "I said something similar to him once."

"What did he say?"

"'But what good would that do?'"

My heart squeezed. "Is he a saint?"

"You might think so."

Amin grunted from the back.

The man's mouth turned into a teasing grimace as he tacked on, "Unless you know him."

I chuckled, then grew quiet. "Thank you. For telling me," I added when he gave me a questioning look. "It's been a lot, everything I've seen today so far. I'm taking it all in."

"You're welcome."

I admired all the meticulously crafted things and sighed. "I want so many of these, but none of them will fit in my bag." The weight of the casing had become comfortable in my hand, the metal warmed by my skin. "But I think this will do just fine."

He plucked it from my fingers with an approving nod, and I followed him to the small cash register. I waited until he finished wrapping it in paper to ask, "What's your name?"

He handed me the souvenir tied with a bow of twine. "Emil."

"Mallory," I offered. "Thank you for this and for the other night. You saved me."

"I suppose that means you owe me." His voice was casual, but still I faltered a moment.

I turned the package over in my hands, considering it and his words. It was powerful for such a small object. Its symbol of perseverance had struck a strong chord in me, and I gripped it tightly as I raised my head with determination.

"Of course I do," I said at last, fixing a smile on my face. "Did you have something in mind?" I didn't intend for it to come out flirty, but I was glad to find a sliver of the old me still lurking in wait.

"I didn't mean—" he floundered.

"But I did," I cut him off, my resolve strengthening. This was my chance to get the trip back on track and refocus. I could—would—put this ugliness behind me. *Experiences, people, out of my comfort zone,* I reminded myself on repeat, then added out loud, "Plus, I could use your help again. I have no idea where to eat dinner tonight, so it's my treat if you take me to your favorite spot."

In mock-seriousness, I held out my hand with the solemnity of a blood oath.

Conflict fought what I hoped was desire as he carefully considered me and my terms.

"Nonnegotiable, I'm afraid," I added, trusting my instinct, keeping my face unreadable as I toyed with him.

The gamble paid off. With a hesitant shrug, he took my hand gently and gave it a shake before letting go. "Meet me here at eight?"

I finally cracked, grinning like a cat, and said in my sweetest voice, "See you then."

My stomach was so full of butterflies, I practically floated back to the street, only held down on earth by the tiny chink of heaviness in my heart that I obstinately ignored.

CHAPTER SIX

THE REMAINDER OF THE day passed in a blur as I wandered about town, eager for eight o'clock to roll around. The devastation of the war remained fresh in the outlying buildings where bullet holes had bitten into the stone structures, windows still spider-webbed with cracks. I even saw a faded sign warning of undetonated landmines, so I didn't stray too far from the town center. In my mind, I kept wandering back to Emil's words about the war. With the signs of it so close by, I wondered if it really was so simple for Mostar's residents to forgive and forget as making art from the remains of the violence. The obvious answer most certainly was that it was complicated and, I suspected, would remain so for a long time to come.

Intrigued by my good Samaritan, I arrived early outside the shop, settling in to people-watch. I had only been there perhaps ten minutes before a woman carrying a quiet child approached me. Her face was youthful, but her stooped shoulders and careful countenance spoke of years of hardship.

She said something in Bosnian, I assumed, but I waved my hand at her apologetically.

"Sorry, I don't understand."

She held out a tin cup, battered and tarnished.

"Oh." I bit my lip as my eyes found the infant, who was still fast asleep in the crook of her arm. A few euros in her hands were certainly worth more than in mine. I dug into my purse and dropped a few coins into the cup with a clang.

"Mallory!"

Emil stood outside the shop, closing up. He wore a crisp, white button-down shirt, slacks, and black leather shoes, cutting a fine figure, if I did say so myself. I straightened and waved, the excitement automatically returning for our evening out, but my hand faltered as his expression didn't match my enthusiasm. His eyes were hard as he looked from me to the woman. I twisted back toward her, but she was already several houses away. She shot a worried look at me before scurrying around the corner.

Emil's footsteps clapped softly against the stones, and I stared at him curiously.

"Is something the matter?" I asked.

His jaw was tight, and he gave a little jerk of his head. "You shouldn't have paid her."

I bristled, instantly on the defense. "She had a baby. It seemed like she could use any help she could get."

He sighed, his expression easing. "Her name is Elena, and she's not from here. She comes back almost every summer during the height of tourist season, carrying a new child. She is sent here by her husband or her brother, whoever can take advantage to earn extra cash."

My stomach flipped. "Oh."

"Sorry, I didn't mean to sound angry. You meant well." He turned, gesturing for me to follow, and continued. "The problem isn't just why she's sent. She could also get into trouble for begging. It's a large fine for someone who only makes very little each day. It's better to leave it next time."

I nodded, still feeling a bit ill. "All right."

He led me across the river and turned right. All along the street waited bustling restaurants and cheerful patrons. The charred smell of fire from a grill and the clink of glassware jump-started my appetite. I'd been so excited about the evening, I'd forgotten how hungry I actually was.

With a gentle brush of his fingers across my lower back, he guided me toward one that I couldn't have picked out from the rest. Of course, that meant it was as gorgeous as any, emanating that same soft, warm glow while an arbor of vines enveloped the outdoor seating area. The host directed us to an open table in the front, which overlooked a small square. Several children kicked a ball around as he handed over menus.

"Do you like wine?" Emil asked.

"Please."

I stared at the menu and unfamiliar names, then looked at Emil.

"I'm willing to try anything," I said. "I don't know what's good here. Do you mind?"

He smiled softly at my open-mindedness and turned to the waiter to order for us.

Everything was delicious. Emil explained the variety of dishes, which included sides of warm pita bread, a platter of various finely sliced and minced meats, and grilled vegetables, all of which burst with novel spices and flavors. The bottle of wine we shared was silky and full-bodied. With busy hands and captivating cuisine, it was easy to pass the time. Once the waiter cleared the last of the plates, however, an awkward silence descended.

I shifted in my seat and took a sip of water for something to do. His eyes were focused on his lap, watching his fingers twist. I cleared my throat, which finally dragged his gaze to mine.

"Chilly," I quipped wryly, trying to break the ice.

"Are you cold?" he asked, concerned.

It was dry and warm, even long after the sun had set.

Instead, I tried a different tack. "Have you lived here all your life?"

He hesitated before giving a simple, "Yes."

"What do you do for fun?"

He shrugged. "I enjoy things outdoors, swim in the river, fish. A group of us go hiking most weekends." He gestured toward the steep hillsides.

My eyebrows rose, impressed. "That's cool." I wasn't a hiker, but even I could tell any trail up those ridges wouldn't be a walk in the park. "I don't know the area at all. Are there other towns close by? I couldn't see much on the drive in. It was too dark."

"A few. Smaller, not like this."

A solo guitar twanged, the sound coming from somewhere within the restaurant.

"What kind of music do you listen to?"

"I'm fine with most anything."

"So long as you can dance to it, right?" I joked. The sarcasm was lost on him.

"I don't really dance."

I nodded. And waited...in vain.

"Okay, break time. It's your turn."

He looked down, staring at his lap again. "Sorry. I'm not good at conversation."

"You did fine earlier," I countered.

"I'm not good at small talk."

"Then don't do small," I encouraged.

His gaze turned to me again before he leaned toward the table, resting his elbows there, his beautiful face tilted closer. I stared into his toffee-green eyes, then glanced along his strong, stubbled jawline. The thick coarseness of his hair made me guess he had a constant five-o'clock shadow, no matter how often he shaved.

"All right," he said, his soft voice alluring. "Tell me about your life, Mallory—?"

"Roth."

"Mallory Roth." He let the letters slip across his tongue like he was tasting a fine vintage.

Wow, hadn't this man been as nervous as a boy just a moment ago?

"It sounds like a fairy tale."

I laughed a little. "Surprisingly, you're not the first person who has said that to me."

"Really? And who is my competition?"

I choked on my next sip of water. "I think you can take a ninety-pound old lady."

He blinked. "What?"

"She wasn't coming on to me," I said, then added with mock-seriousness, "At least...I don't believe she was." I stroked my chin for effect.

Emil looked nonplussed for a moment before the crease in his brow lifted. "You're joking?"

Finally!

I dropped the pretense and grinned. "Yes."

"Very well." He grew serious once more and prompted me back on track. "Your life."

I thought it would be difficult, speaking to a complete stranger about my history. I talked about where I was from, my silly hobbies, and even a little about my family. Emil listened quietly for the most part, only interjecting a few times with a question or comment.

"So I worked and hoarded every penny I could for school," I concluded. "I graduated in May."

"How old are you?" He looked at me as though I were some strange species.

"I'll turn twenty-six when I'm in London in a few weeks. I finished high school early by taking some advanced classes and summer courses, but the time off I took to save for the nursing program..." My words faltered, tainted with regret. I hated that it had put me so far behind.

"Why are you in a hurry?"

No one had ever asked me that before. I paused, considering.

"Because...of all of this." I waved my hands around. "The world, life, seeing things, experiencing them. I didn't want to wait. I want to do things now. Four walls and a chalkboard might fill your head with knowledge, but it can't teach you what it's like beyond them, not really. Plus, the quicker I could become a nurse, the sooner I could help people and could start really living. I just wanted to have the job-part figured out before I went out and lived a little myself first."

He watched me, barely blinking, never moving except for the small smile slowly growing on his face.

I responded before he could. "Go ahead, laugh. I know how idealistic and naive I sound." I hesitated, my own words sending my good mood dropping in an instant. "I know that now." I felt like a different person than the bright-eyed optimist I'd been at the airport back home only days ago. Idealistic and naive, that's exactly what I'd been before...

"Hey." His hand urged my face up, concern etched across his own. "What just happened?"

His touch was distracting. Apart from running into him the first night, and the brief graze of fingers in the shop, this was new. His skin was warm, with a slight toughness of callouses on his index finger and thumb, but still gentle. My head told me to pull away, but this was one command I would not be following. It felt good, secure, reassuring.

But this subject wasn't a bridge I was ready to cross yet. So I smiled, even as tears pricked the corners of my eyes. "It's nothing."

The slight cock of his head and look of reproach told me he wasn't about to buy it. I held my breath, trying to force the tears from falling. Traitor tears. It wasn't working.

"Breathe," he whispered. I exhaled slowly and took a steady breath back in. He released my chin, and my skin was suddenly cool from the slight breeze wafting down the street. I already missed his warm touch.

Without it, though, I turned instantly on guard. Would he press the matter?

He removed the napkin from his lap, and my stomach plummeted. I'd ruined the moment. Perhaps he wanted to wrap this up. I grabbed my purse from the back of my chair as he stood. The happiness I'd felt before had taken a headfirst dive into the river, everything running cold inside me.

"What are you doing?"

My wallet was in my hand, already halfway out of my purse. "Paying."

He shook his head, standing at my side. "Not yet." He held out his hand once more. "Come."

He led me through the restaurant and down several steps to a second terrace where a few tables and a square of open space overlooked the river. Beside a lush, flower-draped railing sat a guitarist, who was plucking out a remorseful, soul-stricken tune. Emil stopped and turned to face me. His hand was still in mine.

"Would you like to dance?" His voice had all the enthusiasm of one about to have a root canal, but his expression held firm.

"You don't have to do this." My fingers were ice cold.

"That's not an answer." He stepped forward. I could feel the heat from his body, we were so close. Except for our hands, we weren't touching. He waited.

"Okay." I sucked in a breath as I closed the distance. His right hand slid along my lower back, the fingers of his left settling between mine. I brushed my free hand down his neck before stopping at his collar. My face pressed against his shirt, and I breathed in the clean, natural scent of him. I was practically lying on him, comfort and calm slinking back through my body.

We rotated in a nondescript circle, swaying gently to the music without any kind of talent or proper form. But neither of us cared. Eventually, his cheek rested against the top of my head, and I felt the stiffness in him melt a little.

This didn't happen. You don't go out for one night and immediately dissolve into the ease most people take months or years to achieve. It wasn't natural.

I froze. What was I doing? Why was I letting this stranger so close? I wasn't being careful. Had I learned nothing? He knew where I was staying. He knew I was alone. It was history on repeat, and it wasn't even ancient history!

I began to pull back when suddenly an ethereal voice joined the guitarist. Emil must not have noticed that my movement had begun too early, because he was smiling when I caught sight of his face admiring the newest addition. I followed his gaze. An elegantly dressed, middle-aged woman stood by the guitarist, both of whom were watching us with warm eyes.

Why were they staring at us like that?

I looked around the tables to find the exact same expression on other people's faces. As the singer and musician struck a harmonious chorus together, I turned back to Emil. He'd been affected by the good-will bug, too, it seemed. His tender gaze thawed my fears, and I forced myself to remember that I had been the initiator, not him. I was in control, I tried to convince myself.

"This is an old song," Emil said. "My mother sings it sometimes."

"It's beautiful," I said. "What is it about?"

"What slow, haunting songs are usually about. Love and loss."

"And it's still your mother's favorite?" I wondered aloud at the sadness in the singer's voice.

He lifted a shoulder as we swayed. "Isn't that what music is supposed to do, connect with the moments in our lives when we need understanding the most? Why else would there be such a variety?"

He was right. Sad songs helped during a breakup or through grief. Upbeat songs boosted a road trip or party. Others had the power to lull you to sleep on a dreamless night.

The song drifted to a close, and there was a smattering of applause. Emil and I parted to join in, and the singer and guitarist each gave a bow. Soon, he was plucking a more cheerful tune, and some guests began clapping along.

"I'm not good at this pace," Emil said with a grimace.

I laughed. "Me neither. But it's about the spirit of it, not the skill."

"Hmm. I have a suggestion...one with a more age-appropriate scene."

"Oh dear, have you been holding out on me? I thought I'd seen the real you, but you're a partier?"

He rolled his eyes. "You caught me." He waved me ahead, so I lead the way back through the restaurant to our table. "No, this is not usually my kind of place. Too touristy."

"Wait, what?" My hands planted on my hips as I spun around. "I told you to take me to your favorite spot to eat. I wanted genuine, not touristy. That was not our deal!"

His shoulders tightened infinitesimally, his cautious look peeking back through. "No, it wasn't, was it? I apologize. Where I go—it's not the same." He waved his hand around vaguely, which I took to mean the setting.

There was something strange in his tone, as if I was asking him to reveal a closely guarded secret. I didn't press it. "Fine. But I would still like to try it."

His mouth quirked. "Maybe I'll owe you someday."

My foot tapped as I stared at the surrounding patrons. He was right. We were surrounded mostly by older people. They had a certain cruise-ship vibe about them, and I couldn't help but laugh.

"So why here, if this isn't your normal crowd?"

He seemed to sense he was forgiven. "Let's just say you encourage me to try unexpected things."

Hopefully I didn't give off the vibe that this was *my* kind of scene. I pulled my purse onto my lap as we sat, digging inside for my wallet. "Well, I'm intrigued, Mister...I don't know your last name."

"Bajrić."

"Well, Mr. Bajrić, what did you have in mind?"

His face filled with reproach as I set bills on the table. I raised an eyebrow. "Nonnegotiable, remember?"

"All right, then. Since this is my idea, my treat."

"You're on!"

CHAPTER SEVEN

THE THUMP OF HEAVY bass enveloped us as Emil and I climbed to the fifth floor of a building a short walk from the restaurant. He led the way with me following close behind. When the door opened, the blaring noise blocked out any other sound.

Emil's hand reached for me, and I grabbed it as he pulled me into the thick sway of the crowded club. He guided me toward the crammed center of the room where the mirror behind the bar reflected back the laser lights cutting erratic patterns through the blackness.

Emil paused. I could see his mouth move, but that was all.

"What?" I yelled.

"Drinks?" he said, leaning in to shout right next to my ear.

I spoke directly into his as I squeezed his hand. "I'll get them."

He shook his head. Playing the "who pays first game" was going to grow old fast in this din.

"I don't want to lose you in all this," I bellowed instead. "Let's just go up together."

He responded by yanking me along, his warm hand easily encircling mine with room to spare. We moved with the crowd and squished against the bar.

I couldn't hear what he ordered, but he turned to me, gesturing to the bartender.

"Gin martini," I told Emil, and he passed it on.

As we waited, I surveyed the club. People pulsed to the rhythm, dripping in sweat. The closer to the epicenter, the more sensual the bump-and-grind became. I raised my eyebrows at Emil with a questioning look.

He ducked his head, shrugging.

Our drinks arrived, and we both downed them purely out of thirst in the dead heat. When the last dregs were gone, he was pulling me forward again.

Maybe I should buy him a leash. I held back a bark of laughter at the thought.

Thankfully, he was drawing me outside onto a terrace with views of the shimmering town below. It was still busy, but much quieter.

Emil found a small space along the railing and let me go ahead of him so I could get a better look. He stood behind me, both of his hands resting on the barrier, circling me in with his body and tanned arms. A shiver that had nothing to do with the breeze five stories up tickled my skin.

"So, this is your scene, huh?" I teased.

"You sound surprised."

"I don't know you. I have no right to be surprised."

He sighed. "I'm not sure why I like it. I shouldn't."

"Why not?"

"Masses of people aren't my thing."

I twisted my head around enough to reach his eyes. He looked down at me, completely serious.

"You're right. This is an odd choice for a hermit."

The corner of his mouth lifted into a smile at his own expense, and I returned a coy smirk before facing back toward the view.

"I wouldn't go that far," he replied. "I do enjoy solitude and get it where I can. I don't always have the time to go away from town to find it, but here..."

"Lost in a crowd," I realized.

He nodded, his chin brushing against the back of my head.

I spun around, my elbows and butt pressed to the cold railing. "It makes sense."

He was so close, and for just a moment, his eyes wandered down to my lips. "Do you want another drink? I can go."

That same twist in my stomach pulled tight.

"It's okay. I'll get them this time. What would you like?"

His gaze was unblinking, making me uncomfortable. I tore my eyes away, clearing my throat quietly.

"Beer is fine," he said at last. He raised his arm so I could duck under, and I wove back inside.

It didn't seem possible, but the gathering had grown even more cramped. I kept my hands clamped to my thighs to avoid touching others, but it was inevitable as bodies pressed against mine. I finally made it to the edge of the bar and was waiting for our drinks when a man approached and grabbed my hand, trying to coax me out onto the dance floor.

I flinched, then offered a nervous laugh. I waved him off, but he wouldn't take the hint. His pulls became more insistent. I dug my heels in, my arm becoming the rope in a tug-of-war between us. Panic ripped through my chest, and my breathing quickened.

"No!" I yelled, giving a furious yank.

Suddenly, I was flying backward as I was released. Luckily, I hadn't been dragged too far from the bar, so I simply landed against its sopping-wet surface. I pushed my hair out of my face in time to watch Emil take the man by the shoulders and shove him toward the terrace. They were both swallowed by the crowd before Emil was fighting his way back through to find me.

"Are you all right?"

My heart was still racing. Sweat beaded along my feverish skin. I didn't even try to rearrange whatever telltale panic was surely still flashing across my face, and instead covered it with a quick nod.

"Do you want to leave?"

Part of me wanted to go, but no, I wasn't going to let this be the end of our evening. I shook my head. "No, I'm all right."

I tried to compose myself as the bartender handed over our drinks. Emil sipped his while I finished mine in a few gulps. He watched me carefully as I set my glass back on the bar. He followed suit, though his was only a third empty.

He held out a hand. "Come with me."

My gaze swooped over the crowd for any sign of the man from earlier. I couldn't even remember his face, just the impression of his hand on my wrist. I eyed Emil's waiting fingers, and my heart calmed a little as mine intertwined with his.

Wordlessly, he cut a path through the faceless people. The room was curved, shaped like a jelly bean. He led me to the inside bend, close to the wall, and stood still as everyone moved around us. I wondered what came next, but Emil just watched me, waiting.

I shook my head, perplexed.

His eyes ticked up, and I followed their direction, staring at the ceiling.

It took a moment. The laser lights mounted on either end of the room shot out beams toward the opposite wall where the bar was. But because of the curve, they didn't quite hit the center, so our little slice of the dance floor remained dark, out of the spotlight.

Lost in the crowd.

I looked down.

Emil leaned in again. "It's just us."

His fingertips skimmed hesitantly down my arms, halting above my wrists. His look was a question, and my hands answered. They moved his down to rest at the top of my hips. With one step forward, I forced them to move around to my lower back, my body resting against his. His chest was firm, solid against mine. Not the bodybuilder kind, but athletic, toned from an active life. I could feel the hum of music outside and the buzz of drink inside as they coordinated to take over my body. We joined in with the disconnected crowd, uninhibited by worries of being watched here in our little corner of solitude.

For the second time tonight, we danced, each step a little smoother, each move heating the beautiful tension between us. Suddenly, he spun me on the spot so I landed with my back to him, his hands moving along my hip bones. I swayed beneath them and felt, rather than heard, a slight groan rumble in his chest. My hands reached overhead, winding behind his neck. Without thinking, my fingers raked the hair at the base of his skull, and he pulled me against him gently. One of his hands ventured up, skimming across my ribs.

And I froze.

My body, my mind, my heart came to a breakneck standstill.

Catapulted out of the moment, he mimicked me, his hands stopping their trail. In the next second, they were gone entirely, along with his warm heat. My heart resumed at a rabbit's pace. I turned in a slow circle, but he was right there behind me, mere inches of space between us. His gaze was a mix of caution and worry.

"Are you okay?" I asked. Whatever had caused me to respond was snuffed out with the absence of his touch.

He watched me closely. "Are you ready to leave?"

I nodded, not sure, but anything to break this icy moment. He motioned toward the exit, and I led the way downstairs.

My head felt clearer on firm ground and away from the heavy music. We walked side by side, but not touching. I hoped he might offer his hand once more, but both were tucked deep into his pant pockets.

"Did I do something wrong?" I asked when the silence stretched.

"No." He sounded surprised.

"Okay."

He turned toward the river, but I stopped. "Where are you going?"

"Walking you to your room," he said, like it was obvious.

"You don't have to go out of your way," I said, uncertain if it even was. "I know where it is from here."

His jaw tightened. "What's wrong?"

"What do you mean?"

"Something has been bothering you."

"It's been a long trip," I justified. I offered a consoling smile, trying to lighten the mood. "I'm just a little tired."

His feet remained firmly planted toward the bridge. "Then I don't want you getting lost so you can sleep well."

Apparently he was stubborn. Duly noted.

"All right, thank you."

He walked me to my building, saying a simple, "Goodnight," before turning back the way we'd come.

"Emil?"

He stopped, glancing over his shoulder.

"I had a wonderful time." The eagerness in my voice was thick as I grasped to hold on to the magic of the evening before it had turned sour.

His back straightened, his eyes narrow. "Me, too."

I wanted to ask him if I'd see him again. I *wanted* to see him again. But his body language was cold, closed off. After what must have seemed erratic behavior on my part back at the club, I guess I couldn't blame him. I wasn't prepared to share my why with someone else, even if just to explain. A piece of me wanted to, but...not yet. Not even to a stranger as nice as him.

"Goodnight," I said, my voice small.

He nodded and left.

CHAPTER EIGHT

WARMTH SEEPED BACK INTO my bones. I lay just downriver from the bridge, soaking in the rays, my towel spread over the flat bed of stone next to the burbling water. The new day had dawned overcast and chilly at first, but now the late morning sun had banished the clouds. With it went the quiet of a sleepy town on the brink of waking up.

Shops opened for tourists, and cafés clattered with the sound of breakfast service. Across the river from me, a man climbed a diving platform erected atop the rocky bank. Its height was modest compared to the towering Stari Most. For a while I'd watched him practice, admiring his form in every way one could construe that statement.

But eventually he left, and the mellow sunlight had turned me lazy. I'd kicked off my shoes and removed my cover-up from my bikini in hopes of getting a little tan. The bridge arched to my left, and it appeared much higher from down here. A few people had joined me on the shore, but most remained lined up above at the bridge's pinnacle.

There, the first crowd of the day gathered. I recognized the same long-haired, twentysomething-year-old man I'd noticed fleetingly from the tower in the Stari Most museum yesterday. His bright-red swim trunks reminded me of a flashy insect crawling along the lip of the bridge. I still couldn't guess what it was he was selling up there, but his animated body language drew the visitors in like bait. His companion today was young, probably in his mid-teens, with short-cropped hair and beautifully browned skin.

I smiled as the crowd's laugh trickled down. Whatever the elder boy was saying now, he seemed to have refined the art of charm. He was a born entertainer, earning hefty cheers and claps as his voice grew louder.

"Is he going to jump?" came a woman's hushed question from behind me.

My eyelids flew open, and I sat up, leaning on my elbows as I looked to the crest of the bridge. His red trunks made it obvious he was on the wrong side of the railing. His hands held on behind him as his arms stretched straight, his body hovering over the void as his long hair swept past the barrier of his wide shoulders.

What the hell?

He pulled himself back straight, and his audience responded audibly.

His arms waved as he egged them on more, and I could just make out the younger boy moving through the people, collecting tips or bets, I wasn't sure. More cheering, more teasing, but then finally he let go.

My throat constricted as he plunged toward the depths. He shot like an arrow, entering the water gracefully with barely a splash.

My mouth was hanging open.

What an idiot!

Clapping from the crowd greeted him as he broke the surface, a huge smile on his face as he turned toward them, raising a fist in triumph. The people behind me joined the applause, too.

I shook my head, lying back and closing my eyes again.

The sound of splashing alerted me that the insane diver was climbing the rocks on my side of the shore. I stayed where I was and ignored it when his feet spattered icy droplets onto my legs as he approached.

His shadow fell across me as he said something in Bosnian.

I pretended to be asleep.

He sat down next to me anyway, his tone flirty as he spoke once more in Bosnian.

I whipped off my sunglasses, propping up on one arm. "I don't understand you."

"Ah, American!" His eyes brightened.

I sighed. "How do you know? What if I'm Canadian?"

He cupped a hand around his ear playfully. "Eh?"

His mocking accent was pretty good, I had to admit. "You got me."

"Do I get to keep you?" He waggled his eyebrows suggestively.

I put my sunglasses back on and returned to tanning.

"Did you like my dive?"

"On a rating of what? Sane to suicidal?"

He laughed. "It is Luka's first jump today."

I peeked to see him pointing up at the bridge and his young colleague. Luka, I assumed, was now in the same position, his body hanging over the drop.

"Why?"

"It's a sign of manhood. If you don't, you will never have a girlfriend."

"You're kidding?" I scoffed.

"It is no laughing matter," he said solemnly, holding back a smile. "Do you want Luka to be alone forever?"

"Better alone than dead from falling off a bridge."

"Is it?"

I didn't respond, turning instead to watch Luka just as he let go.

Immediately, I knew something was wrong. A shiver ran up my spine as his arms struggled wildly through the air, growing ever closer to the pavement of water at an awkward angle.

The diver beside me uttered what sounded like a curse. He was moving before his friend even hit, jumping into the pristine water and fighting against the current.

A splash towered high as the smack of Luka's body reached my ears. My hands flew to my mouth as I stood, wading into the water up to my knees. I breathed a sigh of relief as Luka returned to the surface. But even at a distance, I could see the grimace of pain on his boyish face. I hoped it was simply from the sting of impact, but when he struggled to swim, my nursing instincts kicked in, certain it was something more.

The other boy swam Luka to shore where I waited.

"Don't touch his right arm," I said, noting its unnatural slant as I helped pull him up the slippery slope. His shoulder was obviously dislocated. We sat him down on the rocks as he wobbled, and I scanned the rest of him. Even with his dark tan, his skin was flushed along the right side of his body. There were no apparent broken bones or abrasions as far as I could tell, so I moved instead to his face. The vacancy in his eyes set off alarm bells.

"Luka?" I said, trying to get him to focus. His gaze grabbed on to me, but he blinked rapidly. "Luka, I need you to follow my finger with just your eyes, okay?"

"Šta?"

I turned to his companion, who looked alarmed at Luka's confusion. He spoke in Bosnian again, and Luka straightened. I moved my finger from one side of his face to the other and wasn't surprised at what I saw.

"He seems to have a concussion," I said to no one in particular. "Dislocated shoulder, too."

"Can you help him?"

I blew out a breath. Luckily, it wasn't the first dislocation I'd seen.

"Okay, you," I said, pointing at the other boy. I shook my head. "What's your name?"

"Dani." He watched me curiously. "Are you a doctor?"

"Nurse," I said. *Technically.* My hand was lightly supporting Luka's arm by the elbow, but at my slightest movement, he hissed.

"Sorry," I muttered. I looked back at Dani. "Okay, this is going to suck for him for a moment, but we need to get this arm supported so we can move him." I warned him with a look, and he nodded.

"Luka," I said, forcing his eyes to meet mine. "Deep breath." I pulled one in, waving my hand in front of my chest to encourage him to mimic me. His face paled, but he did as I asked.

As gently as I could, I shifted his arm so it spread across his chest. Luka moaned, but his teeth ground to hold anything else back as his hand splayed against his opposite shoulder.

"Good job," I soothed him, and Dani gave me a grateful smile. We weren't finished.

"Dani, can you grab my top over there? I don't want to let his arm go."

He fetched it. "What do you want me to do with it?"

"We're going to tie his arm to his chest. Use the sleeves to go around his neck. Yes, like that." I searched the crowd as I yanked my bag overhead and slipped on my sandals. "Which way is the nearest doctor?"

He finished the double knot. "There's a clinic not too far. I'll show you."

He slung Luka's left arm over his shoulder, and we ascended toward the street. Luka was still moving sluggishly, and my concern grew. Our slow pace made the trip last an eternity.

"So, where are you from in America? Is it California?"

I shot Dani a look of pure disbelief. "Really? Now?"

He shrugged, but remained silent until, "It's here, on the left."

The building looked identical to the houses around us. I threw open the door, a small sitting room waiting just inside the entrance. The familiar smell of antiseptic stung my nose, snapping me to attention. The woman behind the counter stared open-mouthed as Dani and Luka struggled in through the doorway ahead of me.

"Zdravo, Amina," Dani said to her, followed by his lazy smile.

I cut in, all business. "He jumped off the bridge," I said to Amina. My words tripped over one another. My heart hammered as the realization finally set in—I'd just treated my first official, out-of-school, real-life patient. And I hoped to any god above that I hadn't done something wrong, minimal though it had been. "Is there a doctor available?"

She spun in her swivel chair and disappeared through the interior door. In moments, she was back, followed by a bristly-mustached man. His gray hair had thinned to a wide stripe traveling around the back of his head from one ear to the other.

"Hello," he said as he entered the waiting room. His kind eyes locked with mine. "I'm Dr. Tanović."

And that was the end of English for the tourist. Dani and the doctor launched quick words between them as we walked down the hall into a narrow room. Dani and I helped Luka onto the examination table, and they grew silent. The doctor checked Luka's eyes and his shoulder before straightening.

"You're a nurse?" he asked, once more including me.

"Yes. Well, barely."

He smiled. "Your assessment was correct."

I released a shaky breath.

"He does have a concussion," the doctor continued, "and you handled the arm well. I'll set it and you can have your clothes back." As he said this, he kept his eyes on his clipboard.

And that was when I realized I was still only in my bikini.

Wonderful.

"You can wait outside while I finish," he dismissed us.

Dani and I sat in silence for a while before voices wafted down the hall. We stood expectantly as the doctor, Luka, and a man helping to support him entered the room.

Our eyes met, and I nearly laughed out loud. "Hi."

"Mallory?" Emil's accent caressed my name in a way that made it sound exotic. For a second, his eyes danced across my exposed skin. His cheeks flushed, and his gaze fixed back on my face, but not quite meeting my eye.

"What?" Dani said, stretching out the word in disbelief. "*This* is Mallory?"

Of course *they know each other.* I sighed. Whatever Dani said next to Emil in Bosnian didn't leave much to the imagination. The words were unintelligible to me, but the teasing, lewd tone translated perfectly.

"Šuti," Emil snapped.

Dr. Tanović cut through their banter. "Thank you for helping." He stepped forward and handed me my cover-up. I slid it on, blushing furiously.

"Of course," I said once securely clothed. I grabbed my purse from the chair. "I'll go, then."

"No, wait," said Emil.

"Yes, *please* stay," Dani flirted.

I rolled my eyes at him, but my attention quickly reverted back to Emil. Things had ended so abruptly last night. Maybe he didn't want to see me again, but his intense look now, even uncomfortable with our audience, made me hope I was wrong.

"I'll help with Luka," I offered. It came out like a question, but he gave me a slight nod.

"We've got it, Dani," Emil ordered. Dani groaned but smelled defeat.

"All right." Dani offered soft words of encouragement to Luka as he escorted him forward, along with one last obvious dig at Emil. Then Dani spoke to me. "Thanks, Ljepotice." He made a phone with his fingers and mouthed, *Call me.* Emil merely rolled his eyes, then turned his attention back to helping Luka.

I laughed as I held open the door for Emil and Luka with my foot, folding my arms across my chest as they struggled through. "Don't hold your breath."

Dani sucked in one anyway, his chest puffed out like a rooster, and stuck two thumbs-up as I let the door swing shut.

"How did you end up involved in this?" Emil asked as he led the way.

"I was at the river when he jumped."

"He's lucky, then."

"I barely did anything," I said with a shrug. "He'll be okay, so long as he gives it proper time to heal."

Emil nodded.

"So how did *you* end up involved in this?" I countered.

"I was already at the clinic."

"Are you hurt?" I scanned him, but couldn't find anything out of place.

"No." He shifted Luka for a better grip before he answered. "I brought Omar lunch. He's family."

"Who?"

"Dr. Tanović."

A prick of wonder sparked inside me. "That's a coincidence."

"That's one way to think about it."

My heart skipped. "How do you think about it?"

His head turned, looking across Luka at me. "Too many coincidences mean something else."

My lips twitched as I hid my smile of pleasure. "I suppose you could say that."

Poor Luka. He was playing puppet between us, being dragged every which way through the streets, suffering the ping-pong of flirting going on around him. Thankfully, as it turned out, he didn't live far away.

His mother answered the door, her eyes wide at the scene waiting for her. It was a rush of quick questions and worriedly flapping hands as she tried to help Emil with her son. With Luka tucked safely into a plush chair, she kissed Emil on each cheek. Whatever he said to her had her planting kisses on either side of mine, too.

"You're welcome," I smiled. "Did you tell her what the doctor said? He needs to be checked tonight to make sure he wakes up."

Emil relayed the instructions, and she nodded fiercely.

"Thank you," she repeated again and again.

As we left, I waved to Luka. He returned it grumpily as his mother began to rather aggressively tend to him. I snorted as Emil closed the door.

"What?" he asked.

"I think Luka might've preferred if I'd left him by the river."

Emil grinned. "Mothers and sons around here have a complicated relationship. What do you call it? Mother hens, I think?"

I chuckled. "I get it."

"Of course, for us, we would do anything to protect them," he admitted. "Nothing is like a mother's love, even after we're grown."

"That's beautiful."

His eyes narrowed. "You're teasing me?"

"I'm really not. I think it's nice that's the norm here instead of the exception."

We were walking again aimlessly, simply following one another nowhere.

"Are you and your mom close?" I asked.

"Yes." It was a simple answer, but the quiet hitch in his voice spoke volumes.

"Why did you leave so quickly last night?" my words burst out without segue.

He stopped. "I thought you wanted me to."

"I didn't." I crossed my arms, staring at the ground. "Not like that."

He shoved his hands into his pockets. "You were acting like you did."

"I'm sorry. I didn't mean to. I had a great time." The one exception had nothing to do with him.

"Me, too." He took a step forward. "Did you know that Luka is also a relative?"

"Really?"

"He's my mother's sister's...honestly, I don't know, but he is."

"Big family?" I guessed.

He shrugged from one side to the other. "A bit."

"Have I met anyone in this town you don't know or aren't related to?"

"Probably not."

"And Dani?" I prompted.

"Is a friend I've had for forever," he dismissed lightly. He took another step toward me. "But with Luka...that means you saved a member of my family."

"I hardly saved him," I protested. Dani had done most of the work by getting him out of the river.

"Still, that's a debt that needs to be paid." His gaze was pointed, even as his mouth twitched with a smile. "I now owe you a debt, Mallory Roth. What can I do to repay it?"

I fought to remain business-like. "Depends. You broke our bargain last night. How do I know I can trust your word?"

He bowed his head in mock-shame. "I promise I'll follow through completely this time."

It was my turn taking a step forward, putting less than a foot between us. "Then make a believer out of me."

"Name it."

Memories from our evening's conversations swirled, and I latched on to the first winning thought. "You said you enjoy nature, right?"

He nodded.

"Show me the most beautiful place you've ever seen."

He pulled his hand from his pocket and held it out. "Deal."

I took it, giving it one decisive shake.

CHAPTER NINE

THE DEAL ENDED WITH a plan for Emil to meet me at the bus station at 6:00 a.m., hiking shoes on, swimsuit at the ready in my bag. My nights were still fitful, though the calls to prayer weren't the problem. Nightmares plagued me, one never quite the same as the other, but all ending with ominous, twisty streets, the press of hands along my skin, and the flash of a pair of dark eyes.

After waking just before 3:00 a.m. with a start, I'd scribbled off a two-page note to Gail when I couldn't fall back to sleep immediately. I did my best to not gush about Emil and failed entirely. There was a pitifully short section near the end about the city before highlighting the mystery of my outing the next day. Eventually, I fell asleep somewhere in the wee hours before dawn.

Despite my lack of rest, excitement still had me out of bed before my alarm sounded, so I was early and munching on a granola bar when a compact red car pulled up to the station.

Emil bent to see me through the passenger-side window.

I bounced forward, getting in. "Morning!"

"Good morning."

I strapped myself in as we set off. The radio was playing electronica softly in the background. The car's interior was worn, but clean, smelling of faded peppermint. We sat in comfortable silence, taking in the landscape blurring past the windows as the little villages began to wake.

"So are you going to tell me where we're headed?"

"You already know that. The most beautiful place I've ever seen."

I crossed my arms, shooting him a pointed look. "That tells me nothing."

He hid a smile. "Exactly. Don't you like surprises?"

I used to.

I swatted the errant thought away. "I do, but that doesn't mean I'm not curious."

The radio faded to static as we lost our station.

"Pick something," he said. I fiddled with it until pop music blared through, crystal clear. I waited for him to tease me, but his fingers tapped the rhythm out across the steering wheel.

"Tell me about when you first found this mystery spot."

He scratched at his chin thoughtfully. "I think I was about ten? My family went there to camp. It was the hottest summer I can remember, so it was busy, but it didn't matter." He was quiet for a moment. "I'd never seen anything like it." His eyes darted to me before returning to the road.

"Sounds amazing." I bit the inside of my cheek, questions about his family burning in my throat. It would be natural, where I was from, to ask more about them, but I wasn't sure if it would be impolite here. That and my few questions so far had been met with vague responses at best.

"What are you thinking?" he asked.

"What do you mean?"

"I can sense you chewing." His eyebrow raised.

"I don't want to be rude."

He didn't say anything, so I continued hesitantly.

"I was curious about your family? I know you said Dr. Tanović and Luka were family and that you were close to your mom, but..." I left it open-ended, allowing him take the lead on whatever he cared to share.

He stared out the window quietly for a beat. "Luka is my cousin—somehow—I don't know exactly. My mother still lives in Mostar. My sisters, Mia and Asja, too. Dr. Tanović is my stepfather."

The weight of his missing family member hung between us.

"Younger or older sisters?" I asked instead of the obvious follow-up question.

His smile returned. "Mia is thirty-eight, six years older than me. Asja is nineteen and my half sister."

"So you're the in-betweener," I teased. "How is that?"

His shoulder raised. "I manage. Too many women." His tone was affectionate.

"I'm the youngest," I offered. "Just me and my sister, Sydney."

"Are you two alike?"

I wrinkled my nose. "Not really. She's very serious. I'm more like my mom, I guess."

"In what way?"

"All over the place?" I chuckled at my own expense.

"And your father? Is he more like your sister?"

"Not at all," I said quickly, a surprisingly strong, angry twinge blazing in my stomach. I tamped it down, continuing, "I love Sydney. She's just more reserved. She's not easy to get to know and keeps a lot locked up, but she's a good person. My dad wasn't around much when I was little, so she grew up too fast, I think. It was mostly only us girls."

"Do you see him now?"

I shifted lower into my seat. "Occasionally." *Very occasionally.*

I'd always felt guilty being the only one that didn't automatically bristle at the idea of him being around. I'd been too young to really remember the bad days firsthand. The mental and, near the end, physical abuse, the abandonment, his many vices that cleft our family apart. The hurt—and fury in Sydney's case—upset me, certainly. But living vicariously hadn't endowed me with the same automatic rage as it had them. So when my temper flared suddenly at Emil's mention of my father, it was surprising in its intensity. That was new.

When I glanced his way, his face was tight.

"How was that?"

"Complicated." I didn't look away until he did.

"I'm sorry."

I gave a weak smile. "Life, right?"

His mouth quirked, but that was all I got in response.

The drive lasted under an hour. Every once in a while, we'd pick up a thread of conversation, but mostly we sat silently in each other's company. It should've been awkward, but it was relaxing. I daydreamed as I watched the tiny towns and vast expanses of nothingness pass by.

We pulled off the main road and ended in an unpaved parking lot with a ticket window. Above it read Kravica Nature Park. We paid the fee, and I followed Emil down a twisting footpath. The foliage had overgrown pieces of the walkway, while little outlets curved for a place to stop if you needed a breather from all the steps. The park had just opened when we'd arrived, so there were only a few other people along the steep, dusty, dry path with us. Curiosity burned through my brain, still wondering what lay ahead that had kept Emil so enamored after all these years.

Then I turned a corner and stopped in my tracks.

Sunlight twinkled down on the vast shelf of water spilling into an emerald pool below. It didn't look real, the waterfall too gorgeous. Only Emil's chuckle tore my eyes away from the view.

"So, did I fulfill my side of our bargain?"

Mouth hanging open, I nodded numbly.

We hiked the last bit of the path, which ended at the brilliant pool. Picnic benches, a restaurant, and cleared spaces bordered the shore, but I only noticed them in passing. I could barely look away from the spectacular sight of the falls.

The water pounded over the ledge, sending a fine mist through the air. The day was already starting to warm, so the spray was refreshing, settling beads of water across my arms and clinging in my hair.

"Thank you," I whispered, reaching for his hand and giving it a small squeeze.

Emil didn't answer, but remained close by my side, and squeezed right back.

Eventually, the promise of coffee and breakfast persuaded me away. I changed so my swimsuit was under my clothes before we filled up in preparation for our hike, which Emil told me would take us up above and around the falls. I followed him through the trees and meadows of grass, the Trebižat River that fed the waterfalls our steadfast guide. It flooded the path in places, even some benches sitting in its stream. Emil explained that they'd had a good year of rain, so the river was full to the brim, making for an unusually spectacular sight.

When the sun hit noon, we made our way down to the pool. Surprisingly, it was still relatively quiet. A few families here and there had set up camp, but otherwise there were only a couple of swimmers. We found a shaded spot and claimed it with our towels.

"Want to go in?" Emil asked, already pulling off his shirt.

My jaw clicked and stuck around my answer at the sight of him shirtless.

His skin was smooth and tanned. His muscles were well-defined, and he was built athletically like a swimmer, his shoulders prominent, as was the small trail of hair leading from his belly button and disappearing into his shorts.

I forced myself to look up as I felt my cheeks redden, which only made them blaze more. "Yes," I managed. I definitely needed to cool off.

He didn't wait for me, tossing his shirt onto the ground and wading into the water.

I shuffled out of my clothes and followed, but quickly skirted back to the shore.

It was freezing!

"Hey!"

Emil turned halfway, already waist-deep. His gaze skated over me, the hooded darkness disappearing from his eyes as he watched the little *I'm cold* dance I was performing.

"Come in!" he yelled.

"Was this your plan all along? To turn the tourist into a human popsicle?"

He grinned and closed a third of the distance. "Come in and I'll warm you up."

Butterflies took flight in my stomach.

Holy hell, had he really just said that?

"Promise?" I called back, calling his bluff.

Some of the heat returned to his gaze as he nodded.

I bit my lip. My toes broke the surface, and I hustled in up to my knees before the shock could take hold.

"Cold, cold, cold!" I puffed under my breath.

He was laughing at me by the time we were even. I shoved my way into his arms, desperation winning over politeness. The relief of contact lasted only for a second. He pulled me into deeper water until it kissed the bottoms of my shoulder blades. I yelped, clinging closer so our chests were pressed together, my arms wrapped around his neck.

I breathed a curse, clamping my eyes closed as all the sensations clashed. His heart pounded against my skin as I spread my legs to circle his hips in my panic to escape the cold.

"Sorry," I mumbled against his neck. Not sorry enough to let go.

"It's fine." His voice was a half step higher than normal.

It took a few minutes before my body grew acclimated to the temperature. It probably would've happened quicker if I'd sucked it up and swam around, but I was reluctant to release him.

"Mallory?"

"Hmm?"

"Are your eyes open?"

My head rose from his shoulder as I looked up and pushed away from him at last.

We were face to face with the falls, just shy of where the water pounded an impressive beat against the surface. The clear, jade hues surrounded us, the slippery rocks visible below. Above, the mist billowed into the sky, a rainbow stretching from the top of the falls arcing down toward the rippling pool. I treaded the crystal water, my hands swirling in front of me, as Emil did the same by my side.

"I've never seen anything like it," I repeated his words from earlier. The same feeling of awe he'd sensed in childhood was the exact one I imagined was coursing through me now.

"I hope it makes up for my broken promise."

"It does. Thank you for bringing me," I said to him sincerely. "This is stunning."

He nodded before moving behind me, gently grasping the curve of my shoulders. I tensed, but he was pulling me backward, far enough away so we could once again touch the bottom. He let me go, but his hand floated on the surface nearby. I licked my lips, looked at the falls, and reached out to hold it once more. His fingers threaded through mine, but his thumb stroked feather-light against my palm. Tingles traveled in shivers across my body. His wordless caress spoke to a carnal part of me that desperately wanted to break free.

When my fingertips were pruny and the sun was dipping closer toward the horizon, we packed up and followed the path to the parking lot. The dry grass glowed golden beneath the late-day sun as we traveled, the warmth fanning through the car making me grow lazy. I propped my elbow on the car door, my head leaning against my fist.

"What a perfect day," I sighed.

Emil nodded, his expression thoughtful. "Yes, it was."

My mind wandered, perusing the figurative road that had brought me here, as I let my tired eyes drift closed. I couldn't have imagined such a place existed all the way back in my room at home. My fantasy had been filled with exotic, beachfront destinations and iconic cities, ones I'd dreamed about since I was little. The idea of me sitting in a car rattling down a pockmarked road with a man I barely knew hadn't even been on the edges of that picture frame.

But if I had to explain it to old Mallory, what would I say? It would be too obvious to declare that life doesn't always go as planned, because of course it didn't. But how would I spell out to her that this place spoke to my soul in a way the clean, spotless streets of Paris hadn't quite touched? Or that the people here, for all their different customs or circumstances, already felt more like friends than some acquaintances I'd known for years?

I shook my head lightly. It was an impossible task. Old Mallory wouldn't understand.

"What is it?" Emil sounded worried, but I waved him off as I opened my eyes again.

"Nothing. Just thinking about how glad I am to be here."

He turned back to the road. "I am, too."

We were quiet for a bit before he asked, "What brought you to Mostar?"

I searched for a simple answer in lieu of the real reason. "Convenience," I said matter-of-factly.

Emil laughed.

"A friend actually suggested Bosnia, so when I...was leaving Marseille, I did some research and read about Mostar. It seemed interesting, plus it looked pretty."

He jerked his chin. "And did it meet your expectations?"

A knot formed in my throat. "Above and beyond."

Above, because I'd had no expectations to speak of, and beyond, because, the more I sat with the knowledge, the heavier the realization grew. Mostar was small and predictable for its now peaceful community, a blessing after so much turmoil. And where they must consider it a hard-won gift, I had looked down on my own home for the exact same things they embraced with grace. I'd endured no bloody road to earn that, hadn't fought for it, but I'd resented it at every opportunity.

Guilt flipped my stomach. Blind. I'd been so arrogant.

He shifted in his seat as the mood in the car changed.

I chose my words carefully. "I think there are probably very few places where both the people and the setting combine into something beautifully, wholly special." I let out a slow breath. "This place, its people? Together...they're paradise."

Out of the corner of my eye, I noticed his head turn slightly, studying my face. Then he nodded. "It's home," he said simply with a hint of reverence.

I chewed my lower lip, thinking of Blackthorn with a fondness I'd never felt while living smack-dab in the middle of it. And it was without sarcasm or resentment that I admitted, "You're lucky."

"That's not always been said about living here."

I considered for a moment. "But I think that's what makes it even more special. It's not just the location. It's what the people here have made it into."

I told him about my visit to the Stari Most museum. Surely my outsider's perspective was overly simplified. Yet he listened quietly, focused. I glossed over some of the most heart-wrenching bits that had stood out to me, wary of hitting any raw nerves or unintentionally resurfacing bad memories.

Finally, I concluded, "From what I've gathered, for those who stayed, it's always been home, even during extraordinarily dark circumstances. It was the love that people poured into it. And they've stood by it, worked for it. That's part of what makes it beautiful, bullet holes and all."

Each of us grew lost in our own thoughts. When he did finally speak, his voice was lighter. "Still, I would love to see it as you do. Fresh eyes. When you're so close to it..." His words caught, and he swallowed, his Adam's apple bobbing. "I want to see places like that, too. I've never ventured as far from home as you." He smiled regretfully.

"Where would you go? What would be the first place you'd check off your list?"

He didn't even think about it. "London."

It seemed an odd choice for this nature-loving, quiet man. "Why?"

"My grandfather was a journalist, and he kept personal diaries. He wrote in them every day, even if it was a single sentence, an event, or a list—anything. My mother showed them to me, and I couldn't stop reading them. My favorite part was a trip he took with colleagues to London." He paused, his eyes growing distant as if they were his own memories.

"He wrote about how strange it was there," he continued. "Clean, precise. The size of the buildings and the heavy traffic. How odd the people sounded, and their food, too. But you could tell he loved it. He saw the Tower of London, walked along the gates of Buckingham Palace and through the gardens, tried afternoon tea, explored Trafalgar Square, browsed the National Gallery. Visited the markets, everything. I was about twelve when I read them. Around that same time, there was this TV show that was set in the UK that we'd get on the few channels we had. I remember feeling this connection, but through him. I never met him, but I feel like I knew him." He half smiled. "Does that sound silly?"

I shook my head. "Not at all. It's sweet."

We were reentering the boundaries of Mostar, and I stared around at the dilapidated buildings with fondness instead of fear, though a new worry had begun to take root. Leaving. I didn't want to. Moreover, I didn't want to leave *him*, which was disconcerting. I sneaked a look at him as he parked, an idea worming into place as we walked the narrow streets to the town center.

Was it crazy? Would *he* think I was crazy? Did I actually want this or was I just wanting a sense of security? I'd started all this to see what I was capable of. Had I proven it? I was alive and whole, at least physically, but at what cost? What did I *really* want out of my time on this trip—an experiment or an adventure?

My jaw locked.

I was done with the experiment. I wanted *this* experience. I *wanted* someone to share it with, someone who would look at this wide world in a way I couldn't see it. To use his words, I wanted fresh eyes. I wanted companionship. I wanted my dreams to come true still, but I didn't want to do it alone anymore.

Maybe that was the fear in me talking. But would that same fear hold me back, too afraid to go out and experience things now on my own? I could live with an altered version of my dreams, but not with never experiencing them at all. An image of me cowering alone from one hotel room to the next, never going out, not exploring, sent a stubborn, decisive stone settling in my gut.

When we reached my apartment, twilight had begun to fall. The now-familiar hustle and bustle of people heading home or out with their friends filled the air with hopeful promise. It was catching and, before my brain could stop my mouth, the words were bursting into the open.

"Come with me."

"Hmm?"

"My last stop is London. Come with me."

At first, he laughed a little. But then he quieted, staring intently at my face with a frown. "You're serious."

I nodded.

"Why?"

I wasn't about to delve into my jumbled reasoning or the root cause, but the more I thought about it, the more certain I became. Plus, every moment that we spent together seemed heightened somehow. Everything with him was just better.

Is it true, or are you only working to convince yourself? that voice doubted in my ear.

I chewed my lip, waiting for the negative thought to collapse, which it did with striking speed.

"I told you how special I think this place is, how rare the combination is between it and the people?" I said steadily.

"Yes."

"If you were with me, I'd always have the best of both." My heartbeat quickened, the raw truth in my own words surprising me. "If the places are beautiful, but the people aren't, then I have you. The balance still checks." I jerked my chin toward him. "You said you wanted to see the world. It's a win-win for us both."

That same curious expression contorted his face as he stared. It was as though he couldn't quite figure out what I was. He seemed to be reading me, barely blinking. It made me nervous, the intensity, but I met it with a level gaze.

His sigh broke the spell, and he gave one of his characteristic half smiles.

"Thank you," he said, and my heart dropped before he even said it, "but I'm needed here. Besides, my budget is quite small."

"I'll bet mine would out-skimp yours," I countered. "I used to think I'd go to all these big cities and those typical, once-in-a-lifetime tourist spots, but..." My lips pressed into a hard line. They didn't seem so important anymore. "But the only thing I have set in stone is my flight back. Everything else is pretty negotiable."

"Why not all those places?" He didn't blink as he waited.

I hesitated again. Then I shrugged, arranging my face with a grin and raising my arms above my head with a flourish. "Spontaneity, baby."

His slight smile didn't quite meet his eyes. "I like that."

"So join me." I was nearly begging, so I switched my tactic. "You choose a spot first, then me, and we keep going until June 28th."

"Why then?"

"It's three days before my flight out of London. That way, we can do that afternoon tea, see the crown jewels, stroll through the palace gardens, and give the royal wave!" I giggled imagining Emil doing a princess wave. "We'll make a bucket list. All the places you always wanted to see. Buckingham Palace, the National Gallery, the works. Yours and mine. What do you say?"

He finally let out a genuine chuckle at that. I could see the yearning and hope flicker on his face, but he remained quietly pensive.

I gave a shrug, looking down at my feet. "Take some time. Think about it."

Time.

One more night before my booking in Venice.

There was no time.

CHAPTER TEN

THE FOLLOWING DAY, WORK took Emil out of town with a round of drop-offs and pickups for the gift shop, and he wouldn't return until this evening. I had my usual breakfast and then explored the outer neighborhoods. Eventually, my internal compass turned me back toward the center, the old bridge drawing me to it magnetically. Around the corner past the tower, I was unsurprised to find the ever-present crowd amassed at its apex.

Dani caught my eye as I crossed the bridge. I gave him a disapproving look, but he only grinned wider.

"Is this all my life is worth?" he egged on his audience. "I'm hurt."

I rolled my eyes, which landed on Luka. He sat on the edge of the bridge, partly hidden behind the people on my left. I worked through them until he spotted me.

He stood. "Hello."

"Hi." I pointed to his immobilized shoulder. "How's it feeling?"

"It's all right," he grumbled. "Thank you for your help. I can't remember if I said that. I guess I was kind of out of it."

"You were, but I'm glad you're okay. And you're welcome." I glowered in Dani's direction before confirming with Luka, "You're not diving today, right?"

Luka shook his head, shame written all over his face. "I don't know that I will again."

"That might be for the best," I said dryly. When his shoulders sagged, I bit my lip. "How old are you?"

"I'm sixteen."

"Would you *like* to live to seventeen?"

He smiled finally, and I lifted a shoulder. "Why do you want to do it, anyway?"

"People say that it's a sign of manhood."

"Oh please," I scoffed. "Not that excuse again. If that's what a guy thinks makes a man, then I'd pass. And I don't believe I'm the only woman who would think that, either." I crossed my arms. "Why do *you* want to do it?"

"It's fun."

"It's stupid."

He sulked, staring at the ground. "I guess, but I still love it."

I let out a puff of air. "Well, maybe after some time spent healing, you'll be at it again. If you want. But don't be surprised if some girl doesn't drool because of it. There are plenty of other reasons they'd choose to be with you."

Hope lit his features. "You think?"

"Of course," I said with an encouraging smile. I sat down on the wall, and he followed suit. We stared out over the town in silence for a moment before I noticed a young woman with flowing chocolate hair and a dusting of freckles making her way toward us. Her eyes were trained on Luka.

"In fact," I said, "I think you might have nabbed one already."

"Nabbed?"

I jerked my chin at the girl, who was only a few paces away.

Luka burst out laughing, his ears flaming red.

"What's so funny?" The girl stopped dead in front of us, looking impatiently from me to Luka for an answer.

"Do you find me irresistible?" He batted puppy-dog eyes at her.

"Irresistible? Yes—irresistibly aggravating!" She patted him mockingly on the cheek.

"What did I miss?" I asked slowly.

"Who are you?" The doe-eyes that turned on me were the same color as her hair.

"Mallory."

"Oh!" Excitement overtook her. "You're Mallory?"

"Why does this keep happening?" I muttered.

"Because the whole town has heard how you rescued me." Luka's voice was a tad bitter. He turned back to the girl. "Yes, this is Mallory, and she thinks you have a crush on me."

She pretended to retch. "Maybe that's how they do it where she's from."

Luka laughed, having mercy on me as he explained, "We're cousins."

Oh!

"Sorry!" Was everyone in this town related? But wait, then that meant... "So, you're related to Emil, too?"

"You know him?" she asked as she shaded her eyes with one hand. The blazing sun was making us all sweat. I was almost tempted to take a leap off the bridge just to cool off.

"Yes, we've hung out a few times."

Her eyebrows shot up. "Well, *there's* a first."

What did that mean?

"So how are you related?"

"Glad to hear he's such a fan of mine that he didn't mention me. I'm his sister, Asja."

"Of course. He did tell me about sisters, actually." I held out a hand. "It's nice to meet you."

She grinned, gripping it hard and swinging it between us like a toddler. "You, too. He also didn't mention you back."

My spirit sank. "No?"

"Nope." She shook her head. "He must really like you."

I turned a questioning look on Luka. He just pressed his lips together.

"Luka," Asja said, "Mia is meeting me here, then we're going to Alina's. Want to come?"

"I told Dani I'd help collect on the next run," he said with a groan. "Maybe after?" His eyes slid past Asja. "Mia's here."

I followed his gaze, and my mouth popped open. There was no question. The woman approaching had to be Emil's other sister. While her slender face and bowed lips were different, her hazel eyes were a dead match for Emil's. Her serious expression was the polar opposite of her vivacious sister, though, a parallel with which I was all too familiar. Her hawk eyes cut from Luka to Asja before landing on me, cold as ice.

She spoke only to the two teenagers in Bosnian, her tone clipped.

"Just talking," Asja answered defensively in English for my benefit.

Mia scanned me more thoroughly than airport security. "Who are you?"

I plastered a smile on my face, extending my hand once more. "Mallory. How are you?"

Mia didn't take it. "Fine." She turned back to Asja. "We need to go. Coming, Luka?"

"He's bailing on us."

"I'm not! I just can't come right now."

Asja sighed theatrically. "He doesn't love us anymore."

I laughed.

"Mallory could join us!" Asja interjected suddenly. I froze. There was no mistaking Mia's demeanor, though I wasn't sure what I'd done for her to be so hostile.

"I can't," I said quickly. "Thanks, though."

"Are you going to meet Emil?" Asja asked, waggling her eyebrows at me and making a kissy face.

Mia's look could've set water on fire.

Shit.

"No, not now," I squeaked out.

"You know my brother?"

"Just a little," I said. "He helped me out the night I arrived, and we keep running into each other."

"How nice." She clearly didn't think so at all.

"Yes, he is," I said, a hint of challenge creeping into my voice. What was her deal?

Her eyes narrowed to slits. "What do you want with him?"

"Want?"

"Yes. You women come here, looking for something exotic you cannot find back home."

Oh no, she didn't.

"Hold on. I didn't come here looking for anything. I'm just passing through."

She gave a stiff nod. "Good. Pass."

"Mia!" Luka stood, his tone cutting, his boyish looks suddenly set into stern angles. "She's a good person. Haven't you heard about what happened to me? You should be thanking her."

For the first time, Mia backed off a step. Her guard was still up, but she gave a small shrug. "Thank you."

"You're welcome." My voice was flat.

"You're such a drama queen," Asja moaned. "Can we go now?"

"Yes." Mia brushed past her sister.

"I'll see you around," I said to Asja.

"Yes," Asja called as Mia dragged her by the arm.

The last glare Mia threw at me told me I was clearly pushing my luck.

When they had disappeared over the bend in the bridge, I looked at Luka.

"What was that about?"

He puffed out a breath. "Mia thinks foreign women are stealing all the good men away. Or just checking a box off in their book."

"That's ridiculous!"

"Not entirely," he said. "But, to be fair, some men do like western women, too. It's not so one-sided."

"Well, that's not what I'm here for." I plopped back on the wall, crossing my arms tightly over my chest.

"Don't let her get to you."

"Is she married?"

Luka grinned. "Yep, with two kids."

"They must be delighted." Poor things.

"They're all right," he said lightly. "You just seem to bring out the worst in her."

"Fantastic."

The crowd drew a breath in unison, and I turned in time to see Dani plunge into midair. His drop seemed to linger longer from this angle, a sense of vertigo from watching him descend sending my heart into my throat. He cut cleanly through the water, rising up to give his signature fist pump before swimming to shore.

Luka stood as people began to dissipate, some stopping to toss a few extra coins into his collection hat. "What are you doing today?"

"I'm not sure." I bit my lip. "Any suggestions?"

"Hmm." His face lit up. "Do you have your bathing suit?"

"It's in my room."

He nodded. "Get it and meet me here at three."

"Okay?" I asked, waiting for more.

His answering grin reeked of mischief.

In the afternoon, I found myself back on the bridge just as the swell of tourists dispersed from the latest jump. Luka was easy to spot as he organized their take from the hat, portioning the money out between himself and a diver I didn't recognize.

"Hey," I said as I approached.

"Hello. One minute."

"Sure."

The other diver gave me a thorough once-over before diligently turning his eyes back on the cash.

"Good day?" I asked when Luka joined me.

"Not bad."

"So what are we doing?"

"You," he corrected. "What are *you* doing?"

"Okay, what am *I* doing?"

"You're following me."

I let him lead me to one side of the bridge. He ushered me up a small set of stairs, where I spotted a sign for the diving club. I twirled around.

"No, nuh uh," I said, waving my hands in front of me.

"Oh, c'mon. I'm not asking you to jump off the bridge. We're going to the practice platforms."

I eyed him suspiciously.

"Honest. It'll be fun."

"I've seen what your idea of fun looks like," I reminded him.

He held up a finger. "One jump. If you hate it, then we'll leave."

I sighed. "Fine. One jump. But if I die, let that be on your conscience."

"I'm okay with those terms."

The men inside welcomed Luka warmly, chatting away in rapid Bosnian. When Luka waved me forward, they greeted me like I was some kind of savior.

"Ah, Mallory, welcome!"

"Hello," I said with a smile. Their excitement and warmth were contagious.

"She wants to practice diving," Luka told them, shooting me a *keep your mouth shut* look.

"Great," said the oldest of the group.

"Is there a fee?" I asked, opening my purse, but the man swatted a hand at me.

"Not for you. When you jump off the bridge, come here so you can be in the books."

I raised an eyebrow at Luka, who was dutifully avoiding my gaze as he awkwardly gathered up some gear into a bag with one hand.

"Thanks! We'll be back when she's ready!" He practically pushed me out the door and down the stairs.

"I'm not jumping off that bridge," I said when we were outside.

"Maybe you're a big baby and you opt out. It wouldn't be the first time. They don't need to know that yet."

"I'm not a baby! And I believe I made it quite clear that I wouldn't from the start."

"Yeah, yeah."

He led me through the narrow streets, working our way to the diving platform. He kicked off his shoes and sat at the edge of the rocks, dipping his toes in. "Are you also a baby for the cold?"

Heaven knew I was, but I wasn't about to admit it. If I'd made it swimming with Emil, I could handle this for my pride, even if it meant enduring without his shared body heat. The warmth of the day had seeped into my skin anyway, so I could do with a little cooling off—or so I told myself. I set my flip-flops to the side and sank down next to him, plunging my legs in up to my mid-calf.

It was freezing!

Instant gooseflesh popped across my body.

"You all right?" Luka egged me.

"Mhmm." I clamped my teeth together to prevent them from chattering right out of my mouth.

"It's cold, I know. I got you a wetsuit."

"Luka!" I yelped, yanking my feet out of the water.

He shook with laughter. "I couldn't help it."

"This is the thanks I get!" I huffed in mock-anger.

Once I was fitted in the wetsuit, Luka began to explain the appropriate technique for the jump. We did trial positions on land, the watchful eyes of tourists across the river making me anxious. At last, Luka nodded with approval.

"You got it. Now, just do the first one." He pointed toward the platform, the lowest jump still seeming to tower over my head.

"I don't think I like this," I balked.

Luka began to protest, but the words never left his mouth. His body relaxed, and he gave a casual shrug. "All right. If you can't handle it, I'll take the wetsuit back." He held out an expectant hand.

I ground my teeth, let out a childish huff, and made for the steps. They complained beneath my feet as I climbed up and along the lower platform. My heart thumped as my eyes sought out Luka. He offered me an overly zealous thumbs-up. I shook my head, urged my body past the point of no return before I could think twice, and plunged toward the steady river.

I was airborne for what seemed both an eon and an instant. The crowd became a blur of colorful clothes, while the turquoise river moved in slow motion. Tendrils of current swept below me, the water ominous and beautiful from this angle. My hair whipped across my eyes, making me want to push it out of the way, but Luka's clear instructions forced my hands to remain where they belonged, preparing for the plunge. And yet, even as my body went through the motions of anticipating entering the water, an exhilarating sense of joy set my insides alight.

This was freedom.

This was exhilaration.

This was abandoning all semblance of control.

Moving, keeping going, not stopping.

No thinking.

No past.

No future.

Just now.

It was peace and anxiety and release, all at the same time.

Damn it, Luka was right.

It was also insanely fun!

The shock of raw cold quelled the mix of fear and adrenaline, my mind gloriously blank as I drifted suspended beneath the water. The river had a stronger than expected current, tugging my body down as if it didn't want me to go yet, either. But even as I struggled toward the surface, inside I was lighter than I had been in days. I emerged, drawing in a deep breath that felt more like an exhale. I grinned as I fought my way back to the bank where Luka waited, his hand outstretched.

"Are you all right?" he asked as he helped hoist me onto solid ground.

I nodded, shaking all over. He threw a towel around my shoulders.

"You did good. Nice entry."

"Th-thanks."

"How was it?" He knelt next to me, his forehead creased with worry.

I sighed, shivering. "You win."

His concern was wiped away by a huge grin. "I told you!"

"Save the gloating for later. I want to go again."

He barked a laugh.

I spent the next few hours alternating between jumping and the two of us relaxing beside our little bend of the river. Luka was a quiet soul, not a chatterbox. Long silences stretched leisurely, followed by bouts of insane glee as I flung myself off the higher platform. Finally, the sun dipped to hide behind the hills while summer thunderclouds gathered as rapidly as a sped-up movie. We packed everything and made our way back up to the street.

As we crossed the bridge to return the gear to the club, I hesitated, Luka wandering ahead of me unaware.

What would it be like to jump from up here? my reckless mind wondered.

I leaned over the railing. It was still impossibly high, but I'd grown a little more accustomed to the sensation of vertigo. My skin tingled with a mad desire.

"Mallory?" Luka had stopped and was watching me carefully.

"What do you think?" I said. "Am I ready?"

He closed the gap between us. "It's late," he said hesitantly. "And a real instructor is supposed to be present."

"I don't know if this will last. I feel...brave." I shook my head. "Do you know what I mean?"

His throat worked as he swallowed. "Yes."

"Am I ready?" I asked again.

Even though he looked like he'd rather not, he nodded.

"I'll still want that wetsuit," I warned, tossing down my bag.

CHAPTER ELEVEN

It was the quietest night I'd seen in Mostar, probably due to the threat of summer rain and the lure of dinner. I changed right on the bridge with no other witness besides Luka. I struggled to pull on the damp wetsuit, my hands shaking as I finally managed to zip it up. Luka hopped over the railing one foot at a time before helping me do the same.

"You okay?" he asked.

I hoped pure terror wasn't emanating from every inch of my body as I nodded mutely.

New experiences. Going out of my comfort zone. These were what I'd wanted all along when I'd started this journey.

"Okay," Luka continued, nodding his chin toward the diving platform that now looked like a child's playground. "So it's the same as down there, nothing changes. When you come up, you just head for the bank on your right. Well...you remember."

Holy hell, did I. The image of Luka's doomed jump flashed in my mind. Fear fought back against my stubborn pigheadedness.

I ground my teeth. My choice, my rules.

"Are you sure?" he asked, as though he could hear my internal conflict.

I opened my mouth, but my answer was drowned out.

"Mallory!"

My feet slipped against the polished stone as I spun toward the sound of my name, crouching to hold on to the railing. He was up the street, but even still, my eyes zeroed in on Emil in an instant. He broke into a run.

"Shit, he's going to kill me," Luka said, panicked.

"No, he's not. This is on me."

Luka didn't look convinced.

"What are you doing?" Emil asked, his voice bleeding with worry.

"It's fine," I said lightly, soothing relief spreading through me. "Just going for a little late-night swim."

His eyes shot to Luka, who cowered beside me. "What did you do?"

"Nothing I didn't ask for," I countered, driving Emil's hard gaze back to mine.

"Please come onto the bridge."

"Pretty sure I'm still am." For emphasis, I stood straighter, desperately trying to ignore how far up I was and on the wrong side of safety. A giddy high rose inside me, fueled recklessly by the spike of adrenaline.

Emil froze like I was preparing to end my life.

"Relax," I said. "Luka taught me everything I need to know."

Luka groaned.

"He did, did he?" Emil's voice was soft and dangerous. Poor Luka.

"Have you jumped?" I was honestly curious.

"Me?" Emil asked.

I waited, an eyebrow raised.

He shifted from one foot to the other. "Yes, a long time ago."

"Girlfriends?" I teased, my tone bone-dry.

Even in the growing darkness, I could see his cheeks flush.

"Look," I continued, attempting to sound as carefree as I could while my toes gripped the cold ledge, "I've been practicing all day, and I haven't had any issues. I can do this."

"I know you can," Emil said, his voice changing to one of surprise.

"But that doesn't mean you should. It's dangerous, nothing like those practice jumps when it comes down to it. I don't want you to get hurt."

Hurt.

Hurt used to be a boo-boo after a fall or something you felt when you found out your first crush didn't have feelings back. The hurt gnawing at my insides since Marseille was different. Even though the past few days had begun to alleviate it a little in a growing line of tiny sutures, it was still wide and gaping.

But what was this act, this stitch? Was I fooling myself that this was living in the moment or was it actually denial? A temporary balm, like a hit for a junkie? Whatever it was, its immediate urgency was helping, and I wanted it again—the rush, the control—and then the utter absence of it. Nothing I'd tried so far had made it go away, not until today, even if it was just for an instant. I had one more chance to feel all that before I had to leave. The reminder sent a sharp cut through my chest. Each second standing here, wavering on the precipice, was sapping my determination, fear quickly taking over to fill the void.

"It won't hurt me," I responded finally, my voice firm.

Emil stopped at the edge of the bridge, right below me. Conflict warred across his face, his thick eyebrows set into a deep V. "People have died before, and you saw what happened to Luka. It's not worth the risk."

"Some things are worth risking."

"*You* aren't worth risking."

"What if *I* think I am?"

He stared down at his hands, growing still.

"What are you running from, Mallory Roth?"

A different kind of fear twisted my stomach, but I didn't answer. I focused on the concern behind his eyes. His honest eyes.

I hovered in limbo. Part of me wanted nothing more than to fling myself into the wide expanse, to feel the rush of complete and utter freedom. No going back, just letting go.

But the other part of my brain regurgitated all the things I'd thought the first time I'd watched Dani jump. And that sane part of me was desperate to climb over this stupid railing keeping any distance between me and Emil, to lose myself in his arms again where it was safe, sound, and warm. The urge toward the latter was a fine wine versus iced tea, comforting and rich instead of thin and cold.

"I'll go with you."

It was like hitting the water in a belly flop, the air slapped from my lungs.

"What?" I breathed.

His words were slow, measured. "I will go with you tomorrow when you leave." He moved away a few steps, his eyes cast down as though he were backing from a wild animal.

"Are you sure?" I didn't want a pity companion.

"I talked to Amin about it at the shop today," he admitted hesitantly. "He said he would be fine."

Luka's hand on my back steadied me as I scrambled over the barrier too quickly. My feet touched down on the slick stones, and I slipped on my way to Emil.

He caught me, but his relief at having me down from the ledge quickly shifted to uncertainty. "You haven't changed your mind?"

I laughed. "I nearly wound up in the river just now out of excitement. Of course I haven't."

Finally, Emil let loose the ghost of a smile. "Good. Because when I asked, Amin practically threw me out of the shop."

"Mia's going to hate you," Luka warned in a singsong voice as he climbed over the railing to join us.

"Mia can suck it," I answered, my tone cutting. I shrugged out of the vacuum-sealed wetsuit, chilled to the bone.

Emil, who'd been studying my bare shoulders as they emerged from beneath the neoprene, was distracted by his sister's name. "Mia? What's Mia got to do with this?"

I shook my head pointedly at Luka, who looked ready to dish. "I'll tell you later."

Luka's mouth shut with a disappointed snap.

"All right," Emil said. "Can I walk you home?"

I nodded and handed the wetsuit to Luka, quickly pulling on my shorts and top. "Thank you again for today. I'll take a rain check on the bridge another time."

Luka glanced toward Emil, then laughed at the warning glare he was sending. With a wave, Luka headed back to the club, disappearing around the wide arch. Emil and I set off at a leisurely pace.

My still-wet hair dripped a narrow stream down my neck into my T-shirt, making me shiver. "How was your trip?"

"It was fine."

"Where did you go?"

"Several villages."

I guess elaboration was not on the menu tonight.

"Doing what?" I prompted.

"Some other shops sell Amin's work, so I drop them off. Others give supplies."

"That sounds nice."

"Yes. What happened with Mia?"

I sighed. "I met both your sisters today, actually. Asja is adorable, but let's just say Mia isn't my biggest fan."

Emil stiffened. "What did she do?"

"Nothing overtly bad."

"Mallory."

I huffed. "She basically accused me of seduction," I admitted. "Warned me to stay away."

"She didn't," Emil whispered, his voice venomous.

"In so many words."

Whatever Emil wanted to say, he bit it back. His jaw clenched as a vein ticked near his temple. If we'd been in a cartoon, steam would've been shooting out his ears.

"I'm sorry she did that. She had no right."

I shook my head. When she heard Emil was coming with me, she was going to be righteous as hell. "Luka's right. She's going to hate me for this."

Emil stopped abruptly, his hand ripped from mine.

"I don't answer to Mia." His quiet voice held a warning.

I backpedaled. "I didn't think you did. It was just an observation."

His eyes flashed to me, softening in an instant. "Sorry."

I shrugged it off. "It's okay. Siblings."

He started walking beside me again. "So where do you want to go?"

"Tonight?"

"Tomorrow."

Oh, right. "Well," I said, "I kept things pretty open. I did book Venice already. That's set for tomorrow. I would love to see it if you don't have anything against it. And London at the end, of course."

"Have you been to Croatia yet?"

"No, but it is on my wish list. Have you?"

He nodded slowly. "It isn't far. We could cut over and drive along the Croatian coast on the way to Venice."

"Okay." My stomach lurched. This was really happening.

We arrived once more at my apartment, but as he turned away, I stopped him. "I have a map and list upstairs with everything I thought I might hit during my trip. Do you want to take a look? Maybe it could be useful for ideas." My heart thrummed in my ears.

"Sure."

He followed me up the steps, nervous tingles skating across my skin. I took in several deep breaths, hoping he'd chalk up my loud breathing to me being out of shape (thought a girl for the first time ever). When we reached my door, I slid in ahead of him, doing my best to appear at home. As I dropped my bag next to the bed, I noticed he left the front door cracked open behind him.

"Nice view," he said, making his way to the balcony.

"Yeah," I agreed, rummaging haphazardly through the messy pile of papers on the coffee table in search of the map. He let himself outside, his forearms pressing into the metal bar as he leaned against it. I accepted the space and slowed down, my fingers finally skimming over the frayed edges of the map.

"Found it," I announced, joining him on the balcony. He took it, unfurling the paper and pulling it taut between his hands. I stared out across the city, watching the lights pop on as people arrived home from work.

"That's quite a list," he commented.

"Yeah. I might've been a little ambitious."

His fingers traced over the circles and notes in the margins. "Did you go to Florence? I've heard the Duomo there is amazing."

I bit my lip. "No, I never made it to Florence."

He peeked sideways at me. "Why not?"

"Because I came here." I plastered on a smile.

Emil studied my face a moment before returning to the map. "Lucky me," he said gently.

I cleared my throat. "So? Anything interesting?"

"Mhmm," he murmured. "Prague could be a good one to keep. You have Germany here, so it would be easy to see some of it on the way to Prague from Venice." His eyes floated to the top of the map, which was decidedly more absent of my untidy scrawl. "Have you considered Belgium?"

"I hadn't, no. Did you have somewhere in mind?"

"Bruges."

"Wasn't there a movie about that place?"

He chuckled. "Yes, but I don't think most people who saw it would see it as an invitation to visit."

"What do you mean?"

"Never mind. Don't watch it before we go. If you want to go, that is.

You should see it and then watch the movie."

"Why?"

"Because, fresh eyes, remember?" He tapped the side of his brow teasingly. "After. Then we can compare notes."

My eyes narrowed. "What are you hiding from me?"

He feigned innocence. "Nothing, I only want your unbiased perspective. I can never have that for Bruges, not now." He leaned toward me. "Our bargain, yes? What do you say?"

His light tone took on an undercurrent. He was being honest, damn near poetic, in his desire to learn and see the world with me—through me—just as I was with him. It was what I'd always hoped this trip would be, an awakening of sorts, even if it looked different than I'd expected. This added layer was an opportunity I could never have imagined throwing into the mix.

"I think...it's a deal," I said.

He folded the map conclusively. "Let the adventures begin."

CHAPTER TWELVE

Sunlight burned the backs of my eyelids. I indulged in its warmth, caught in the last glorious moments between sleep and waking. Finally, my whole body stretched the length of the bed, a few joints popping, relieving any remaining tension. I smiled, eyes pressed shut.

I hadn't woken once all night and beamed at the realization. It meant I would be raring to start this new leg of the journey bright-eyed and bushy-tailed. I opened my eyes as I sat up, throwing back the sheets, and froze.

It was morning. As in sun-filled, birds chirping, people already going about their day kind of morning.

No!

I lunged for my phone. My heart stuttered at the time. I was late. Over an hour late. I scrambled out of bed, stubbing my toe violently on the coffee table leg. Cursing, I wrangled on a T-shirt and shorts at random. I was running a comb through my hair while simultaneously attempting to brush my teeth when a knock stopped me from flying about the room.

"Coming!" I garbled around the toothbrush. I hopped a path through my discarded clothes, slid the dead bolt, and opened the door.

"Sorry, sorry," I rambled. "I overslept. Or my alarm didn't go off.

Or—I don't know."

I went mute as I watched Emil's expression shift in quick succession. Anger and worry gave way to relief, which settled into intense focus, probably because I was babbling at the rate of a high-speed train. But, even then, what lingered in his eyes was caution, of all things.

"Are you okay?" I asked when my brain and mouth restored their connection.

"Yes." His hard gaze searched behind me, and I mirrored him, wincing at the disaster zone I'd left in my wake.

"I really am sorry." I stood to the side, offering him entry, while still taking the temperature of his mood. "I'll finish getting ready as fast as I can, then we can go."

At last, he relaxed a fraction. With a tight nod, he entered. I kicked stuff out of the way.

"Help yourself to anything," I volunteered over my shoulder. "There's a kettle for tea or coffee and...well, that's it." I grimaced as I gripped the bathroom doorframe.

"It's fine, Mallory," he said, his voice quiet. "I'll be here when you are done."

I shut myself in, sucking in a breath before going to the sink to rinse. Toothpaste rimmed my mouth, making me look like a kid who was still working on their technique.

Cute. Really cute, Mallory.

My reflection rolled her eyes at me as I dutifully went about making myself as presentable as possible within a five-minute deadline. When I emerged, Emil was carefully folding my scattered clothes. My stomach flipped.

"Oh god, please don't," I moaned.

His hands continued to work. "I don't mind helping."

Internally, I prayed he hadn't found any discarded underwear. I did a thorough search for anything left behind. When I was sure I had everything except for a few stray bathroom items, Emil patted an impeccably neat pile of clothes.

"Are you good?" he asked.

"Yes," I answered. "Thank you for your help. I'll grab the last of it."

"Sure." He scratched absently at his chin. "I'll move the car and meet you at the bus station lot. What can I take down for you?"

"Nothing. It'll all fit in Bertha."

"Bertha?"

The heat in my face raised to third-degree flames. I pointed halfheartedly to my pack beside him.

He lifted an eyebrow at it, but made no comment. "Okay, see you down there." He hesitated for a moment at the door before he walked out, closing it behind him.

I could practically feel my blood pressure drop when I was alone again. A few deep breaths steadied me. Then I focused on the task at hand. One thing at a time, one step at a time.

I left a heartfelt thank-you note to Ivan on the table, along with a tip. With a pang of sadness, I dropped the key into the lockbox, wishing I could have said goodbye to him in person. My shoes pattered down the familiar path, and I hesitated when I reached the street. I couldn't help taking a final look at the bridge while I was here. I hurried to it, closing my eyes a few times to be certain I had it picture-perfect in my memory. With a sigh, I turned on my heel and retraced my way to the station.

Emil's car sat idling, but he stood at the open rear hatch. He wasn't alone.

Mia.

My steps faltered, watching as he took what appeared to be an intense tongue-lashing from his irate sister. She pointed at the car before shoving the same finger into his chest, then gestured toward town. A few of her words reached me through the gentle breeze, but it didn't matter that they were foreign. Her hands snatched at thin air, emphasizing whatever point she was making quite clearly, even from a distance. Anger and fear melded as one within me. What the hell was her problem with me? And would she make him reconsider?

As she grew still, Emil's arms crossed. His eyebrows rose in a challenge, his words too soft to hear. She shook her head. Not in defeat, but in disbelief. She turned on her heel without another word as she stomped off—of course, straight toward me.

Our eyes met, and the fury in hers was alarming. I wondered if I was in for it next, but her quick stride brought her right beside me, and she simply kept on going. She muttered something unintelligible, but her tone said everything. Annoyance flashed through me, but I quickly bit back the retorts on the tip of my tongue. Lashing out wouldn't help, and she was leaving, so whatever Emil had said to her, it was done, for now.

I drew in a shallow breath, studying the pattern of cobblestones beneath my feet, until I found the courage to look up. He watched me carefully. Even still, the tightness around his eyes released a little when I offered a small smile.

"Hey," he said, shifting a few things in the trunk to make space.

"Hi." I stuffed Bertha in. "Sorry again for the late start." I shifted uncomfortably.

"Don't worry about it." His hand waved dismissively, but he didn't quite meet my gaze.

Elephant meet room.

"Is everything okay?" I asked. "You know...with her?"

He busied himself with organizing the already sorted luggage situation. "Mia is overprotective sometimes. She means well."

"Does she think I'm kidnapping you?" I said with a laugh, trying to lighten the mood.

He lifted a shoulder. "Something like that."

"Didn't she notice we're taking your car?"

He nodded, but didn't elaborate. "Ready?"

Drop it, Mallory, the voice in my head insisted.

"I suppose." Longing moaned in those two words. He looked at me curiously, and I smiled. "I really like it here. It's sad to say goodbye."

His stoic mask wavered slightly. He followed my gaze, staring back at the now-bustling town. It was just another average day for everyone else.

"Yeah." Emil turned away and headed to the driver's side. I held on to the view a moment longer before joining him in the car.

Our road was familiar at first, swerving down the same route we had already taken to the Kravica Nature Park. But soon enough, we passed the turn and found ourselves in new territory.

"Which way are we going?" I had the detailed country map he kept in his car spread across my lap, tracing the tiny lines with my finger.

"I thought we'd head toward Split, then take the coast up along northern Croatia and through Slovenia. From there, Venice is not too far."

I nodded. "Last night I checked my reservation, and it said the desk would be open until 11:00 p.m., so we've got the day to do whatever we want." I folded the map with satisfaction. My job was done. Emil seemed to know the way. Now I could simply go along for the ride. A deep breath filled my chest. I let it out with a content grin.

The car cut through the sharp mountains, their jagged peaks gradually filed down to rolling hills covered in scrub brush. Knee-high brown grasses billowed in a delicate dance, courtesy of the nearing sea breeze. When the edges of the Adriatic finally swam into view, it was somehow more perfect than the filtered photographs in a magazine spread. Twinkling hues of emerald and sapphire melted into taupe as the ocean gave way to sandy beaches combined into nature's artist palette.

"Wow," I breathed.

"Wow," Emil agreed.

The coastal town of Split glimmered as our first official destination together. At this point, we had been driving for two hours and were both grateful for an excuse to stretch our legs and explore.

We parked near the Riva promenade and wandered away from the sea. Beautifully polished stone streets and buildings surrounded us. The flow of the crowd led to a market pitched beneath wide-brimmed trees. Emil pointed out fruits and fish, which were specialties of the Mediterranean coastal region. We sampled a few items, including honey-sweet figs and mouthwatering plums, buying some to take with us in the car for snacks.

From there, we roamed the streets of the old town, stopping first within the towering remains of the Peristyle of Diocletian's Palace. It wasn't hard to picture it in its heyday. People still gathered in the square, much like I assumed they'd done for hundreds of years. Even with the modern clothes and cell phones, the well-preserved ruins catapulted us right into the heart of the city's long history.

Eventually we moved on, braving the harsh sunlight after the shade, following the wide streets into the belly of underground cellars running beneath the old town. Merchant stalls filled the space as we escaped into the cool reprieve of the subterranean market. Many shops showcased jewelry, trinkets, clothing, and artwork, but the vast caverns stretched far beyond the spots of light flooding the entrance.

I perused a stand selling delicate mesh pouches filled with dried flowers and herbs, the variety of scents tantalizing. The woman behind the counter approached after a few moments, pointing out her favorites.

"And this?" I said, picking up one to read the handwritten label: lavender.

"This comes from the island of Hvar," she explained. "They are well known for it."

I weighed the petite bag in my hand. Easily transportable and, a bonus, would make Bertha smell amazing. "I'll take it," I said, handing it over to her with a smile.

"Good choice," she complimented as she rang me up.

Emil had wandered into a different section on my left, which held antiques and other more "manly" souvenirs. When he found me again, it was with my nose practically pressed against the glass display in a jewelry shop. In one case, repurposed spoons and forks were twisted into elegant bracelets and rings, some inlaid with colorful resin or sporting leather bands. The cabinet in front of me showcased handcrafted jewelry straight from a storybook, delicate and light, glittering with rough-cut gemstones.

"I see you've done well," he joked as he eyed my gift bag.

"It's small!" I countered with a laugh. I looked at his hands, but they were empty. "Nothing catch your eye?"

It took a second before he looked away from my face and into the glowing display case. "Which one do you like?"

My nose wrinkled. I didn't need anything else, though the prices were more than reasonable. "They're all pretty, but I'm just looking to look."

The salesperson's shoulders slumped.

Emil leaned over the glass countertop. "That one?"

How had he guessed?

It was a silver necklace, the twisted metal forming the pendant as thin as twine. It looped around the chain into a dewdrop shape, and, at its center, tiny crystal gems surrounded a dainty pearl.

I shrugged. "Maybe."

The merchant stood straight again.

"But I already got something," I insisted. "I don't want to buy too much. We still have a ways to go." I spun on the spot, moving toward a tunnel I hadn't ventured down yet.

Emil followed me, but he kept fidgeting as I moved from a stall with purses, then to another with sun hats. As I sifted through an array of beautiful scarves, I glanced up, hidden behind my eyelashes. His eyes were locked on a wicker basket in a blank stare, clearly bored.

"Go ahead and look around," I urged him.

He jumped a little before he looked at me, his face sheepish. "Are you sure?"

"We can't get too lost. If I can't find you, we can meet at the stairs."

"All right."

When we reconvened at the sun-drenched staircase, his hands were once again empty.

"Still no luck?" I asked.

"Not today."

We ascended to the street level, the brightness blinding after the dark labyrinth, but it was the late afternoon heat that pulled us to a stop. Behind me, Emil's stomach grumbled. I smirked, and he ducked his head in embarrassment.

"Should we find food?" I suggested.

"Probably a good idea."

Full-fledged restaurants lining the streets bursted with tourists, so we wandered farther outside the town center. Eventually, Emil spotted a takeout window selling cevapčići, which it turned out were mouthwatering sausages tucked into a warm, soft pita. Served with it was a roasted red pepper sauce, which added a bright zing to the rich meat.

With our hunger satiated, the heat was now our immediate adversary.

"Want to head to the harbor?" Emil's body shifted before I answered, but I followed eagerly.

I swiped my hand across my forehead. It wasn't just the heat. The humidity was stifling.

I jerked my chin at the sea. "I want to dunk into that and not get out until nightfall," I quipped with a laugh.

The ocean dazzled beneath the sun slipping lazily toward the horizon. Along the shore, we joined the crowd strolling the bone-white promenade at a relaxed pace, breathing in the briny air.

"Can we sit?" Emil asked after a bit, stopping in a narrow patch of dappled shade.

"Yes, please," I agreed, plopping down on the warm, bright walkway.

We settled on the ledge, our feet dangling over the water. A refreshing breeze wafted off the surface, occasional gusts spritzing us with salty drops.

The setting was bliss now with the puff of wind. The view was hard to abandon, and we lingered longer than intended. When we had finally said our silent goodbyes to Split, we headed back to the car and continued our journey along the shores of the Adriatic.

Despite the late hour, we stopped often to revel in the quaint beauty of the villages and admire the pristine white-sand beaches. Fluffy clouds moved at an impressive pace as we turned the corner into night, barely on the edge of leaving Croatia and entering Slovenia. There, thick trees and lush undergrowth lined the roads as we wove inland for the first time in hours. It felt like we had just passed one border before we reached the next, arriving in Italy before I could even fathom having already driven through Slovenia. The countries were all so close to each another, tied up together into a perfect gift.

Darkness closed in on all sides. The sleepy towns and rural roads blended outside of time and space. No indications other than the rare street sign pointed to our location. Eventually, my mind started to wander, swept away into the night.

CHAPTER THIRTEEN

OUR LEISURELY PACE THROUGH Croatia had taken its toll, and we arrived late in Venice. By the time Emil parked the car in Piazzale Roma and wakened me, night had fallen hours ago. We set out for the hotel, which I'd marked on my phone near the Rialto Bridge.

On slow, stiff legs and with several wrong turns, it was at least a half hour before we finally stumbled upon it. Warm light spilled out the narrow entryway, my tired feet eagerly crossing the threshold. The tiny space featured a deep mahogany counter, behind which waited a hawk-eyed receptionist.

"Buonasera," she said.

"Buonasera," I parroted back.

"Reservation?"

"Yes, under Roth. Mallory Roth."

Her fingers sped across the keyboard. "Three nights?"

"Yes."

She nodded, leafing through sheets of paper.

"I need to book a room as well," Emil spoke up.

Her hands kept working as her eyes slid to him. "We are full."

"Oh." I bit my lip, grimacing at him. How stupid. Why hadn't I thought to call ahead?

"That's all right," Emil said quickly. "I can find someplace else."

The woman's gaze darted to the clock. "It's summer, late at night. It will be hard."

"Do you have any recommendations?" I asked.

She sighed. "No, but your room has two twin beds. For twenty-five euros more, he can take it. We include complimentary breakfast."

Nerves spiked my heart rate, but there wasn't another option.

"No, that's—" Emil started.

"All right," I cut in.

The woman was quick, adding the details to my reservation and printing out a receipt.

"Are you sure?" Emil whispered.

"Yes," I said, my hand trembling a little as I signed the bill. He slipped the woman the extra money, and I gave her a tight smile as I handed over my paperwork.

I barely heard her as she spoke about nearby attractions, when breakfast would be available, and the checkout time. I scooped up the information pamphlets she offered with the room key.

We walked upstairs to the second floor, pivoting in the cramped space to avoid hitting the picture frames decorating the walls. I stopped in front of number twelve, working the antique key into the lock.

"Thank you," Emil said softly.

"Of course," I answered before letting the door swing inward.

The room was lovely, splashed in swaths of pastel colors. Old-fashioned floral wallpaper added to the cheerful ambiance. The honeyed ceiling reflected light from the upward-facing sconces, which hung on either side of the beds. Lacy curtains draped around the opening to a balcony. Shining beyond through the French doors waited Venice in all its romantic intrigue.

I moved inside, past the bathroom, and dropped Bertha to the ground. She landed with a thud at the foot of the bed closest to the entrance.

"You don't want the bed by the window?" Emil offered as he followed and gazed out across the balcony. "It's quite a view."

"That's okay. I'll probably sleep better away from the light." I swept a lock of hair behind my ear as I busied my hands with my toiletries.

"Are you hungry? We could go get something before turning in."

I let out a small breath, meeting his gaze gratefully. "Starved."

Night lights flickered off the undulating waters of the canal outside our hotel. A steady, but not packed, flow of fellow late-night wanderers guided us around the corner. There, waiters bussed tables along the canal edge, one restaurant stacked after another.

"There are so many," I said with wonder.

"And more where they came from, I'd bet," Emil said, smiling.

"Do you want to look at menus or just pick one?"

"Ladies' choice."

I grinned, moving toward one with a charming green canopy.

After we were seated, the waiter promptly approached. "Buonasera," he said, handing over menus. "If you have any questions, let me know. We have two specials: the Risotto al Nero di Seppia, which is a risotto with cuttlefish and ink sauce, and our Fegato alla Veneziana, which is liver cooked our Venetian way. Would you like anything to drink to start?"

"Wine with dinner, I think," Emil said, "but one moment to decide our order first, please." The waiter nodded and disappeared. "What sounds good?"

"Everything," I laughed. "The risotto seems interesting. I've heard about it before. I might try that." I closed my menu with finality.

"Hmm," Emil mused, returning to the list of delectable dishes. Eventually the waiter returned, took our order, poured the wine, and left us to our people-watching. Gondolas danced up and down the canal, some with dangling lanterns like a trail of fireflies over the water. One passed close by, and the gondolier bellowed out a soulful melody.

"What do you think of those?" I asked. "Cool or touristy?"

Emil looked at me from behind his wineglass and shrugged. "Both."

"When in Rome, right?"

"I suppose," he said, grinning at my lame joke.

As we waited for our food to arrive, we chatted absentmindedly about our wish lists while in Venice. I added the gondola and St. Mark's Basilica and its square to mine, then turned it on him. "You?"

"I'm most interested in just exploring the city. It's a marvel, how the structures float."

"Floating structures?" I repeated, holding back a smirk.

He saw it anyway. "Did you know that they are built on wood? Big logs stuck into the seabed like toothpicks. That's what they built the foundation on."

"Wood?" It was a surprise. Mostly that the buildings had lasted for so long.

"The salt water hardens them," he said as if reading my mind. "They are being changed for more modern materials as the buildings are repaired, but it is amazing."

I stared across the water at the rainbow of colors the building faces painted, each leaning against the other as if for moral support. It did affect how you saw them, seemingly normal above the surface, apparently anything but from beneath.

"I'd like that. Let's get lost." I raised my glass to his, and he met it with a clink.

"Here we are," the waiter said as he approached and gracefully swept our plates onto the table. My eyes popped at the jet-black dish before me. Grinning like a kid on Halloween, I checked out Emil's carbonara before I noticed him staring worryingly at my meal.

"Is there anything else I can get you?" the waiter asked.

"I think we're good, thank you," I replied, and we were alone once more.

"You really want to eat that?" He eyed the pitch-black color with distaste.

In response, I scooped some into my mouth, my eyes closing of their own volition. It was creamy, pleasantly briny, and deliciously sweet.

"Mmm," I moaned.

"You're kidding?" Emil raised a brow.

I smiled. "Nope!"

His mouth gaped as he watched my reaction.

"Try some," I urged, holding out my plate.

"No thanks." He busied himself with his pasta.

"Emil, are you afraid?"

"Yes."

"Why? I'm not dying, and it's delicious!" I loaded another spoonful and held it out as if I was trying to entice a toddler with an airplane.

Subtly, he pushed my water glass closer.

"Your teeth are the same color."

My grin disappeared immediately. "No!"

"Yes."

I swished some water around before asking, "Better?"

He finished a mouthful of pasta as he nodded. "Yes, but it'll just be back in a moment."

"I don't care," I decided, eating the bite he refused. "It's worth it." Purposefully, I smiled wide after swallowing.

His expression was slightly disgusted even as he chuckled.

We were both ravenous, but the mouthwatering meal poised a difficult decision—to scarf or to savor? We managed both. By the time we'd finished our main courses, we were stuffed and opted to share a plate of tiramisu.

"Hmm," I breathed with my last bite. "Amazing."

"Yes, it is."

I caught him looking away. Propping my head up on one hand, I followed his gaze, basking in the soft scent of the sea in the air. Sleek boats mixed with the gondolas, their lights' reflections skipping across the waves hypnotically. There was a warmth to the scene, even as the cool breeze raised goosebumps along my bare arms. I relished the moment, closing my eyes and listening to the sounds of the water sloshing against the dock and the distant melody of music.

"Mallory? Wake up."

My head jerked. Wow, had I really just dozed off?

"Sorry." I rubbed furiously at my eyes.

"It's all right," Emil said, straight-faced. "I know I'm not great company." I laughed, and he cracked a smile.

"I'm dead," I admitted.

"Me, too." He stood, offering his hand. My forehead crinkled. It was such an old-fashioned gesture, but somehow it'd never felt artificial or forced when he did it. Slowly, I slid my hand across his calloused palm. His warm fingers encased mine, and we walked hand in hand to the hotel as though it were the most natural thing in the world, like we had done it a thousand times before.

Then the bedroom door shut behind me.

The two beds were innocent enough, yet my stomach squirmed all the same. We readied ourselves for sleep, passing by each other awkwardly for turns in the bathroom. When he pulled the curtains closed, the gossamer only dimmed the flickering light outside to a dull throb.

"Good night," he said as he slid beneath the covers.

"Night." I rolled over to face the wall, taking steady breaths to calm my racing pulse. Almost instantly, the room filled with Emil's soft snores.

Knowing Emil was lost in slumberland alleviated some of my tension. As tired as I was, though, I wasn't sleepy anymore. Carefully, I flipped over on the creaky bed. His face was shadowed, the light from behind turning him into a silhouette. But as my eyes compensated, his relaxed mouth, worry-free brow, and delicately fluttering eyelids became clear.

It's strange how people asleep look so unlike their everyday selves. Is it as simple as unconsciousness stealing away their cares, joys, and burdens, transforming the person into a blank canvas, the purest version of their physical selves? Or is it more the things that make them *them* are wiped away? Their signature smile, the perk of attitude, the life behind their waking eyes?

Emil's mouth and nose twitched like he'd smelled something particularly foul. I stifled a giggle.

I watched his uninhibited reactions, insatiably curious about his dreams. As my own attention grew foggy with an irresistible, drowsy pull, I promised myself to ask him in the morning.

My mind wandered lazily across the wonders of the day and luxurious evening, committing to memory the feel of the Adriatic swishing over my toes, the dry heat of the sun reflecting off polished stone, the pungent scent of ocean in the canals, Emil's skin brushing against my palm...

His thumb skimming my lips, fingertips along my throat, sharp nails pressing into my hips.

My breathing hitched, my body clenching, ready to spring.

Hot breath fanned across my collarbone, trailing a path down to my chest.

"Please, don't."

Heavy hands gripped my arms, holding me down.

I struggled wildly. "Let go!"

"Shh..."

Angry tears ran fiery rivets down my cheeks.

"Mallory."

My name sounded sweet, making it all the more perverse.

"Get off!" I jerked, trying to lash out.

"Mallory, wake up!"

My wrists were clenched between two strong hands. I opened my eyes to darkness, except for the streaks of moonlight searing across the whimsical wallpaper. I gave another violent tug, and the hands disappeared. I kicked out wildly, using the momentum to fly off the bed and into the bathroom. I flung the door closed, my back bracing against anyone coming in.

"Mallory?" Fear strained his words. "Mallory!"

Panic choked me, even as my dream began to dissipate. I took a few breaths. "It's nothing, I'm fine. Go back to sleep."

A thump and slide came from the other side. "Lock the door."

"What?" My voice trembled.

"Do it."

I twisted on the floor, reaching up to flick on the light to find the old-fashioned bolt. I slid it into place, the solidness of it comforting. "Okay."

A beat, then, "Are you all right?"

I hugged myself, holding in a sob. "Yeah, it was only a dream. Go back to sleep."

"Stop saying that." What I imagined was his head thudded against the door. "You need to tell me what happened to you or this isn't going to work. It wasn't just a dream. I know the difference. Since the night I met you, I..." His words faltered, laced with a sorrowful ache.

The throb inside me deepened. This wasn't fair to him. But if he knew the truth? Would I be something pitiful to him? Would he be as disappointed in me as I was that I hadn't been brave enough, that I'd simply run away? Or would he think I was blowing things out of proportion, just being dramatic?

On the other hand, I'd chosen to trust him, time and time again. He hadn't let me down so far. *One more time*, I prayed. *Please*.

"Okay." It was a little word. It sounded as small as I felt.

"I went from Marseille to Mostar," I began haltingly, "but that hadn't been the original plan." I swallowed hard. "Something happened there. Or...someone, I guess."

Silence waited as I paused, but it wasn't empty. I could feel his presence through the barrier. Steady, secure.

"The man who ran the apartment I was staying at," I continued, sucking in a breath, "he offered to take me out and show me around. I thought it would be fun, to see things from a local's point of view. And it was, for a while."

My heart hammered in my chest so loudly I could barely hear myself.

I rewatched in my mind's eye as he let himself into the apartment. I felt the too-familiar touch of his arm slinging across my back.

How could I have been so blind?

Disgust twisted in my gut, and I pushed on, anger lacing my voice. "We were at the beach and he—he tried to..."

Tried to what?

The same conflicting thoughts washed back over me again, fresh as the night it had happened.

He'd kissed me. So what?

But then he'd followed me. If he followed me, he wasn't just going to let it go...let me go.

Right?

I battled against the confusing swirl, skipping over panic to the release.

"I fought him off and made it onto a bus. When I got back to the apartment, I was packing my things, and I heard..."

I shook my head, trying to joggle the memories into the correct order.

"No, I *saw* him through the peephole in the door." I nodded to myself. Yes, that was right.

Once again, I could feel Bertha pressed between my shoulders as I hurried out of the apartment, and the surge of pain as I jumped the last stretch to the ground.

"I barely made it out before he came in." I shuddered at the memory of his dark gaze, his silhouette looking at me from above. "I went down the fire escape and I just...only I ran to the airport. I didn't know what else to do. I could've..."

I stuttered to a stop, hanging my head. I took a moment, my mind flying through all the things I could've done, but didn't. Because I was too weak, too scared...too selfish.

"I just left."

The silence draped like a blanket along the other side of the door.

"Emil?"

"I'm here," he answered softly.

I bit my lip as the quiet stretched. "Can I open the door now?"

He shuffled to his feet, his shadow hovering beneath the gap in the door as he moved away. I stopped at the sink first, sloshing my face with a slap of cold water. One breath in, one breath out. The fluffy towel swung limply on the drying rack as I pulled back the lock. The door creaked open, revealing him leaning against my bed.

The heels of his hands pressed deep dents into the edge of the mattress, his long legs extended straight out and crossed at the ankles. At first, I thought he was relaxed. But as I stepped from the bathroom, the harsh light threw his body into sharp relief. His muscles were tensed, veins popping along the insides of his arms and the side of his neck. When his eyes finally met mine, they were a flat black.

"Are you okay?" I asked, suddenly wary of him.

He nodded.

I couldn't quite decipher his attitude. "Are you mad at me?"

"Mad at you?"

I lifted a shoulder. "I am, so I'd understand if you are."

He didn't even appear to breathe, he was so still. Then he pushed off the bed, closing the distance between us down to a foot. A shiver ran along my spine, rooting me to the spot. The same deep V I'd seen when he talked me down off the bridge formed once more between his eyebrows. Slowly, he raised his hand. It stretched toward me, stopping just shy of my face, and waited.

"Why would I be mad at you?" he whispered.

I came back to life, my head tilting so his hand grazed against my cheek. I closed my eyes, sighing into his gentle touch. Relief washed through me, warming every icy chink in my armor. My hand covered his, the other lightly clasping his wrist.

"Why are you mad at yourself?" His tone held a note of bitterness.

My eyes drifted open. "Because I didn't see it coming." A breath shuddered from me. "And I didn't fight."

I could've done something. Stayed. Reported it. Fixed it. But instead,

I'd run. I'd played along to gain an advantage...and then I'd just fled. I shook my head. Naive coward.

Emil's other hand came up to cup my face as he took another step forward. "Yes, you did. You *did* fight." His forehead pressed to mine. "You were scared. Don't you dare feel guilty for it." Tears stung my eyes as the rage coursing through him hit me. "I'm so sorry."

"You have nothing to be sorry for," I countered.

His head shook. "No," he agreed, "but I still wish it hadn't happened. For that, I am sorry."

My heart gave a painful squeeze. "Thank you." Hesitantly, I pulled close, laying my head on his chest, and circled my arms around his lower back. Slowly, he followed suit, one hand stroking my hair down the back of my neck.

"Do you want me to go?"

I stiffened. "What? No."

"I can sleep in the car. You need to rest."

He pulled away, but I grabbed his hand.

"You helped me from the moment we met. And it's all you've done since." I swallowed past the knot in my throat. I didn't have a right to ask, but I didn't want to let him go. "Please stay. I can't promise I won't dream again or freak out, but know it's not because of you. In fact, if it hadn't been for you, I don't think I *could've* slept."

And in this place, this room? I'd grown accustomed to Mostar with its sounds and smells and spaces, even in just a matter of days. Here, it was all new and strange again, somehow foreboding in the night, despite its beauty.

His jaw locked, but he gave a nod. He padded back to his bed.

My stomach twisted. "Emil?"

"Yes?" He stopped fixing his covers.

"Will you...I mean, you don't have to, but...will you lie with me? Until I fall asleep?" It was stupid, maybe even selfish, but his touch was a tonic.

He peered at me. "That's what you want?"

I nodded mutely.

He rose, and we climbed onto the bed facing each other. I curled tighter, unsure where to look.

He sighed. "Turn over."

I did as I was told.

"If you want me to stop, all you have to do is say it."

I concentrated on breathing slowly as he shifted closer, waiting for his arms to close around me, but they didn't. Instead, his fingers worked across my scalp and through my hair in slow, soothing strokes. Carefully, they drew lower, pressing the tight muscles along my neck and shoulders, urging me to relax.

"Is this okay?"

"Mmm," I murmured peacefully.

With every prod and press, each stroke and release, my body began to release its tension. My mind went graciously blank, losing myself in the feel of his hands. His lower body spooned around me, warm and secure.

"Can you sleep?"

Some garbled version of yes was as good as he was getting out of me.

"Sleep, Mallory. You're safe."

And, mercifully, I did.

CHAPTER FOURTEEN

I WOKE NOT WITH a start, but with a luxurious, deep-boned sense of calm. I had slept. Like, *really* slept. I grinned goofily as I stretched, an unladylike grunt sounding from my chest. And then I remembered I was not the only one able to hear it.

With my senses on high alert, I rolled onto my back, peering sneakily through half-closed eyes. But Emil was not by my side. Nor, indeed, in his own bed. My fingers curled around the sheet, pulling it up to my chest as I knelt forward to peek into the open bathroom.

Nothing.

I looked down and spotted a folded note on the nightstand between our beds.

I went to breakfast, it read. *I will be there or close by outside when you want to join me.*

A soft smile tugged at my lips as I set the note back in place. I jumped out of bed and stepped onto the balcony, rubbing sleep from my eyes. Already, tourists flocked the narrow streets below. Boats churned a foamy trail as they darted through the canals. The summer sun tickled my skin just before the humidity whacked me in the face. I spun back into the relatively cool room and snapped the doors closed, drawing the curtains, too, for good measure.

The tousled sheets reminded me of my nightmare, of the secret I'd shared, and falling asleep in Emil's arms. I took a moment to collect myself, to shower off just a little of the mortification from last night down the drain. I towel-dried my hair roughly, threw on some mascara, and donned a flowy dress. Steam still clung in a sheen across my skin as I made my way downstairs into the simple, quaint dining room. One look around told me Emil wasn't there. I piled together a plate of pastries at random, accepting an offer of espresso from the roving waiter. I scarfed it all down, suddenly eager to go out and explore.

I slung my bag over my body as I stepped out into the brilliant sunlight. It didn't take long before I spotted Emil to my left. He was speaking with a family, a man and woman in their early forties, with two disinterested-looking, gangly boys in tow. I leaned against the edge of an alleyway, keeping out of sight to watch.

Emil's face was set in that now-familiar expression, landing somewhere between concentration and curmudgeon. His head turned to follow the woman's pointing as she clearly asked for directions. He gave a small shrug as he spoke, shifting from one foot to the other. Then he turned toward the smallest boy, who sported a bright green jersey. Emil pointed to it and the boy's face lit up as he spun to show him the name on the back. Whatever they were chatting about—soccer, I assumed—relegated the woman's request for directions to the background.

But the parents didn't seem to mind. Their group all smiled and chatted until the woman gently ushered the boys forward. Emil gave them a genuine smile as they walked away, but it disappeared as he was left alone again.

He searched in the direction of our hotel, but didn't spot me. He turned back and looked out across the water, his posture shifting from relaxed to stiff. His hands rested in his pockets as he eyed the gondolas parked as densely in the canal as the scooters were up on the street. As I made toward him, he moved in a small circle, wandering along the walkway at an unhurried pace.

He stopped abruptly, his shoulders loosening, and I paused, following his gaze to a scaffolded building. The fascination grew on his face as his head tilted, scanning up its side. Suddenly, his eyes dropped and whipped toward me, as though he finally felt he was being watched.

I blushed at being caught, covering my embarrassment with a smile and wave as I jump-started my feet again.

"Hi," I said as we met in the middle, tucking a wild piece of hair back behind my ear.

"Hello." He watched my fingers before his eyes studied my face. "How did you sleep?"

My stomach swooped. "All right. You?"

He nodded, then gestured toward the city. "What would you like to do first today?"

"Hmm, I know we talked about going to the church, the gondolas, all the *touristy* stuff," I said, setting up the tease, "but if you're going to get mistaken for a local, I don't know that you'll want to be seen with me."

His mouth opened and closed for a moment, completely at a loss.

"I saw you with the family," I gave in. "Nobody's asking me for directions. I never pass under the radar!"

Understanding lit his face. "It's the hair."

"There are blonde Italians."

"Then the pale skin."

"Again, not all Italians are super tan."

"And the clothes."

My eyes shot down to my dress. "What's wrong with what I wear?"

"Nothing." The shake of his head clearly bemoaned "women" before he chuckled. "And then there's your voice."

"Well, that's just going a step too far," I said curtly. "How can you not appreciate my *incredibile accento*?" I spoke the last bit in my worst attempt at an Italian accent, accompanied with an over-the-top flourish, and received an eye-roll from a passerby.

"I don't think that's right."

"Shut up, it's incredibile!" I tried again, managing to sound even worse.

"Incredibly bad," he chuckled. "But honestly, I don't think it's any of those things. Well, maybe the accent."

"What, then?"

"Americans, you have a"—he paused, trying to put his finger on it—"a certain attitude about you. It's easy to see."

"Attitude?" I wrinkled my nose. "A bad one?"

He gave a soft sigh. "It depends on the person. You? No...but still obvious."

I lifted my hands, resigned. "So be it."

"Just don't start wearing long white socks with sandals, and we'll be okay," he said, his voice playfully dark.

I snorted. "Not on your life."

We moved toward the centerpiece of the area, the Rialto Bridge. I glanced in either direction as we walked up its arch. From atop its vantage point, Venice sprawled invitingly, ripe with possibility.

"It's beautiful."

Emil rested his forearms against the ledge. "More bridges," he commented.

I chuckled. "I have a feeling there's quite a few more to come."

"In a city full of canals?" he joked. "They wouldn't dare."

As we stared out at the city considering our options, the rising call of a man perched at the stern of a boat caught our attention. His powerful voice carried up to us, his English heavily accented.

"Visit the beautiful Venetian islands. Only a few seats left. You don't want to miss this day at sea!"

I nudged Emil with my elbow, pointing toward him. "What about that?"

He followed my finger, listening to the man's sales pitch. "Sure," he agreed.

We hurried down the slope to the other side of the canal, slowing our pace as we neared the boat. Emil held out a hand, warning me with a look. He led the way in front of me, his tall frame earning the attention of the man.

He leapt up at our approach. "Signore, welcome. I am Capitan Zanetti." He bent into a theatrical bow. When he straightened, his gaze shot past Emil toward me with a devilish grin. "Take the bella signora out with us and win her heart." He spoke in a pointed, loud whisper to Emil, his ploy obviously meant to include me. I ducked my head to hide my smile.

Emil's chin jutted. "How much?"

The man feigned surprise. "Could you really put a price on her affections?"

"Try me."

The captain's jaw tightened, then he curled a finger to bring Emil in closer. Their harsh whispers bit the air as they spoke under breath. Emil sighed, looking at me as if to question whether I was worth it. I cocked an eyebrow and, hidden from the captain, Emil winked before turning his serious expression back on. With a solemn frown, he shook the man's hand.

"Come aboard, signora!" Zanetti called, jovial once more. He took one of my hands while Emil held the other. The boat's deck was slippery, but I wasn't so much of a dunce as to fall into the sea just yet, especially with the boat still securely moored.

"Well, did you get what you wanted?" I whispered in Emil's ear as we took our seats alongside a handful of other passengers.

Emil kept his face unreadable as the captain readied the boat. "I would have taken his first price, so we did well."

"Kudos!" I congratulated him, holding up my hand for a high five. He clapped it as Zanetti gracefully slid out into traffic and steered to the mouth of the canal.

Our initial stop was the island of Murano. The group rapidly dispersed from the boat, feathering out along the main canal or side streets as Zanetti shouted out at us, "Be back by eleven o'clock!"

"Any preference?" Emil offered, glancing left, then right.

"Not really."

We followed one another, exploring aimlessly, at ease. Well, at least I was.

Emil's hands were once again stuffed in his pockets, walking close by my side.

"What's wrong?" I finally prompted.

"Hmm?"

"You're all..." I waved generally at him up and down.

He followed my hand, looking himself over. "I don't..."

"You're all stiff, like a robot. We're literally walking around one of the most drool-worthy locations, one that people have on their once-in-a-lifetime bucket lists, and you're acting like you're on the way to get a prostate exam."

His eyes flew wide with shock before he laughed, his shoulders drooping. "I'm not used to this, I guess."

"Being in Venice? Yeah, me neither."

"Not just Venice. Being somewhere..."

I spotted the problem immediately.

"Other," I finished for him.

How well I'd known that feeling. But while the same notion had excited me, I'd been prepared for it, planned for it, counted on it, in fact. The idea of this trip had been sprung upon him. It didn't matter that he'd admitted to wanting to travel. Dreaming about something and walking those steps were two entirely different things, and he'd had no time to mentally prepare for what it would be like.

The crowds, new smells, unfamiliar languages...they were still culture shocks, even in their beauty. Whether coming from sleepy Blackthorn or peaceful Mostar, the hustle and bustle of the sheer quantity of tourists, the boisterous Italian locals, and the strange settings were a lot to take in.

"I get it," I finally said out loud. "But you didn't seem so worried this morning when you were with that family."

"No," he admitted. "I was distracted."

"So I just have to distract you, huh?" I toyed, my tone devilish.

He raised an eyebrow. "That won't help."

"No?" I said, pouting, then dropped the sugar-sweet voice and laid a hand on his muscled forearm. "Don't worry, I'll protect you."

He shook his head with exasperation. "Said the tiny American girl."

"But you forget," I said. "I've got *attitude*."

"I didn't say it was the kind that would make people afraid."

"Do I scare you?" I teased.

His body tensed again as my fingers brushed up his skin, goosebumps appearing in a trail left by my touch. But then he swallowed and held his arm out to me. I linked mine with his, and he shot me a grin before responding, "Constantly."

We wandered past shop after shop displaying dazzling glass, from giant sculptures to delicate figurines set among the glassware and shimmering vases. At one bend, I noticed a group enter a building through a pair of sliding doors. Looking in, I spotted a master in action and crept into the workspace. The cavernous room was dim except for where a skilled glassmaker worked his craft with deceptive ease. People sat on benches lined around the room, transfixed, as though they were watching a stage play. Emil settled by my side as the man pulled here and cut there, the molten glass radiating like a miniature sun.

I couldn't be sure how long we stared in awe, but four pieces later, I felt Emil shift next to me as he glanced down at his watch and flinched. "We need to go," he whispered urgently.

I checked my phone. We had five minutes to get to the boat.

I muttered a curse and ducked out after Emil. The sunlight burned across my skin. In retrospect, I probably should have packed my tube of sunscreen.

"Which way was it?" I twisted on the spot, nothing looking familiar now that the crowds had grown exponentially.

"Here." Emil guided me to the left, and we set off in a hurried walk. The town had come alive with both tourists and locals. Now we were crammed in like sheep with the rest of the flock. Ahead of me, Emil looked back, his expression worried.

"I don't think we're going to make it," he called above the thrum of the crowd.

"They won't leave without us," I scoffed.

He looked at me with an arched brow. "Take my hand." I did as he said. For a brief moment, my skin tingled pleasantly. Then, I was being yanked forward in what seemed to have become a pattern.

"Emil," I complained as he wove a sharp path through the thick sea of people. A few threw angry glares at the back of his head before turning them on me. Eventually, I gave up tugging and let him pull me along. At least I was tall enough to peer over people's heads when the boat came into view.

"See?" I called. "They haven't gone anywhere."

Which was when they began towing in the ropes.

"Oh, I see all right," Emil said, smugness still managing to seep into his anxious voice. Suddenly, he dropped my hand. "Run!"

Competitiveness flooded my body, triggered by some animalistic need. With a laugh, I pumped my arms, legs working double time, each of us picking our own line through the crowd.

"Last one there's a rotten egg!" I called as I came up on his left side. His look of surprise lasted an instant, allowing me precious seconds for a head start. But his long legs moved in fluid, graceful strides, quickly gaining any lost ground. Visitors now ducked out of our path with equal parts annoyance and amusement on their passing faces.

I couldn't remember the last time I'd run just for the fun of it. I was flying. The hot air turned cool with the breeze of my speed. My feet pounded a sure, steady rhythm beneath me, my equivalent of the *flap-flap* of wings. I chanced a look over my shoulder as the mob thinned, but Emil was already right there. He tossed me a sly grin before turning his attention back to the boat.

"Wait!" he shouted, waving his hands overhead.

"Wait for us!" I joined in, but my voice didn't carry like his. The pinch in my chest eased when a fellow passenger pointed out our ridiculous spectacle and turned to someone out of sight.

We sped around the corner, still at full speed, Emil cutting it finer and gaining an extra foot at the last second. His hands slammed against the hull where the annoyed captain waited to help us on board. He muttered under his breath in Italian, shaking his head.

As I lead the way to two empty seats, I caught the eye of the person who had spotted us and gave them a grateful wave. I still couldn't speak as I sat and gulped for air.

"So, what do I win?" Emil asked as he slid down next to me, drawing in long, slow, steady breaths. Was he trying to rub it in, or was I just that hopelessly weak?

"The glory," I managed to wheeze.

"Hmm." His lips pressed into a line as he judged his prize dubiously, but he quickly let the facade drop, leaning against the railing as we pulled out again to sea.

Soon, the candy-colored buildings of the island of Burano were greeting us with a smile. Capitan Zanetti, on the other hand, turned a scowl on me and Emil for an extra beat as he reminded the entire group of our next departure time. I grinned innocently, pushing Emil ahead of me off the boat.

"Would you mind?" I asked, holding out my phone to Emil for a picture.

He took it, glancing around. "Where?"

I led him away from our slowly dispersing group to the bright-green backdrop of one building, which perfectly contrasted my dress. I couldn't help my grin. Everything was so cheerful, even me.

After Emil had taken a few, I said, "Okay, your turn." I held out my hand for his phone.

He hesitated. "No, it's okay."

"C'mon," I pressed. "You have to have some photographic evidence. Otherwise you won't have them to look back on when you go senile."

He snorted. "Nice."

"Honest," I countered. "Now give it over."

"The camera on my phone doesn't work," he admitted.

"Oh no," I murmured, letting my hand drop.

"It's okay," he said. "Asja has been after me to get a new one, but everything else still works. And I never did use the camera much, anyway." As he spoke, he pulled an ancient flip phone from his pocket, turning it over thoughtfully in his hand.

"Emil," I laughed, "I think you are due for an upgrade."

"Maybe," he agreed halfheartedly, "but I believe in a certain value of things. Too much is disposable these days."

It was commendable, though it didn't help in this current predicament. He couldn't go the whole trip with nothing.

"Okay," I said, my voice stern. "Stand over there." I pointed in the opposite direction from where my picture had been taken, this one with an ocean backdrop to complement the sunny yellow and deep-blue buildings along the canal's entrance.

"No, really, it's fine." Was that embarrassment flushing his cheeks?

My hand rested stubbornly on my hip. "You might as well give in now, because I won't stop."

His grimace was not unlike a kid facing their most hated food.

I shooed him toward the spot. He slouched over, hands awkwardly linked behind his back, but his wince didn't quite meet his eyes.

Playing along, I frowned and called, "Smile!"

As soon as the corners of his mouth lifted, I clicked the photo.

"Perfect!" I said as he slunk toward me. "One down, a million to go."

He sighed heavily, but I detected a flicker of gratitude.

That he hated having his picture taken was clear. Not uncommon, but the last look he'd tried to hide told a different story.

I grinned. "Come here."

He stood up straighter, moving closer to me with a little less reluctance. "Another?" he asked, a pleasant lilt in his voice.

"Your arms are longer than mine," I said, pretending to struggle to hold the phone out far enough for a selfie. "Could you?"

He took it and twisted the angle just right. His other arm curved around my shoulder, his fingers light on my heated skin. "Ready?"

I snuggled into his side and, at the last second, squished him in close. "Now!"

At my sharp command, he snapped the photo out of pure reflex.

I pulled away, holding out my hand expectantly. He handed my phone over, and I brought up the image. My heart squeezed. By catching him off-guard, there was an innocence to his face I'd never seen there before. His smile was full, surprise brightening his eyes. He appeared younger, lighter.

"Can I see?" He looked over my shoulder, and his mouth opened ever so slightly.

"Keeper?"

When he looked away from my phone, his expression was warm. "It's perfect."

The rest of the afternoon was full of exploration and delicious bites—pastries, sampling a variety of cheeses and meats, and gelato. Always more gelato. I found myself buying little knickknacks, touristy trinkets to treasure as mementos. We even made it back well within the time limit for the boat, much to the relief of the captain.

The lazy return ride to Venice grew choppier as the light crested toward the horizon. The captain kept eyeing the sky with worry. I followed his gaze, but the few puffy clouds seemed innocent enough.

I was sorely mistaken.

CHAPTER FIFTEEN

WE MADE IT SAFELY off the boat, but the clouds opened by dinnertime and rain pelted the roof throughout the night. Water cascaded from our balcony down to the stone pathway and into the canal. The next morning rose slate-gray, but dry. At least, for a while.

Emil and I walked to St. Mark's Square, stepping over puddles as the sun fought the ever-darkening clouds. By noon, it had lost.

Perhaps fittingly as we exited St. Mark's cathedral, the heavens let loose with a torrent, the raindrops pelting the hood of my jacket. I pushed it back enough to raise my eyebrows in question at Emil.

"Should we go to the hotel?" he asked.

"I suppose so." My heart sank. "Maybe it'll let up later."

By the halfway point, our shoulders were soddened, our pants drenched from the knees down. Screw it, if I was to be cold and wet, I might as well enjoy it. I grabbed Emil and pulled him down a random street.

"Where are you going?"

"*We're* going exploring!"

"Aren't you cold?" he asked, clearly trying for an excuse to head to the room.

"Yep."

He shook his head, but let me drag him along for a change.

Down a narrow canal, a row of disheveled buildings sat ruined in their scaffold cages. Emil slowed, his gentle tug guiding me to a stop. A conglomeration of tools and equipment waited abandoned beside an entrance's doors, paintbrushes dripping diluted rainbows into buckets. The weathered exteriors, once surely grand and rich, waited for their chance to return to their former glory.

"I wonder what they'll do with these?" I mused.

"Depends on the damage, I imagine. Probably restore them if they can...tear them down, if not."

I frowned. "Really?"

Ahead of me, Emil stopped one building farther and pointed to the home across the way. A hand-painted sign was set on its door. I stepped back as I read it.

DEMOLIRE, it said, surrounded by a slashing red X.

"That's sad."

"It is," he agreed.

I shifted to the alcove of the first house, watching Emil. I couldn't quite gauge his expression. His gaze roved the faded paint and weathered wood as he slowly moved toward me. It was as if he was doing calculations in his head, measuring between the eaves, down this wall, the width of the fogged window.

"What's going on up there?" I asked. I meant through his mind, but when he answered, he was still staring high above.

"Not sure." He was far away, thoroughly distracted.

I bit back a smile and ran my fingers over the rough, rotting door. With the lightest of pressure, it wheezed open, the handle and bolt long gone. I smiled at the invitation.

"C'mon."

Emil quickly pulled at my arm. "No. You don't know if the structure is sound."

I pushed the door open wider, peering in. A crisscross of planks, clearly meant for walking, staggered up through the stories. I slid from beneath his touch, holding my hands out toward him as I backed inside, step by step, but out of reach.

"Live a little."

He grunted in protest as my invisible rope dragged him forward, but couldn't help his gaze from darting up. The vast space was filled with a hazy light, the interior larger than one would expect based on its slim profile outside. The floor was completely stripped away in the center of the room, angry waves slapping against the old wooden posts Emil had told me about before. I stared at them with respect, their resolute figures remaining stalwart after all these years.

"Whoa," I breathed. Delicate artwork adorned the walls. A careful, talented hand had painted the scrolls and patterns around the crown molding, the colors dull with age. Arched windows looked out over the canal, the white paint chipped and bubbled. Even in its dilapidated state, it was stunning.

Emil moved swiftly through the room, his earlier concern about safety forgotten. He looked like a kid in a candy shop. His head tipped as he stared skyward, eyes flitting from one feature to the next. His fingers brushed a caress over the carved pillars framing the living space. The world seemed to have dropped away for him, so engrossed in the structure that he didn't notice the steady drip of water pooling in the hood of his jacket.

I mirrored his movements around the perimeter, keeping a careful distance on the narrow path to avoid taking a bath in the canal. "What do you think? What should our move-in date be?"

Emil snapped out of his reverie, confused at first. Then he played along, a slow smile sliding across his face. "By Christmas?"

I snorted, shaking my head. "I would have never expected it of you."

"What?"

"You're an optimist," I said with a mocking note of disgust.

He laughed. "Guilty."

I followed the light up to the hole in the roof, water cascading in drips and drops back to the sea. "It's definitely roomy."

"Yes, very spacious."

"Where would you suggest I put the Christmas tree?"

We met at the far corner of the room. He looked around a moment, then pointed over his shoulder to the window. "There. That way, anyone passing by outside could see it."

"But not see *in* here," I said knowingly, and he nodded. "Smart."

A particularly large swell battered the beams and boards, creating a rogue wave that lapped at our already sopping shoes. The house let out an ominous groan.

"I'll call and tell the builders our plans," I said urgently.

"Good idea," he responded, grabbing my hand and pulling me to the entryway.

"Wait," I teased, straining against him, "I want to get a color sample from the wall!"

"Enough, Mallory," Emil insisted, his voice tense with worry as the floor gave another grating note of warning.

I snickered as he shoved me out into the sturdy stone alley.

"Too soon to be picking colors?"

He shot me a look of reproach as he secured the door.

"C'mon, you know you wanted to go in there as much as I did," I pressed.

At first, I thought I was in for a talking-to. But he stepped toward me into the middle of the sidewalk and looked again up at the building face. I watched as water beaded in his thick curls before overflowing and breaking into trails as they flowed around his brow bone and nose.

"Yes," he said, barely audible. "I did." The tightness in his eyes didn't make sense, nor did the slight break in his voice.

I shifted uncomfortably. "Is everything all right?"

His face fell. "Yes. I'm sorry."

A shiver that had only partly to do with the damp slithered down my back. "For?"

He opened his mouth, but only a trembling murmur caught in the wind.

"Do you want to head to the room now?" I clenched my jaw as gusts whipped the otherwise mild air into a sharp bite.

We traveled the short distance in silence.

The warm protection of the lobby pulled a sob of relief from my lips. Somewhere along the way, I'd gotten bone-chilled. I bounded up the steps with Emil on my heels.

Inside, I stripped off my jacket and boots, chucking the former into the bathroom sink. I danced in place.

"Go ahead," Emil offered, shrugging out of his wet clothes more slowly. "Take the shower first."

"Are you sure?" I asked, desperate.

"Just go."

He didn't have to tell me a third time. I scurried away gratefully.

I soaked in the heat as long as I could before getting out to give Emil a turn. When he emerged in a white T-shirt and pair of sweatpants, I was tucked in up to my chin in bed.

"Better?" he teased.

"No," I said, my feet and hands still freezing. "I can't get warm."

The joke faded from his lips. "Would you like help?"

Heat flooded my insides, but didn't extend to my extremities. "You don't have to turn into an iceberg with me."

His shoulders twitched, playing it cool. "I'm fine."

"Well..." I pondered. "If it's not too much to ask?"

He tossed his towel to the bathroom floor and ducked into the bed. "Move over."

I obliged, waiting for him to get comfortable before sliding my feet to touch his legs. He sucked in a breath, but didn't push me off. I lay on my side, facing him.

His hands slid over mine, rubbing warmth into them. "I don't get it. It's not cold out."

"I'm from the desert," I reminded him. "It's cold to me. And I'm not used to humidity. Plus the wind? My body doesn't know what to do with it." I curled in tighter, nose pressed to his chest, his chin resting on top of my head.

An unspoken hush had fallen over the room, disturbed only by our breathing and the rhythmic pattern of rain coming from outside. The sound was hypnotic, and I found myself dozing with the steady rhythms as my body steadily warmed with his touch. Gentle fingers grazed my hairline, and I nuzzled in close without thinking. His fingertips stilled a moment before resuming their path across my head, lulling me to sleep.

Warm arms.

Hot breath.

The grit of sand upon my skin.

I jerked awake.

"You're okay," Emil whispered.

I couldn't have been asleep for long. In an instant, I knew where I was and who held me, my heart already slowing to a more normal rhythm.

"Mmm," I sighed against his chest. "Thank you." The words were a mumble.

He smoothed a hand down my spine. "Go back to sleep. It's still raining."

But I was too awake now. "Why do you know about the Venetian architecture?"

His hand stopped at my mid-back. "Just something that interests me."

"It was beautiful," I admitted. "I wonder what it was like. Before."

His fingers resumed their course, traveling up toward my shoulder blades.

"Can I ask you something else?" I ventured.

"Of course."

I tucked my chin against my knuckles. "What was that about, at the house? You were…upset."

"It wasn't safe."

"Nothing's safe," I countered.

His lips pursed. "No, I suppose that's true. But there's a difference between that and recklessness."

"I'm not reckless," I mumbled.

"No?" he challenged.

I bit my lip. "I guess I just never wanted to live in fear," I explained thoughtfully. "Sure, bad things happen sometimes. Being cautious in life could help avoid some of them, but no one makes it through unscathed. I'd rather get banged up a few times than always be too afraid to let anything happen at all." Doubt clouded my voice.

Did I still believe that? I wanted to. The ideology had served me well through life until recently. I would be a bona fide hypocrite if I didn't take the good with the bad. Issues with my dad were easier to relegate to the background, distant memories, small things I barely remembered. Marseille was fresh—raw—but should a single negative event really be able to shake my beliefs to the core? Whether I wanted it to or not, it had, at least a little. It had changed me to some extent. How much, I wasn't yet sure.

"That's brave," Emil said.

I rolled my eyes. "Or really stupid."

"Maybe it's both."

I fixed my face to hide my worry, tilting my head to meet his eye. "Very generous of you."

He frowned, a dark, but teasing look obscuring his gaze. "I said maybe."

I shrugged. "Maybe is as good an answer as any."

I turned my back to him and stared over his bed toward the balcony, the wet rooftops of Venice glistening in the night beyond the railing.

"Did I say something wrong?"

I looked at him over my shoulder. "No." I faced the opposite direction again, bumping my hips into his. "I just wanted to look outside."

His sharp breath had me grinning as I made contact. Eventually, he took my brusque invitation and spooned me from behind. The bed was warm now with our combined body heat. A lazy mood took over, and we chatted off and on about random topics, other times staying silent for long stretches. Neither was uncomfortable.

When the sky darkened and the rain quieted to a damp mist, we went downstairs for dinner. We made plans for our departure the following day, and I browsed hotel options in Munich before our next stop in Prague. We dined and then bade a last sorrowful goodbye to Italy by taking a final stroll through the canals. It was dead, only a few people trailing across our path. Gondoliers lined the docks, chatting, their boats empty. A couple passing by waved off one of the gondoliers as he spoke in rapid-fire Italian. As we approached, his eyes locked on to us.

"Solo ottanta euro," he offered, waggling his eyebrows.

Emil slowed to a stop, looking from the boat, to me, and back to the man. "All right."

"You want to?" I asked, surprised.

Emil nodded as the gondolier jumped to attention. The neighboring gondolier raised his eyes to the heavens with a jealous huff before settling, disgruntled, into his empty boat.

Emil got in first, holding out a hand to help me. "When in Rome, right?"

I smiled, accepting it, and stepped carefully in after him.

Drifting through Venice at night was like being carried away into an enchanting scene straight from a storybook. Snuggled beneath a thick wool blanket with Emil only added to the illusion, which was broken when our gondolier began a swooning love ballad. I sniggered behind my fingers, though his singing voice was anything but comical. Emil pressed his lips together, nudging me in the ribs when I snorted.

When we docked back to reality, our savvy boatman bid us a wholesome goodnight.

"Grazie. Buona notte," I answered with a wave as Emil helped me clamber back onto solid ground.

We wandered inside, floating on a magical high.

"Thank you for going," I said. We had changed and were standing out on the balcony, taking in a last glimpse of the city in the moonlight.

"I had to endure it," he sighed dramatically.

I let out a derisive laugh. "What? No you didn't."

"I did," he countered. "It made you happy."

I crossed my arms. "So?"

He watched his fingers twist, his next words simple. "You need happy."

I opened my mouth, but no sound came out. What could I say to that? He knew too much for me to deny it. And yet I had been happy, even before tonight.

"Well, then the joke's on you."

He paused before finally meeting my gaze. "What do you mean?"

"I was already having a ball," I said, turning to lean my back against the railing. "So you endured that for nothing, I'm afraid."

A tender smile played around his mouth. "Then it's time for payback."

"What do you want?"

He straightened, then held out his hand to me. Hesitantly, I took it.

"To sleep," he admitted. "I'm exhausted."

Without waiting for a response, he led me inside. He let go after depositing me on one side of the bed, then clambered in on the other. He patted the space reserved for me. Grinning from ear to ear, I jumped in. The bed bounced, its groan of protest matching Emil's. He pressed up against me all the same, and I curled into place with a sigh.

CHAPTER SIXTEEN

EARLY THE NEXT MORNING, we left for Munich, aiming to avoid a repeat of our late arrival in Venice. We stopped along the way, turning our Italian visit into a Shakespearean trio by briefly exploring both Padua and Verona. Their picturesque streets and facades were fresh to my eyes, unlike the touristy images of Venice I'd drooled over for so long. No pre-existing expectations, only the enchanting awe and joy while exploring their beauty.

Beyond the cities, vineyards and flat plains gave way to walls of steep cliffs framing the valley floor. Sometimes they were hidden behind large swaths of thick hedges or trees. During a particularly lengthy stretch, the radio had cut in and out so frequently, we'd given up and shut it off completely. The silence wasn't uncomfortable, but it made time stand still between the quiet and the monotonous spread of indistinguishable scenery.

I snatched my bottle from the console's cup holder, the warm plastic crinkling. One gulp of the hot water was enough to cure my thirst, but not my momentary boredom. I watched the water inside sway and tremble with the movement of the car, and inspiration struck.

"Never have I ever drank something and had it come out my nose," I said.

I grinned at Emil as his head turned slowly in my direction. His look clearly questioned if I'd finally lost it.

"Excuse me?" he asked before his eyes returned to the road.

"Never have I ever drank something and had it come out my nose," I repeated plainly. I had to press my lips together to fight off my laughter as I watched his face work.

"That's what I thought you said." He leaned forward, gripping the steering wheel a little tighter. "Are you all right?"

My laugh burst out. "Yes."

"I don't understand."

"It's a game."

"Drinking things until they come out your nose?"

"No," I scoffed. "Never Have I Ever. You haven't played?"

"No."

"Then you say, 'Never have I ever played Never Have I Ever.'" I shrugged as though it was the simplest thing in the world.

He processed a moment. "So it's a game to learn about the other person?"

I nodded. "Well, you can do it in a group or whatever—and usually there's drinking involved—but yes, that's the gist of it." I cocked my head to the side. "Wanna play?"

"What do I win?"

"It's not that kind of game."

His smirk told me all games were that kind of game.

"All right." He mulled over the possibilities. "Then never have I ever swam in a swimming pool."

My mouth popped open. "What?"

"Did I do it wrong?"

"No, that was a *WHAT* what," I explained before gaping at him. "Never?"

"Never. Just rivers or lakes."

I feigned outrage. "The chlorine smell! Swimming in kid pee! The mass of bodies crammed in together!"

Disgust twisted his lips. "Those are good things?"

"They're *terrible* things."

"Why are you upset I haven't done it, then?" he asked.

"Because I'm jealous," I said cheerfully, dropping my affronted attitude with a smile. "Good one."

He shook his head, trapped between bafflement and amusement.

We kept going for a while. Apparently Emil had also never been on an airplane, broken a bone, or gone on a blind date. I teased him that the last was because he knew everyone in Mostar, so it wouldn't be possible anyway.

I admitted I'd never ridden a roller coaster or gotten a tattoo. Eventually I'd run out of ideas and embarrassingly blurted out, "Never have I ever gone commando," then had to explain what going commando was.

Emil had burst out laughing.

As we moved north, closer to the Austrian border, the villages became distinctly more Alpine. Wood cabins dotted the grassy knolls, surrounded by cows and sheep. I watched their listless grazing, glimpsing the tips of snow on mountains in the distance.

I noticed my phone had a couple bars of service and pulled up the map of our surroundings to poke around. I was clicking on various towns and nature areas, and my jaw dropped when one image in particular stopped my scrolling.

"Have you heard of the Dolomites?"

"The mountains?"

"Yes," I breathed, returning to my phone. "They look gorgeous."

"How far away are they? We could stop for lunch near them if it makes sense."

I did some research and discovered the closest point, the Odle Group, was only a half an hour detour off our planned route. We stopped beforehand in Bolzano, where we gathered together items for a picnic feast.

At the register, I thumbed through postcards, selecting a few showing off the mountains we were about to meet in person.

Back in the car, I set up the directions on my phone before pulling out a pen and starting to write. I started with a bulleted play-by-play to my mom that excluded any mention of my new road trip companion, then completed a novel for Gail with every detail from our days in Venice.

"Who are you writing to?" Emil asked. He sneaked a look at my lap as I filled up the last bit of white space at the bottom.

"Gail," I said, blowing on the ink so it wouldn't smear. "I met her on the plane coming over here. I think I mentioned her before on our first dinner date."

Date?

I wanted to smack my hand across my forehead.

Emil's expression went vacant as he stared out at the road. "The old lady you said was hitting on you?"

I choked, having forgotten the context. "The one I *joked* was hitting on me, yes."

His lips twitched as he fought back a grin. "*Was* she hitting on you?"

"No," I said, drawing out the O playfully, then sighed. "She's far too cool for me." I shook my head. "Pity."

He coughed out a confused laugh. "But you barely know her. What do you say? In your notes?"

I was thoughtful as I considered. "Everything, kind of," I admitted. "I don't write like I'm speaking to a stranger."

Maybe I should.

My face flushed with embarrassment as I pressed on, but my words felt right. "She seemed to get me. I didn't have to explain myself around her. It was easy, so I just say what I've seen and done and experienced so far."

His eyes searched my face for a moment. "All of it?"

My heart stuttered. "No," I said softly. "No, not all of it." I pushed my shoulders back, resetting with a breath. "But everything else. All the good stuff."

"So does she know you've taken on a travel partner?" he asked curiously.

The corners of my mouth lifted, knowing what he was asking. Yes, he was included in the good stuff. I tapped the postcard against my thigh. "She does now."

His brows relaxed, his chin dipping in a single nod with a small smile.

The narrow road leading us deeper into the mountains alternated between thick, lush forests and wide grasslands. Then, we were climbing. The switchback roads twisted up the hillsides, my ears popping a few times. The dense forest grew sparser of its broadleaf trees, the evergreens taking over completely with the higher altitudes. Eventually, without fanfare, the road ended near what I believed was a home until I saw a roughly carved sign declaring it a bed-and-breakfast. But my attention didn't linger there.

Instead, it was drawn up. And up. And up. Up to the pointed peaks of the Dolomites towering over us.

It felt like that scene from *Jurassic Park*, where the characters first see the dinosaurs at the same time and gape in open-mouthed awe. Emil and I mutely left the car, not even bothering to close the doors as we stopped in front of the bumper to stare. The midday sun drenched the bright limestone faces of the sharp pinnacles. They stabbed toward the cloudless, azure sky from a blanket of boulders and shale at their base, which stretched down until hidden by a line of trees. The mountains seemed so out of place, so unlike any others I'd seen. I imagined an alien landing on Earth would feel something akin to what I was now.

They were undeniably spectacular.

I scooted closer to Emil, who leaned against the hood of the car, ogling the same as me. A cool, crisp mountain breeze ruffled my hair. I breathed it in, my eyes closed, before I squinted at Emil.

"Worth it?" I prompted him.

He looked away from the sight to give me a lopsided grin. "Very."

"Are you hungry?" I asked, moving to grab the food from the car.

"Yes, but I'm afraid that, if I look away, they might disappear."

I laughed. "Okay, you watch them to make sure. I'll get the food."

No matter how many times we glanced down to fill another cracker with lusciously creamy cheese or to take a sip from our overly-warm water bottles, they remained right where we'd left them. As we packed up lunch, a man from the bed-and-breakfast walked outside and greeted us with a wave.

"Buongiorno," he said, stopping at the end of the walkway. "Are you lost?"

"Only in amazement," I teased.

He smiled vaguely. "It's a little late to start hiking. Do you need a room? I still have one available."

It was barely after one o'clock, so we had plenty of time to get to Munich, but the offer was tempting. I wasn't ready to leave.

I pursed my lips and looked at Emil.

His eyes sparkled, reading my expression in an instant. He winked before turning his attention back to the man. "How much?" he said, his bargaining voice returning.

As it turned out, there was a reason this particular room hadn't been taken. I'd managed to sneak a glimpse inside another while we walked past an open door. It was spacious, and I spotted the large log bed, a TV, a hutch with a kettle and tea fixings, and a rocking chair next to a balcony overlooking the mountains.

Ours was lovable in a summer camp kind of way, decked out with rustic, rough wood walls. Beside the sink sat basic amenities for the morning. A tiny table and stools were shoved into a corner on the right as a makeshift dining area. Against the far wall, a set of bunk beds waited immediately across from where we stood in the doorway. If I had to guess, in a former life, the room had been a large, walk-in storage pantry. I could easily picture it stuffed with seasonal items and knickknacks.

I laughed.

"Umm," Emil said, the sound drawn out with uncertainty.

"I get the top bunk!" I yelped, running into the room to throw Bertha atop the thin mattress. The bed was so narrow, I wondered if I'd need to sleep exclusively on my side. I tried to hurl myself onto the bunk using only my own momentum, but failed.

"Darn it," I grumbled. I turned to Emil, whose face was hidden behind his hand. "I wanted to do the run-and-jump thing I've seen in the movies. It looks so cool."

His hand passed down his brow to his chin. His fingertips tapped over his mouth, which was clearly lifted in a smile.

I stuck out my lower lip. "Never have I ever done the *Dirty Dancing* vault onto a bunk bed."

He finally laughed out loud. "I don't know what that is, but I get the idea. Turn around."

"Why?"

"I'm going to make your dreams come true," he said in a playfully stern tone.

I arched a brow at such a frank remark coming from him, but did as I was told. He crossed the creaky planks before his hands were on my hips. I sucked in a breath at the contact, my pulse kicking into overdrive, my stomach swooping with a tingle of excitement.

"One, two," he counted—"three." On three, I pushed off the floor, and he lifted in unison. I twisted so my butt was at the edge, my legs dangling over the side between his hands, which rested on the bunk's frame.

"Better?" he asked.

I grinned giddily. "Yes. And now I can check it off my never list."

He gave a nod, his gaze dropping to my knees, which were at eye level to him. His thumbs brushed against my outer thighs in a caress. Tingles danced across my skin at his soft touch, and I looked up. His eyes bore that hint of darkness I'd spied a few times before, captivating me in their grasp. The moment held, then broke as he took a step back.

"Want to go out and explore awhile?" He cleared his throat as he checked the time. "We've got a few hours before night."

I swallowed, working to subdue the heat that had risen through my body, and nodded.

Our host, Albert—"Just call me Bert"—gave us rough directions to a few trails leading off from the meadow across from the bed-and-breakfast, as well as a reminder that they served dinner at 7:00 p.m. With no other options in the area, I set an alarm on my phone so we'd return in time.

Through the forest, we found ourselves in a wide field. Despite the blistering sun during the day, the wild grasses were still a verdant green from being fed nightly by dew. Wildflowers in pink, white, and blue blanketed the meadow in patches, adding to the cheerful scene. Staring at the mountains during the easy hike was an optical illusion. They were huge, yet always seemed distant, giving the impression that we were walking in place. One vista view to the next provided breathtaking angles, and it was only as the sky began to fade into a burnt orange that we turned back with regret.

Dinner was a simple affair, but delicious, an interesting mishmash of Italy and the region's former Germanic roots. A crisp white wine was served first with the antipasto consisting of crostini, cheese, and cured meats. For the main course, we each dug into a bowl of crescent-shaped ravioli, filled with potato and drizzled with a brown butter sauce and topped with a sprinkling of parsley. Some sort of apple fritter dusted with cinnamon and sugar was our divine dessert, and I ate more than my share when Emil pushed his last slices toward me. I didn't argue.

On second thought, maybe I should have. My stomach squirmed as we went upstairs to our room. But the taste of the tart apples and sweet toppings still lingered on my tongue.

Worth it.

The bathroom we were to use was shared, but it was late enough that there was no line. When Emil returned from it, I was already tucked into my bunk, one elbow on my pillow propping up my head as he entered.

He tossed his bathroom things into his bag before walking to the light switch. "Ready?" he confirmed.

I flopped onto my back, pulling the covers up to my chin, though it was quite toasty inside. "Check," I said seriously.

He snorted, but switched off the light, plunging us into utter darkness. Not a streetlight to be found, not even a sliver of moon through the single window.

I heard him cross the room, then a *thunk* and groan.

"You okay?" I asked, leaning up and over the edge of the bed. A rush of air slapped me in warning before my eyes had adjusted, and I reared back. From the sound of his voice, I knew we'd just avoided an in-line collision with our heads.

"Yeah," he said, completely oblivious to the close call. "Hit my shin on the bed frame."

"Sorry." I winced in sympathy.

A rustle of clothes, then sheets, then the creak of the mattress sounded as he got in. I settled back with a deep sigh, already dreaming of the stunning views we'd seen throughout the day.

The bed beneath me squeaked as Emil moved once. Twice. A beat, then a third time.

"Everything okay down there?" I asked.

"Yeah." The word was hesitant.

"What is it?"

"It's fine."

"Emil."

"I think there's a board missing beneath it or something. It's sagging weird."

"Should I go down and talk to Bert?"

"No, no, I just need to..." Sounds of him shifting, a scraping noise along the floor, then silence. "That'll work."

"What did you do?"

"Moved my pillow and pack into a sort of brace."

I pressed my lips together. I could do it. I could not meddle...

Nope.

I sat up, shoved the covers off, and swung my legs out. "I'm going to talk to Bert."

A hand grabbed my ankle. "I swear, if you make me get out of this finally comfortable position to stop you, I'm gonna..." The warning hung waiting in the air.

It was cute he didn't want to be a bother, but honestly, these beds were not the best, even when fully outfitted.

"You're going to what?" I taunted him, softly swinging my feet.

He slid a light nail up the instep of my foot.

The sensation simultaneously tickled and sent a hot zing of commotion to other parts of my body. My breath caught as I felt things in places he hadn't even touched.

But my ticklishness won out. I yelped, yanking my legs up and giggling involuntarily. "No fair!" The words shook as I gasped.

"It worked, didn't it?" he said, his tone knowing. The bed groaned as I imagined him lying down with care.

"I don't want you to be miserable all night."

"I won't be."

"We could share?" I offered.

He barked a laugh. "How? With me taped to the wall next to you?"

I couldn't argue his point, so I bit my lip.

"Don't worry about it, Mal. If I was so uncomfortable, I'd go speak to Bert myself. Just get some sleep."

"Okay," I gave in unhappily. "Goodnight, Emil."

I was already half asleep when he said it back.

CHAPTER SEVENTEEN

IN THE MORNING, BERT'S wife whipped us up a hearty meal of eggs, fruit, and a potato fry, along with strong, strong coffee.

The second strong was at the request of Emil.

He didn't complain, didn't say a word about it, but the redness of his eyes and swoop of darkness beneath them told me he'd lied. I wondered if he'd slept at all. I was watching him cautiously, and he caught me while taking a sip of coffee.

"What?" he asked, looking down at his shirt and running a hand over his mouth, searching for stray crumbs of food.

I pursed my lips, then gave a knowing shrug. "Nothing."

We finished breakfast and readied for the second leg of our journey, bidding Bert a heart-felt thank-you before we drove off with a wave.

The familiar stunning scenery greeted us as we wove a return journey through the same route, though it looked different going than it had coming. The new perspective shifted and revealed things I hadn't noticed from the opposite side of the car. Another thing that'd changed? Emil's driving.

He didn't drive aggressively normally, but now we were cruising at granny speed. At first, I ignored it. Then, I fought against saying something. Until...

"Where's the fire?" I asked.

He blinked, his expression unfocused. "Huh?"

"Be careful, Speedy McGee, or we might end up in Munich *before* tomorrow."

"I don't understand."

"Probably because you didn't get any sleep last night, Emil," I finally said softly.

He frowned, but gave in. "Yeah."

"I wish you would've let me get it fixed."

"It's my own fault," he said, rubbing his eyes with his free hand. He winced. "Would you be able to drive for a while? Just so I can nap a little?"

My gaze zeroed in on the gear shift like it was a venomous snake. Technically, I knew how to drive stick. My mother had owned a manual car when I was learning to drive, but, lucky for me, the thing had given up the ghost a few weeks in (I took no responsibility that my atrocious skills had killed it outright). Her next car had, mercifully, been an automatic.

I cringed at Emil. "Never have I ever driven a stick?"

His eyebrows rose in surprise. "Never?"

"Well..." I explained, but made it clear that, while *theoretically* I could, maybe I shouldn't.

He licked his lips, contemplating how much of his life he was willing to gamble. "Want to try it while we're still on the back roads?"

I bit the inside of my cheek, worried. How much of his life was *I* willing to gamble? With one more desperate look from his bloodshot eyes, I caved.

"All right, if you really want me to," I sighed, "but you do so at your own peril."

He pulled over so quickly, I think I underestimated his exhaustion.

Ten minutes later, after stalling the car during my first five attempts to get it into gear, we were rolling down the narrow road. My hands gripped the wheel convulsively, my muscles taut. I didn't risk looking at Emil, but his lack of movement in my periphery told me he wasn't any more relaxed.

"Good," he complimented me as I managed to find my way into third. He breathed with relief as he eased further into his seat.

"Don't get too comfy yet," I warned him.

He scoffed at the possibility.

But soon enough, soft snores floated through the car and, without an audience, I did loosen up a fraction. There were practically no other cars around, so all I had to do was focus on keeping us on the road. That much, at least, I was pretty confident I could handle.

Signs for the freeway started to pop up, growing closer and closer. One name suddenly set off alarm bells.

Autobahn.

Even I knew of that legendary stretch of highway.

"Emil," I whispered, worried as the sign warned me of the entrance ahead. He didn't answer. "Emil!"

He jerked awake. "What? What's wrong?"

"The Autobahn!" I practically screeched.

"So?"

"No speed limit!"

"Only some parts don't," he said calmly, though I wondered if it was solely to stop the impending freak-out on my part.

"Oh, great." My knuckles turned white on the steering wheel.

"Freeway driving is the easiest kind to drive a stick." Was that amusement in his voice?

I aimed a sideways glare at him.

"Do you want me to take over?" he offered.

Too little, too late. We were already taking the gentle curve of the on-ramp.

"Emil…" I worried as cars raced past me.

"You're okay," he encouraged, looking back to help me assess traffic.

"You've got it."

I pressed hard on the gas. The car lurched, but picked up speed to match the oncoming vehicles.

"You should be good here," he confirmed as I inched between two long gaps. And then we were sailing along the famous highway. I released a breath.

"I'm staying in the slow lane," I bit out.

"You're okay?" He rested a hand on my arm. "We can trade places if you're not."

I licked my dry lips. I didn't want to risk our lives, but he'd barely gotten twenty minutes of sleep yet. I reminded myself that all I had to manage was brake, gas, and switch lanes for the most part here, the same as regular driving. Unless some jerk cut me off or a deer ran out into the road or...

"I've got it," I managed to say, sounding somewhat sure.

"If you aren't, just tell me."

"I will."

Eventually, my panic dimmed, and we cruised along with the minimal traffic. Emil also was able to fall back asleep. It wasn't until I started seeing Munich climbing up the list on the road signs that I woke him.

"Sorry," I apologized.

He stretched. "It's fine. Where are we?"

"Not sure exactly," I admitted, "but I think we're getting close. Is it okay if we switch?"

We did at the next opportunity, the last vestiges of adrenaline fading from my body as he took over. I found myself grinning at finally having conquered that monster from the past.

Emil's smile touched his still-tired eyes. "You did good, Ljepotice."

My eyes narrowed. "Dani called me that, too. What does it mean?"

Emil cleared his throat, staring out the window. "Ljepotice?" he said, stalling for time. "Uh...it means beauty. It's used in a...something you call someone you care for? I can't think of it."

"Girlfriend?"

"No. Well..." he corrected quickly, "Ljepotice, it's often used in that way, yes. But the other expression I'm trying to think of doesn't have to be. It can be what a grandparent calls a grandchild or...something affectionate? I can't think of how you'd say it."

"A term of endearment?"

"That's it."

"But Ljepotice...it does translate to beauty?" I pressed. "As in a beautiful woman?"

He shifted uncomfortably in his seat. "Yes."

My insides warmed pleasantly while I let him sweat it before offering him a lifeline. "Dani's a major flirt, isn't he?"

Emil chuckled. "You have no idea."

"I might," I said, lifting a brow.

His next laugh had an edge to it.

"What's the Bosnian word for rascal?"

"Rascal..." Emil repeated, sounding it out into a question.

"Rogue, hoodlum, womanizer, flirt," I provided. "You know, so if I ever see him again, I can have a comeback in a language he'll have no problem understanding." I grinned sweetly.

"Hmm. Ženskar, I suppose?"

He helped me to pronounce it correctly, along with other options ranging in varying degrees of insult. From there, we continued a back-and-forth game of saying this and that in English versus Bosnian before entering the outskirts of Munich.

The urban sprawl of the city surrounded us as we maneuvered our way toward the old town center. Sweat beaded down my back as we parked and walked through the bustle. We were headed to a hotel I'd scouted online and showed availability before I lost reception in the mountains. The lobby was sleek and modern, decorated with a minimalist white-on-white color palette. An elegant marble countertop cut a graceful arch across the back of the room, hiding the row of computers where the receptionists worked. One of them looked up as we approached, and promptly assessed us.

"Welcome," she said pleasantly. "Two rooms?"

"Uh," I mumbled uncertainly, glancing at Emil.

He lifted a shoulder noncommittally. "It's up to you."

I chewed my lip. On one hand, his presence was welcome. On the other, my unpredictable nightmares had to be a disturbance. And after last night, he might as well get a proper, full-night's sleep in peace.

"Two, please," I decided.

When everything was in the system and paid for, she printed off our receipts. "Here are your keys," she said, passing them and the paperwork over the cool counter. "Would you like any brochures or maps for your stay?"

"Yes, I have a few questions," I began.

"I'll take the bags up," Emil offered as he took his keycard, easily hoisting up Bertha and heading for the stairs.

"How can I help?" the receptionist encouraged me after he left.

"Neither of us have been here before," I said. "Do you have any recommendations? Food, sights, activities?"

"Where are you visiting from?" she asked as she pulled pamphlets from beneath the counter.

"I'm from the US and he's from Bosnia."

"Very nice," she responded, laying the folded papers out flat, and began circling her top picks for places nearby to eat, good spots for shopping, and several art galleries and museums. She paused. "Have you ever been to a German bathhouse?"

"First time in Germany," I laughed, "so no."

"They are very relaxing," she said, a twinkle in her eye. She indicated one on the map that didn't look too far away. "This is my favorite. They've got all sorts of baths, mineral, hot and cold, saunas, and so on. A little more adult-focused, though there is a main pool for families."

"Do I need to book in advance?"

161

She shook her head. "No, it's all quite casual."

I thanked her for her help and made my way to the third floor. Emil was waiting outside my room with Bertha.

"Thanks," I said, grabbing her by the handle and sliding the plastic card into the slot. "I would like to clean up, and then we can talk about what to do, if that works for you?"

"Sounds good," he agreed, glancing at his watch. "Half hour?"

"Perfect."

With that, he let himself in next door.

Inside, my room was clean and simple, with a balcony overlooking a quiet street below. I showered and was patting my hair dry when there was a soft knock. I slipped on a fluffy white bathrobe and opened the door.

"Come on in," I said, standing to the side. Emil's eyes briefly skated down the low V of my robe before snapping up and away. He walked in, looking around, though the room was probably a mirror image of his own.

"Did the receptionist help with ideas?" he asked curiously as he turned to me again when I shut the door. His focus stayed trained upon my face.

"Yes." I went to the nightstand and spread the brochures across my bed. I pointed out some of the sights and restaurants. Emil nodded agreeably until I got to the bathhouse.

"She was telling me how there's all these options, and it sounds so nice," I sighed.

"Are you sure you want to do that?"

I frowned. "You don't?"

"I don't know how comfortable I am with it," he admitted.

"Really?" My excitement plummeted, followed by confusion. "But you were happy to swim at the waterfalls. I thought you'd like it?"

He nodded slowly. "Yes, but this is different. And there are probably a lot of people there." His attention dropped to his finger, which picked at the pattern in the comforter, his body stiff and uncomfortable.

"Emil, are you shy?"

He swallowed. "No."

"You are!" I teased. "You know you have nothing to worry about, right?"

"I don't?"

I shook my head.

"Why don't I?" His bashfulness dissipated as he stared at me.

"Because you are gorgeous."

Oh god, did I just say that?

It was my turn to hide. I ducked my head, only to notice my bathrobe was nearly falling open. I crossed my arms.

"Gorgeous?" he prompted.

"Handsome," I amended. There, that sounded more manly.

His fingers pinched my chin, forcing me to look at him. His eyes were like flashlights, light pouring in to search through my hidden secrets. "Hmm," he murmured, seeming satisfied with what he found there.

My skin was already warm from the shower, but it flushed crimson. My body tensed beneath his touch with excitement. A breath whispered between my lips.

"You do look as if you could use some relaxation," he assessed. His gaze slid down my neck and to my chest before it locked again on my face, which he gently released. "Is this what you want?"

"Yes." I wanted so much more.

Quietly, he nodded. "All right."

"Tomorrow?" I said.

"Tomorrow."

―――

The next morning, we absorbed the picture-perfect window view of our corner of Munich while sipping coffee and munching on crisp ginger cookies out on the balcony. I sighed with contentment as I stared out at the city, listening to it buzz with life. Emil fidgeted with something in his pocket.

We spent the earlier part of the day exploring our neighborhood, browsing through shops and markets. But we stuck close to home so we could return after a quick lunch to change and head to the spa.

The bathhouse was a short, leisurely walk from the hotel and was a beautiful mix of old-style architecture and modern-day function. A grand reception area awaited, along with a genteel smile from the woman behind it. She checked us in efficiently and pointed in the direction of the communal locker areas.

It was quiet as we found row after row of empty aisles. We picked one at random and began to organize our things. Emil pulled his shirt over his head. I couldn't stop from looking down for a second, then forced myself to return to his face. He didn't quite meet my eye as he shoved the T-shirt into our locker.

"Ready?" For some reason, the word quivered.

"Yeah, I'll be just a minute," I said, my voice responding to his nervousness with an octave change. "I need to use the restroom first. I'll meet you out there."

He stared into the locker. "Want to meet in the sauna?"

"Yep, sounds good!" I called, already turning the corner to the toilets.

Once inside, I took several breaths. Why was I so nervous? Why was *he* so nervous? It was counterproductive to the whole experience! And it wasn't as if we hadn't seen one another in a bathing suit before. I shook myself, letting my hair loose before pulling it up into a high bun. I changed into my swimsuit while I was in the privacy of the stall, set my shoulders back with confidence, and emerged.

The locker room was dead. Voices from several rows down were the only sounds besides the distant splash beyond the wide arch to my left. I shoved my clothes into the locker without folding them and slammed the door shut. With my towel in hand, I headed through the arch and noticed a small placard with SAUNA written on it and an arrow pointing the way.

When I turned the corner, a huge cathedral ceiling soared overhead. Stained glass windows met glittering crystal, showering the pools with a heavenly light. I followed the beams down to where they winked in the water. And then my gaze stuck.

My jaw dropped.

Every single person—young and old, men and women—was entirely nude.

I stood still as a statue. But I suddenly realized I was staring, so I wandered toward one of the smaller pools lining the wall for something to do as a distraction. I discarded my towel at the edge and, as I was about to step in, a voice cut sharply through the tranquil space.

"Stop!"

Immediately, my toes withdrew from the tantalizing warmth. I looked up and locked on to the man walking toward me, his eyebrows turned down in angry slashes over his narrowed eyes. He continued speaking in fiery German until he was a few paces away.

"Sorry?" I responded, the word an apology as much as a question.

His expression soured. "No swimsuit allowed."

"Oh." What did he expect me to do, strip on the spot?

He pointed toward the locker room. "In there. Towels only here."

"Thank you." I spun and practically ran back.

I sat on the bench in front of our locker, the door propped open, having pulled out Emil's shorts. Currently, they were lying across my lap. Emil's hesitance all made sense now. He hadn't been afraid of swimming with other people. He'd been afraid of doing it utterly and completely naked.

My face plopped into my hands as I shook my head.

Good job, Mallory. Another gold star for you.

Eventually, I had to deal with it. Emil was out there waiting for me. It was my fault we were here. I couldn't just leave him. He'd done this for me. *C'mon, Mallory, get it together!*

My mouth set into a firm line, determination boiling in my gut. I could do this. I'd survived much scarier things than people in their birthday suits. For heaven's sake, I was a nurse now! Naked people were going to be my bread and butter.

I shut the locker door with a defiant *clack*.

Before I could hesitate, I once again followed the sign for the sauna, moving decisively and keeping focused on the destination. When I reached the correct hall, I had a fifty-fifty shot between two saunas on either side. Instinct pulled me to the right, and I steadied my nerves before I swung open the door.

I walked into the sweltering, claustrophobic room, my skin instantly flushed. The space was packed with naked bodies of every shape and size, but they remained on my periphery as I searched and locked on to only one.

Emil sat at the back, top row, hiding in the corner. His shoulders were hunched as he stared at his feet. But the rush of cool air from the swing of the door gently riffled his curls, so I knew he was aware of a new presence.

Nudity might not be sexual here normally, but when everyone other than the person in front of you faded away, and that person looked like he did, what else was there?

I drew in a breath. It caught in my lungs, now equally ablaze. However, it was nothing in comparison to the inferno when his eyes finally found mine. His gaze lowered, roaming my body from my exposed legs over my torso to reach my face once more. His lips parted as he drank me in like I was a refreshing glass of glacial water. I could have done with a dousing of the stuff myself. Heat pooled inside me, refusing to dissipate through my scorched skin. Time slowed, the whole room frozen, suspending us in this singular moment, book-ended by fire and ice.

Someone snapped, and my head jerked to the sound. A disgruntled looking man pointed at the door, which was still clasped open between my fingers, letting in the cool air. I let it fall closed, and he promptly ignored me once more.

I moved toward Emil, who scooted over to make space on the wooden bench beside him. I noted how everyone had their towels laid out beneath them and matched it. I sat down, trying to force myself to look anywhere other than at Emil.

I failed.

His attention was pointed firmly ahead, looking directly across the space with a determined fixation. I followed his stare to the blank wall by the door, but my gaze immediately wandered. Everyone was silent, save for the occasional shift and rustle of the bodies packed into the stifling room. Luckily, being in the back, I didn't feel as exposed, but still managed to lock eyes with a few people adjacent to me. I ducked my head with an apologetic wince.

It was difficult to breathe, the steam soaking into every crack and crevice. It was tropical mugginess turned up one thousand percent. I was on the verge of suffocating. How did anyone find this relaxing? I tried to take shallower breaths, but it made me lightheaded. I leaned back, focusing only on not dying.

Emil's hand brushed the side of my thigh, and I jumped at how sensitive his soft touch was on my overheated skin.

"Are you okay?" His whisper was directly against my ear and it tickled.

"Mhmm."

The door to the sauna opened, inviting in a luxurious swath of breathable air. My heart leapt. Maybe they needed to clean and were kicking us out.

A lithe woman hauled in a bucket and oversized ladle, a towel strewn over her shoulder. Several people straightened, and I perked up with them, aware something was about to happen. She approached the collection of rocks near the center, dipped the ladle in the bucket, and streamed water over the stones with a sizzle. The pleasant aroma of eucalyptus filled the air. I was inhaling the heavenly scent when she began doing some sort of dance with the huge towel. I watched, entranced, as mist from the rocks billowed and swirled like magic around her.

And then it hit me.

The steam reached its fingers all the way to the back and slapped us with sweltering heat. This was far worse than any triple digits I'd endured in the hottest summer, the humidity adding an extra twenty degrees to the already unendurable temperature.

Instantly, I was at my breaking point.

"Emil," I whispered, close to passing out.

"It's the last part," he murmured. "Two minutes, then it's done."

I wasn't sure I could last two seconds.

"I don't think..." Whatever I thought, it was worse.

Involuntarily, I slumped to my side, but strong arms pulled me in.

"I've got you. Let's go."

CHAPTER EIGHTEEN

STUMBLING AND PARTLY CARRIED, I was suddenly out in the relatively freezing air. I gulped it down, instant shivers wracking my body. Within moments, cold water stung needle-pricks across my feet and legs, before running down my back and arms. One of those arms was slung around a strong pair of shoulders.

"Better?" Emil asked, holding me up against a chilly tile wall with his own body. I squinted at my surroundings, our intimate contact only partially registering.

We were in a shower. When had we gotten here?

I nodded, my head spinning before slowly starting to clear.

"We should go," he suggested.

I shook my head violently. Bad idea.

He huffed out a breath, then shut off the water. We stood there quietly until my limbs stopped trembling.

"Can you stand?" he asked.

I jiggled my legs a little. They seemed sturdy enough. "Yes."

He let me go and returned with fresh towels. One he flipped over his shoulder, then wrapped the other around mine.

"You're sure you want to stay?"

"I'm sure."

"Can you walk?"

Another nod.

Emil held my hand, leading me down a hall toward the adults only baths. He guided me to a glassy pool, lowering himself onto a submerged ledge before pulling me in next to him. The water was luxuriously cool compared to to the hellish sauna. My skin, even after being doused in the cold shower, burned with a dull heat. I sank down into the water up to my neck.

"How could anyone enjoy that?" I blubbered, my words catching over themselves as I lay my head upon his shoulder. His drifted to rest atop mine.

"It's all about degrees of tolerance. For people used to it, it's not a big deal."

"It wasn't too intense in there for you?"

He paused. "It was."

"But you didn't pass out," I remarked.

"I almost did, just earlier."

"How long were you in there before I arrived?"

"About a minute."

I frowned. It didn't add up.

"Not from the heat," he clarified pointedly, at last peeking at me out of the corner of his eye.

It clicked into place, remembering the way he'd looked at me when I walked in. Oh.

"Are you used to this?" I asked, trailing my fingers up his forearm. "Are spas the same in Bosnia?"

"No and no. But you seemed to want to do it, so I went along."

"I didn't know people would be naked!" I exclaimed, twisting in the arm he'd wrapped around my shoulders. "Why didn't you say anything?"

He blushed, which was impressive, considering he was already red from the water. "Honestly, Mal. It isn't a secret."

My face burned. I wondered if it was as obvious as his. "'Spa' means something very different where I come from."

"All of Europe knows the German ideas around nudity."

"Well, I'm not European. I didn't plan for this. That woman..." I fumed, slumping further into the pool as I recalled the receptionist's knowing grin. She understood exactly what she was doing, sending me to the wolves. My hands swished through the water in front of me before I let them sink. My right rested on Emil's knee.

"Are you mad?" he asked as I ran my fingertips absentmindedly through his smattering of hair.

I was embarrassed at being tricked and at being caught off guard. But mad? My hand wandered a tiny bit higher, curious if he would stop me. He didn't.

"Not really," I said. "Are you?"

It was quiet for a moment. We were the only two in this bath, secluded from the others. His fingers traced a pattern on my shoulder.

"No," he replied. "Surprised, not angry."

I lifted my head, and his eyes locked with mine. "Have you ever done this before?"

His gaze heated. "Sat naked with a woman or been to a bathhouse?"

My lips fought from raising into a smile as I nodded. "Yes."

"Yes. And no."

My unoccupied hand swept through the water again, and the movement stirred the air, the faint chemical smell growing stronger.

"Wait," I realized. "Never have I ever been in a pool." I turned so my chest pressed into his side. "Emil, we've checked off something for you!"

He stared at me, nonplussed.

"We're in a pool!"

After a beat, he broke out in a full-fledged grin. Then his expression softened as he leaned back, drinking it in. His hand mirrored mine through the water, and they danced together. They twisted and turned, catching beneath the surface. I held fast, running a gentle nail up his palm.

"So? What do you think so far?" I let go, my hand breaking the surface to gently stroke the side of his stubbled face.

His breath shuddered, but he didn't so much as blink. "I think...I could get used to it if it was like this all the time."

My heart hammered in my chest. Surely he could feel it, I was pressing myself so tightly against him. "Me, too."

I drew in as close as possible without our lips touching. His parted beneath my gaze, and I nudged his nose with my own, staring up at him through half-lowered lids.

"Mallory." My name was a warning.

"Emil." His sounded urgent, needy, in my mouth.

And I did need him. It didn't matter that we were plainly visible to others. They'd paid us no mind before, but at this point, I wouldn't care if they pulled up a ringside seat. My insides ached, my heart clenched, my whole body on fire for an entirely different reason. There was only one release, and he held the key.

"Please..."

And his lips claimed mine.

I melted in his embrace, in his heady touch. The world faded away, the steam drawing around us in an invisible curtain. I was lost and found all at the same time. His hand drifted down my side, resting at the bend of my hip. I whimpered quietly because it wasn't far enough, and I felt his smile.

A decidedly un-sexy grunt permeated our little bubble. I turned to watch an older couple pass by, throwing us disapproving looks.

Emil followed my gaze. We burst out in quiet sniggers, watching their *au naturel* selves sink into a pool across the room.

"Oh, this is too good!" I laughed, leaning into the wall.

"I think we made a problem."

"The audacity," I said, tossing my arms into the air in dramatic, mocking dismay.

Emil's fingers were busy running higher and higher circles up the inside of my thigh. Instantly, the people were forgotten.

He leaned in. "They can't complain about what they can't see," he whispered.

My mouth dropped open, every nerve engaged and at attention. Never in my life had I done anything like this in public, but I'd never desired something so much as his touch on my skin as I did right now. I turned my head, willing him to kiss me, but he pulled away barely out of reach. My brows creased at the denial, but he grinned.

"Tsk, tsk," he admonished playfully. "Out of sight." To drive his point home, his painstakingly slow touch brushed along my ribs. Up. Up. Up.

And stopped, just barely beneath the surface.

I liked this game.

My hands explored, running a line down his abs, and, just as they were about to dip lower, I stilled. My eyes were drawn up to his, and I saw my own hunger reflected back at me. I wanted to devour him.

But this was a game I didn't want to end. With a smirk, my hand changed course, following his preferred path along the inner thighs. I bent my fingers, my nails scraping lightly against his skin. He hissed, and his eyes snapped shut with a shiver. I took advantage, savoring each reaction. I took in the things I couldn't normally without outright staring. His thick lashes. Near his widow's peak, a cowlick turned a section of hair to swirl in the opposite direction of the rest. Beneath his left eyebrow was the hint of a long-healed gash, which appeared and disappeared in the catch of light.

I reached farther toward his knee as a ruse to inch closer and pushed up to place a kiss at the top of the scar.

I sank into the water as he twisted and looked down at me lazily, our noses grazing.

"Cheater," he murmured against my lips.

"All's fair in love and war." The words were out before I thought about what was coming from my mouth—specifically that one, very particular, four-letter word. He stared at me curiously. I pulled back a few inches, breaking the spell with a forced laugh. "Do you know that saying?"

He gave a curious nod.

Darn it.

I sat up straight, bringing my hand into my lap, and searching around for a way to erase my verbal slipup. I locked on to a plain clock in the corner. It was out of place, too modern and slick in this ornate space. It was later than I would've guessed. Did time just move strangely when wrapped in Emil's luxurious embrace? Or had I been passed out longer than I'd thought?

I shuddered at embarrassing thing number 258 for the day and worked to sound cool and casual. "What do you say?"

"About?"

"Do you...want to go back?" I cleared my throat nervously, hyper-aware of what I was implying. "To the hotel?"

He looked at me for a beat with eyes warring between hunger and concern, his face otherwise set with his signature, impassive expression. I was trapped there for a moment before he finally let loose a breath and simply said, "Okay."

I stood, the water spilling from the crooks of my arms and pouring down my legs. I felt every rivulet's path down my sensitive skin. I could hear Emil following behind me, but I didn't look back.

We collected our towels and returned to the locker room where we showered, dried, and dressed in silence. Inside, I was reeling.

Would this ruin things between us?

Or would it make them a million times better?

I wanted this...right?

"Do you have everything?" he asked, scanning the locker to double-check.

I pulled my bag over my head and nodded.

There was a distinct gap between our bodies as we walked through the spa. Even his fingertips didn't quite touch the small of my back, hovering only as he ushered me through their doors into the balmy sunlight.

"Are you all right?" he asked when we were nearing the hotel.

"Yes," I said, leveling a sideways look at him. "Are you?"

"Better now," he joked, running an absentminded hand over the front of his T-shirt. It stuck to his damp skin. My mouth watered at the imprint of muscles in the fabric before jerking my gaze to the ground.

Nerves danced in my belly as we moved through the lobby, up the stairs, and to my door. I fumbled through my bag for my key. He was distractingly close, the near-but-not-touching driving me crazy and doing strange things to my heart rate. Finally, I found it and held it up awkwardly.

"Got it."

"Okay." He turned as if to go to his room, but paused after one step. "I don't—"

I waited, but he seemed unable to continue. "What?"

He sighed. "I don't want to frighten you."

My stomach dropped. "You think you scare me?"

He hesitated, then leaned opposite my room, his legs extending to the middle of the hall, thumbs hooked in his pockets. His head lolled to face me. "Maybe."

I mimicked his stance next to my door, my arms crossed over my chest. "Did I give you that impression?" I asked, trying to keep it light. "Because I don't usually make out with—" It was my turn to grow quiet as the pieces clicked together in answer.

He watched it happen. "The first night when we met, I saw the fear in you. You were afraid of me."

I shook my head, even as I said, "I was. But you know why."

"Yes," he breathed.

"So why do you think I'd still be scared of you now?"

"Not...me," he said, his words faltering. He frowned. "Things...bad things, bad memories, don't just go away. And what can make them resurface doesn't always make sense."

I let it sink in. I understood better than I wanted to, but what I wanted more was him.

"Maybe," I agreed. "But if you remember, even when I was afraid of you, I followed you anyway."

He cocked his head to the side, curious. "Why did you?"

"Honestly? Because the alternative was to keep wandering the streets in the dark without a direction. I told myself that I'd been the one to ask. You simply answered." I chuckled softly.

"What's funny?" He wasn't laughing.

"I was thinking, I guess you could say you've become my direction."

His somber eyes widened in surprise.

Holy shit, why did I keep blurting this stuff out?

I'd called him gorgeous. I'd mentioned the taboo four-letter word. If I wasn't careful, my "direction" would be gone, bolting down the hall to get away from the psycho that was me.

"Sorry," I said. "That probably sounded lame."

"It wasn't. But you can change it."

"Change what?"

"It's your turn. Be my direction." He straightened, winding his hands behind him flat and pinned by his butt. His gaze was insistent, a sultry dare. "Show me what to do."

I couldn't keep up with him. This beautiful, sometimes gruff, sometimes sweet, shy, but always sexy man had too many prismatic facets. It was intoxicating, not knowing which side of him I was about to discover next. But I hadn't seen this coming. As I juggled the array of feelings he evoked with such a simple statement, the picture in the puzzle became clear.

He was putting me in charge, relinquishing control, because he knew this was exactly what I needed. Each moment since we started this journey together flashed by in a slideshow. Where we'd gone so far, the things we'd seen and done—he'd left it largely up to me. Whether it had been a conscious decision on his part or not, I couldn't know, but each little choice had silently fed me back that modicum of power.

But this was a big leap, one we both recognized for what it was. It had to be me to deliberately take this step, and he was unequivocally giving me the deciding say once again.

My heart felt fit to burst with appreciation.

And I was about to milk that power for all it was worth.

I moved slowly, and his pupils dilated, the black swallowing up the brown centers, as he tracked each shift and step. My hands splayed against the wall on either side of his head as I smiled my thank you. As I stared deep into his eyes, I noticed his posture thaw a little, but otherwise he stayed perfectly still.

"Can I kiss you?" I asked.

"Come here and kiss me like you want to."

And I did just that.

My lips grazed his—feather-light, part tease, part nerves. He couldn't help his mouth's response, the slightest purse for an extra millimeter more of contact. Our kiss deepened, and his hands finally released from the wall to snake around my hips, drawing me closer. Things were heating up fast, and he broke away to bury his face in the crook of my neck.

"Mallory..." he murmured along my skin, his face tilting up so the words brushed against the bottom of my ear. The soft inflection of his accent when he said my name in full always managed to do something inexplicable to my insides. Gently, his teeth grazed across my lobe. I was already panting, grappling to wad his shirt into my fists.

Taking the reins a little, he pushed me against the wall opposite, cradling my head as he pressed a series of languid kisses from my lips down my neck to my collarbone. His body pressed into me, and I could feel without question he craved me just as badly.

"Emil, *now.*"

He pulled back. "Are you sure? We don't have to—"

I huffed, cutting him off. "That's sweet, but I *do* need to."

177

His answering smile was erotic as his heavy gaze landed on my lips. I fumbled desperately for my key card again. At last, the slide of the dead bolt unlocked much more than just the door.

CHAPTER NINETEEN

I CLUTCHED DESPERATELY TO the last details of my beautiful dream, wishing I could hold on to them forever as the brightness of morning worked to banish them.

Gentle fingers that had run down my arms, sending a chilled thrill of goosebumps along my skin.

The feel of taut muscles beneath my fingertips.

A gentle gasp of breath upon my neck, followed by a swift, tender kiss.

His face cupped between my palms before I released him and searched further.

My body, my mind, my blood sang through my veins—I felt alive and lazy all at once. My skin still tingled, a deep-set satisfaction in my belly, every part of me utterly at ease.

I flung my hands out to the side in a stretch, and the heel of my left hit something both soft and solid.

"Ow!"

I stopped moving, frozen for a few seconds, before cracking open an eye.

Emil lay beside me, bathed in the glow of the sunrise. One of his arms was trapped beneath my shoulders, his free hand rubbing at a point high on his cheek. He squinted at me, eyes sliding to my mouth, which had dropped open in a thunderclap moment of shock.

"Good morning to you, too," he grumbled.

My mouth worked as reality fought to sink in. "Did we...?"

No, it had been a dream!

"Yes," he answered.

My brain denied it at first, but then it all came flooding back.

After the bathhouse we had returned here...it was all a blur of clothes, soft caresses, and...

I blushed.

Crinkled package remnants from chocolate nut bars, chips, cookies, and paper cups stained with red wine lingered on the bedside table, all courtesy of the downstairs corner shop Emil had run to for our makeshift dinner. We'd talked until after sunset before we'd...

My cheeks must've been crimson by now. I peeked up at him from behind my hands, which were clasped over my mouth in a demure gesture, one they had no right to after all their enthusiastic wandering well into the wee hours.

His eyebrows raised as he stopped rubbing where I'd smacked him below his eye. This time, he didn't hesitate before bringing his fingers to my jaw, running a thumb under my lower lip.

"Really?" I breathed, finally believing it.

"I think so, but if punching me is any indication, maybe I did something wrong."

I laughed, hiding shyly again behind my hands. "I'm sorry!"

"Now she says it."

"Well, I wasn't sure if I was really awake." I pouted playfully. "There'd be no need to admit I'd punched Dream You to Real You. And who knows? Perhaps Dream You had done something stupid."

"So," he murmured curiously, "real me didn't do anything stupid last night?"

I shook my head, dropping my hands and turning onto my side.

"Nope. If last night really did happen, then everything was very, very right."

His small smile spoke volumes. "Is that so?" He stroked the backs of his fingers down my cheek, tucking a wayward strand of hair away from my forehead. I snatched his hand before it could retreat, pressing a long kiss into his palm.

"Do you still doubt it?" I asked against his skin, only raising my eyes to stare at him through my lashes.

"Maybe not." His hand lifted out of mine, clasping my chin between a rough thumb and forefinger, guiding me toward him for a soft kiss. That softness transformed, becoming deep and prolonged. His warmth pressed against me as I drew closer without thinking. Like magnets.

The hotel phone buzzed insistently from the nightstand. We jumped apart at the same time at the intrusive sound. Emil flipped over, answering it and listening briefly before hanging up.

"Miss Roth?" His hair slid silkily across the pillow as he turned, his lips brushing against my ear as he whispered, "Your wake-up call." And, so slowly, his teeth grazed the edge of my ear, sending shivers down my spine.

I whimpered. "They deserve a huge tip."

He pulled back. "Why?"

"Because this is the best service I've ever received."

He smirked, drawing me in close.

Eventually, the yearning to explore lured us from bed. Except for Paris, Munich was the biggest city by far that I'd visited on this trip. It was easy to get lost in its pristine streets. In the afternoon, we wandered through the Munich Residenz, a former royal palace and now a museum. I forced him to take pictures of me pretending to summon my butler and resting against the red-velvet rope barrier like it was my private lounge.

His mouth hung open innocently as he stared at the giant frescoes in one grand space, though it transformed into a smile when he shifted and caught me taking candids of him. The image I captured last as he turned made my heart stop. His eyes, lit with the soft light in the room, looked strikingly right into the camera, accompanied by his gentle tilt of a grin.

I glanced up from the photo.

His brows raised in question. "Good?"

I held the phone to my chest and nodded. This one I was keeping just for me.

By early evening, we ambled back to the hotel, punch-drunk from a full day. Outside our separate doors, we paused, the playful look in his eyes surely a match to my own.

"I'll host tonight," was all he said before using his key and stepping inside.

The *Guinness World Records* book should add a new entry for how quickly I dumped my bag and changed. In what seemed like seconds, I was ready. My hair was pulled up into a messy bun, my teeth were brushed, and I sported my usual evening T-shirt and sweats. I rushed over to his room like a kid excited about a sleepover. When he answered the door, the TV played a faint piano melody through the otherwise quiet room. He'd opened the windows, letting in the gentle breeze.

"Romantic," I teased, sliding in past him, and he gave a lopsided grin.

Next to the window, I spied a bottle of wine and two plastic cups, along with a random assortment of snack items.

"Where did this come from?"

"The downstairs shop again." He moved around me to grab the bottle. "Wine?"

I nodded. "But I was only gone for a second."

"I was quick." The end of his sentence was accentuated by the squelching pop of the cork. He poured and handed me a glass as he asked, "What was your favorite thing we saw today?"

I took a sip as I thought. "The clock in the square," I decided, remembering how the miniature Bavarian figures had danced in a circle to celebrate the start of a new hour. "You?"

His thumb traced invisible patterns up and down the ridges of his cup.

"The modern part of town. I think it can be easy to stay in the historical areas of cities and only enjoy what it has been, but it's nice to see what it has become, too."

I pictured the modern neighborhoods we'd ventured through, including their giant street murals and stark architecture. He was right. It was quite the contrast to the old part of town. Two sides of the same coin, past and present.

We kept our pact, helping one another see the city through each other's eyes, talking about this and that until dusk fell. When the snacks and drinks had run dry, we'd climbed into Emil's bed and grown quiet. His nose nuzzled against my temple, and I tilted back for a kiss. It was slow and gentle, a balance to the fervent energy of last night.

Despite what had happened, the same sense of ease we'd cultivated remained. There was still that calmness and comfort in one another's presence, even in the silences. What *was* different was the invisible little string that had formed between us. I could feel where it had taken hold in my chest, and it tugged whenever he moved too far away, so I tried to not let him.

My guess was that it was the same for him because, after our final kiss of the evening, his arm brought me in closer, neither of us willing to break an inch of contact. With the taste of his lips lingering on my tongue, I rested my head on his shoulder as we lay there together, simply drinking in the sounds of Munich until we fell asleep.

I bolted upright the next morning with a sliver of sunlight slapping me across the face. We'd never set an alarm or arranged for a wake-up call, and I yelped when I saw the time.

Emil practically jumped out of bed at the sound.

We barely made it before checkout, lugging our backpacks hurriedly down to the lobby. I blushed as I handed over our room keys, electrically aware of Emil's proximity, the brush of his arm against mine, the way his hand rested against my back as we exited. Once in the car, my head cleared a little as I focused on the task of navigating out of the city.

The lively streets of Munich were soon behind us. Farm land appeared between long stretches of tree-shrouded freeways, the odd castle glimpsed off in the distance as we wove from Germany into the Czech Republic. The occasional dull sections of the drive were becoming my bread-and-butter time to share all the details of our journey with Gail. Today, I wrote with glee.

"What did you tell her?" He cleared his throat as I signed it, nervously eyeing my smirk. I folded the note with a flourish.

"About what?" I toyed.

"Mallory," he warned.

I slid the paper into my purse with a secretive grin. "You'll never know."

After reassuring Emil that I'd spared Gail the majority of the horny details, I busied myself looking for a place to stay, but everything kept coming up full or outrageously pricey unless I searched far from the old town center. Finally, I found one that seemed promising, but my face fell when I looked closer at the listing.

"Oh," I murmured, then let out a frustrated, "Ugh!"

"What?" Emil's knuckles paled against the steering wheel at my shout.

"This one's a group hostel." I flopped the phone down into my lap.

He laughed, his fingers relaxing. "I don't care."

"But it's a dorm and there aren't bunks together."

"We can share." The sentence ended with a slight question.

Deep down, my stomach clenched pleasantly. "But the beds are tiny. Have you forgotten the last time?" Even with the evidence to prove my point, my counter was weak, no heart in it.

"It'll be fine for a few nights."

"We'll be on top of one another."

His lips quirked. "Does that sound bad?"

My initial knot of worry evaporated with my coy smile. "No, I guess not."

CHAPTER TWENTY

When the boundaries of Prague took over the countryside, I dug through my phone again for the hostel's address. The property was situated on a bustling stretch of road with shops, restaurants, and other hotels. The view down the street dead-ended in a gloriously austere building, which I'd read was a museum.

We checked in (with me surveying the recommended materials from the front desk employee with a more critical eye this time), and the concierge looked between me and Emil.

"Your reservation is for a single bed," she said. "We still have to charge for two people and have available bunks in neighboring rooms, if you'd like?"

I opened my mouth, but Emil cut in first. "No, one is fine."

"Are you really sure you'll be comfortable?" I asked after we'd paid and were walking upstairs. I was all for the arrangement, but we were both sleep deprived...for one reason or another.

But Emil shook his head again. "I prefer it."

And I saw why, at least partially, as we settled in before heading out into the early dusk. His gaze roved over the smattering of our fellow mixed-dorm inhabitants. An uncomfortable wave of anxiety flooded my veins, and I avoided meeting any of the other men's curious looks as we walked through the room toward our bunk. They turned away as soon as their eyes landed on Emil. The warmth that seemed ever present inside of me these days flared with appreciation.

The old square was only a few minutes' walk from the hostel. We passed by street vendors selling roasted nuts and frozen treats, while others offered funnel-shaped pastries crisping over a turning spit. The latter's scent made my mouth water—butter and caramelized sugar with cinnamon. Emil bought one for us to try as we strolled. Impossible as it seemed, it tasted even better than it smelled.

I was devouring my last bite when the vast square came into view. I stopped mid-chew. Gothic steeples of a huge church soared overhead to my right while a towering, intricate clock ticked away the seconds on my left. In the middle sat a grand statue of a man, jet-black and looming over the people gathered around, admiring it from every angle.

Emil's hand slid into mine as we gawked. Natural, without thinking.

My pulse thrummed as we circled the courtyard. "What do you know about Prague?"

We came to a stop in front of the huge, formidable statue and stared up at the figure's sharp cheekbones. "Not much, just what we learned in school. Some history of the place." His mouth twitched. "These days...?" He shrugged.

My gaze scraped down from the proud man's face to his feet where prone figures lay. Was he a hero, a saint, or a conqueror?

"Do you know who he is?"

"Jan Hus," Emil said, pointing at a plaque, his voice thoughtful. "I recognize that name. I think he was a religious reformer who became a sort of martyr at his death."

I nodded like I understood. I *wanted* to understand.

"One of the brochures from the hostel mentioned there's a free walking tour," I offered. "I wouldn't normally want to, but this place..." I drifted off, unable to put my finger on it. There was just something different about it. Whispers from the asymmetrical streets leading off the square promised me they'd tell their tale, if only I'd lean in closely enough to hear it.

He nodded, still pensive as we moved on. "Yes, I think that would be good."

We wandered the streets in search of food and tucked in at a cozy, rustic pub. Overlooking the cobbled road, we ordered a hearty dinner. Emil opted for a slow-roasted pork dish. I just had to try the goulash, though the menu strictly specified theirs was made with all-Czech flavors. Two birds, one stone, as far as I was concerned. It sounded delicious.

When the waiter asked presumptuously if we wanted beer with our meal, Emil glanced at the menu and laughed.

"Yes, two, please," he said, handing both our menus to the waiter.

I wasn't about to complain.

"What's funny?" I wondered after the waiter left.

"It's the cheapest thing on the menu," he chuckled. "Even coffee."

"That sounds dangerous."

It *was* dangerous. Our entrees down and two beers each had me floating in a mellow, mushy fog I didn't normally indulge in. What a lightweight.

The waiter cleared our dishes. "Anything more for you?"

I pointed to my empty pint glass. "I'll take another," I said with a lazy grin at Emil. He cocked an eyebrow, but motioned to the waiter for another as well.

"Is that a good idea?" he asked when we were alone. He had to shout a little. The pub had filled to the brim with the after-work crowd.

As if on cue, I hiccuped. I pressed my lips together, pretending to think hard. "Probably not, but what the hell?" My tone turned dead serious. "I'm on vacation."

He huffed a laugh, and I broke character with a broad grin.

"Have you ever been blackout-drunk?" I asked.

"Blackout?"

"Yeah, like you didn't remember stuff?"

"Ah. Not completely, no. Hazy, but not gone entirely." His eyes searched my face curiously. "You?"

Normally, I wouldn't have offered up the truth, but I'd dug this grave myself by asking. "Once. My first year of college. I'd never drank before, not once, so I didn't know what to expect. It just felt so good...until suddenly it didn't." I winced, the morning after as painfully vivid as the night preceding it was shrouded.

He cringed with me in sympathy.

"Learned my lesson, though, didn't I?"

The waiter arrived with our beers.

I laughed again. "Or maybe I haven't."

"It's just beer," Emil said, taking a sip.

"Did you know there have been studies showing that beer can actually boost your brain power?"

"No," he said. "My experience has shown otherwise."

"I guess it has to do with silicon in it," I rambled on. "Something about improving blood flow."

"Blood flow."

"Mhmm." I took a giant swig, gazing around the pub.

"Just to the brain?"

I choked on my beer, finally gasping, "I don't know!"

He let me get my breath back before mercifully starting a new tangent. "Did you like college? The parts you can remember, I mean."

I shot a wicked glare his way. "I remember all but one night, thank you very much."

His teasing smile soothed my embarrassment.

"Yes, I did," I said. "Though I didn't really connect with any of my classmates. We never became more than casual acquaintances. I don't know why." It had bothered me, yet I hadn't admitted it to anyone until now. I'd never had trouble making friends before, but something kept me at a distance from them.

"You did well in school?" he continued probing.

I watched the bubbles from the bottom of my glass reach the foam at the top, keeping my tone casual. "Yeah, I did all right."

"How all right?"

"Why do you ask?"

"Because I can tell you care."

I winced. "I graduated in the top of my class."

"Near the top or...?"

I groaned. "At the top, top, okay?"

He smirked. "And you can't guess why you never connected with your peers?"

Until now, it hadn't even occurred to me that there was a correlation. We were all going to school for the same thing, trying to snag the best placements after the program we could get. Grades, class standings, and teacher recommendations—it all mattered. Somewhere in my gut, I'd known it all along, so I'd taken things seriously from day one. Professionally, it had served me well. Socially, on the other hand...

"No," I admitted. "I never thought of it that way."

"My guess? You were nice to them, but always too busy to spend much time with them because of your goals. You'd go to a party here and there to show you were part of them, but you were never inside their inner circle."

I gaped.

He nodded, not needing any further response. "You're passionate. It's a good thing. I'd guess they were jealous of your dedication. It's admirable."

"And isolating." I'd never admitted it. Admitted it hurt to be the outcast. It hadn't been an issue in the past. During my undergraduate studies, I'd been the life of the party, the socialite, wanting to be involved. I hadn't stopped desiring those things during my nursing program, but I couldn't afford the time or money this go-around to play fast and loose with my life. So I attained something else. Prestige.

"Have you ever been in that position?" I asked tentatively.

"Which?" His finger swirled over the rim of his glass.

"An outsider."

He licked his lips and was silent for a moment. "Yes." I could barely hear his voice over the tumult, but the hurt was there. I burned inside to know why, but his demeanor had clammed up.

I stared at the dark wood beams reaching overhead for somewhere to look while I searched for a new topic. Something light, something easy...

I grinned. "Never have I ever...snorted cocaine." I sipped my beer as my gaze switched back to his face.

He rolled his eyes, looking down at the table. "Never have I ever been to London."

I frowned. "No fair."

"Why?"

"Because I knew that already."

"And you think I didn't know you hadn't snorted cocaine?" he asked wryly.

I shrugged noncommittally. "Maybe I used to be a rebel. And there are different methods of use, too. You have to be specific."

He sighed, letting it go. "Still, I don't see how it's not fair?"

"You're supposed to kind of try to one-up the other person," I explained. "Like if you know they've done something, and you haven't."

"Seems like it would be the other way around. Wouldn't people who have done something be the better one?"

"Depends on what the thing is," I debated.

"Ah, I see." He considered his transgression. "What's my penalty?"

I pretended to weigh my options. "Not sure yet. I'll let you know when the votes are in."

He smiled as he looked across the room and waved to the waiter for the check. "Never have I ever woken up hungover."

My jaw dropped. "Not possible." I gestured at his practically empty glass. "You're not sober."

"No, I'm not." He made a point by finishing the dregs.

"You were young once."

He choked. "Thanks for that."

"I meant, you had to have partied."

"I did."

"So...?"

He lifted a shoulder. "I don't know what to tell you. I just don't get hungover."

"But..but!" I blubbered. It wasn't fair. "I hate you for never having had to feel the misery of it. It's a shared human experience!" I laughed through my bewilderment.

"You don't hate me."

"That's true," I said, continuing in a singsong voice, "Never have I ever hated you."

His eyes twinkled. "I think I already knew that."

My heart skipped. "Dang. Want our penalties to just cancel each other out?"

He considered me, the playful devil in his gaze boiling my blood. "No, I don't think I do."

I breathed deeply through my nose. "Then what's my penalty?"

His dark grin played with my insides. "I'll figure something out."

After paying, we stood and headed out along the streets, wandering in no particular direction as we continued our game.

"Never have I ever eaten brains," I threw out as a given.

"You really should. They're delicious."

I smacked his arm. "And this coming from the man who couldn't stomach eating squid ink risotto?"

He chuckled, quickly dodging with, "Never have I ever eaten a bug."

My mouth dropped open, and I pointed at myself vigorously.

"You haven't," he countered. "On purpose?"

"At camp, when I was thirteen," I crowed, hands in the air.

"I don't believe you," he challenged.

"Oh, excuse me, Mr. I Eat Brains," I hit back, then cleared my throat, preparing to begin story time. "I met a girl there who was from Mexico, and she brought fried crickets with her after a trip visiting family."

"You ate one?"

"One? I wanted to steal the whole bag."

"You're joking." He didn't sound so sure this time.

"Nope." I mimicked a chef's kiss.

He sighed. "I can't compete with that."

The wide Vltava River slid by on our left as we walked the footpath upstream. Old-fashioned streetlamps cast a warm glow onto the immaculately clean sidewalk. The Charles Bridge gleamed ahead of us in the darkness, sending dots of light dancing across the water below.

I nodded toward it. "Never have I ever jumped off a bridge." The smugness was thick in my voice.

"I knew that as well," he said cuttingly.

"No, only that I've not jumped off Stari Most. But the rest of my life?" I lifted my palms in a shrug.

"I guessed."

"Oh Emil," I sighed behind a pitying smile. "You need to pay better attention to the rules. We already talked about this. Specifics are important."

He pulled me to a stop. I hadn't even noticed we were linked, my hand having automatically slipped into his. His body pushed me toward the railing, my back to the river.

"Still, I think I should get at least half a penalty point." His eyes drifted in a long caress down my face, his voice as quiet as his eyes were dark in a delicious sort of way.

"I don't think there are half points," I managed to squeak out.

His arms wrapped around me on either side, his hands grasping the railing, pinning me in. He leaned forward, whispering, "Then give me an extra confession, and I'll let you off." Electricity sang from the tickle of his words against my skin before he soothed it with a soft kiss to my cheek.

I gasped. "Never have I ever met someone quite like you."

He stilled.

Embarrassment finally blasted through my lack of inhibitions. I twisted toward the river.

He pressed into me from behind. "Not fair."

"Why?"

Instead of answering me, he smoothed the hair from the back of my neck, his lips brushing against the sensitive spot slowly, barely touching.

"This doesn't feel like a penalty," I said, a little breathless, my head bending to the side in invitation. He took a full step back.

That did.

"Hey!" I protested, spinning and reaching for him. But he danced away, my fingers missing him by millimeters. I giggled, but pouted when I missed again. "Now *that's* not fair."

He grinned, walking backward out of reach as I continued to try to catch him. "I played your game fair and square," he said, then winked. "You should pay closer attention to the rules."

I finally caught up to him, my forehead damp after running about in my light jacket. "I suppose." He reached out, taking my hand once more. "But I still have your penalty to deal out, too."

"What penalty?"

I shook my head sadly. "How quickly he forgets."

He thought for a moment, then said, "Ah, London. So what have you decided?"

"Haven't yet. I've got the rest of the night to think of something."

Did I imagine him stiffen?

A flush colored his cheeks as I asked, "Does that make you nervous?"

"Should it?"

I did my best to mimic his mischievously dark gaze from earlier. I probably just looked demented.

We began our return to the hostel, silent, in our own heads. The magic of the spotlights on the towering black steeples and manicured streets cast us out of time and place. We could be in a medieval turn in Prague's history. At any second, around the next corner, there might be a horse and carriage transporting some prince along their way from a night on the town. Or a car's headlights could flash across the square, firmly setting us back into the here and now. It was anybody's guess.

Upstairs, we prepared for bed, taking turns in the communal bathroom before tiptoeing into the dark room. Snuffles and deep breathing cut through the muffled quiet, then the creak of springs as someone turned in the bunk above ours.

"Which side do you want?" Emil whispered.

I snorted, muttering, "What sides?"

The whites of Emil's eyes flashed, catching in the light coming through the slats of the shuttered windows.

"You first," I decided.

He climbed in, his back practically pressed against the wall. Still, only a slight sliver of space remained available for me. I sat down on the bed, then slipped my feet beneath the covers as I lay down and faced him.

Emil hissed when my chilly toes met his skin.

"You could have warned me," he complained as my head settled next to his.

"It's part of your penance," I whispered.

"Only part?"

"Mhmm." I tucked the thin sheets up to my chin, grasping the edge in one fist. The room was icy, the air conditioner on full blast to counteract all the bodies cramped into the space.

"And have you decided on the rest?" he pressed. "Your time is almost up."

"There's no time limit."

"Midnight. It's like Cinderella."

"I didn't spot any pumpkins around," I said snarkily.

"The anticipation is killing me."

I pondered for a few seconds. "Okay, give me another revelation while I think about the ultimate and final penalty."

He thought about it before saying, "Never have I ever sung in front of anyone before."

I let that sink in.

"Never?" I scoffed. "Not even as a kid?"

He shook his head.

"Oh, c'mon," I pushed. "You might not remember."

"Oh, I'd remember." His voice was dark. I raised a disbelieving brow. "Trust me."

I slumped, still not convinced. "Have you ever heard yourself sing? Alone?"

He smirked. "How do you think I learned I should never do it in public?"

I laughed.

"Time's up," he said, his breath ruffling the baby hairs long my forehead. "What do you want, Mallory?"

I flipped over, the bed creaking simultaneously with someone else shifting in their bunk. My back and hips pushed up against him. Sure, I could use the tiny bed as an excuse, but who was I kidding? "Your body heat."

"You've already taken it. And on more than one occasion, I recall."

"I'm freezing." It came out louder than I'd intended in my desperation.

"I can help warm you up," said an unfamiliar, American southern drawl.

I squinted through the shadows toward the sound of the voice. In the bunk opposite, barely a few feet away, lay the murky outline of a fair-haired man I definitely didn't remember seeing earlier.

"Excuse me?"

He propped himself up on an elbow. "Want to cuddle?"

Emil appeared over my shoulder, and blondie's entire posture went ram-rod straight.

"Sure, thanks," Emil said, his tone holding a warning beneath the playful sarcasm.

Without another word, the man flopped down onto his mattress, faced the wall, and feigned sleep.

I followed his lead, turning to Emil again as I worked to keep my donkey-bray of laughter quiet and failed. His hand pressed over my mouth so I wouldn't wake up the entire room.

"Oh my gosh!" The words were muffled by Emil's fingers.

"Shh."

"I can't breathe," I complained.

In response, Emil's arms circled me, my own crossed over my chest like I was about to be buried. Which was appropriate, since I apparently had just died and gone to heaven.

Emil's hands eased along my shoulders, using friction to rub warmth into my skin. One of his legs hitched over my hips, locking me into his heat. His fingers traveled farther afield, grazing my lower back on their way to my behind for an instant before moving up again. An embarrassingly loud sigh escaped from my chest, and I let my head drop into the crook of his neck. The fact we were surrounded by a room of sleepy and not so asleep people made me tense, but any audience was worth this.

"Better?" he murmured.

"Don't stop."

CHAPTER TWENTY-ONE

OVER BREAKFAST, WE SIFTED through the information we'd gathered. Emil proposed the tour could wait until tomorrow. Instead, eyes filled with excitement, he spread open a brochure for the Bohemian Switzerland National Park between us, running his finger along a windy, squiggly line weaving up a steep mountain. The mild weather predicted for today, he insisted, meant it was perfect to go beyond the city to explore the countryside. I pulled a face, picturing myself scrambling up the side of a mountain and transforming into a gross, sweaty mess. He spotted it immediately and used the ace up his sleeve, pointing to a paragraph about a restaurant waiting at the end of the trail.

Good move, enticing me with food. He was a fast learner.

I'd played hard-to-get halfheartedly before giving in. Every sore muscle I was about to endure was worth the price of his childish look of glee at the prospect of returning to the mountains.

Emil steered the car north while I marked up the park map from the visitor center. I added asterisks to the hike the guest services representative had recommended, highlighting viewpoints on the way to the Pravčicka Brana arch.

The hike was a total of eight miles round trip and wove through untouched stretches of forest and sculptured rock formations, the path narrowing the higher we climbed. Plenty of tourists joined us along the trail, and we chatted with others as we paused to catch our breath, munch on protein bars, or simply take in the views.

At one of the overlooks on the steepest portion of the hike yet, I held out my phone in a silent request to Emil as I puffed.

"Now?" he said, lifting a brow as he watched me gasp, my hands pressed to my knees.

I nodded, managing to get out, "This is reality. We have to capture the good and the bad." Tomato-red face, sweat-slicked hair, the whole lot.

He chose not to comment, instead waiting for me to walk to the edge of the trail where the side of the arch was visible past the trees. I plastered on a smile and raised my hands overhead. I dropped them the moment the phone clicked, my arms noodly with fatigue, and stepped to him.

Wordlessly, he handed me my phone and immediately went to the same spot.

"What is this?" I teased in awe. "You want a photo?"

"There's no point fighting anymore," he said resolutely.

I cackled at breaking this stallion.

He rolled his eyes, smiled a genuine grin for the picture, and then we were off again.

It was all perfect—the views, the weather, the company—which meant that I had to ruin it. At the halfway point, I managed to stumble over a camouflaged rock. The same ankle I'd injured in Marseille twisted at an awkward angle, and I yelped as I crumpled face-forward to the ground. Emil, who had been leading the way, stopped at my cry and hurried to me.

"Shit," I cursed through gritted teeth as he helped me scoot to the side of the dusty path.

"What hurts?"

"My pride," I grumbled as I stuck my leg out and rubbed at my ankle. He pulled my stretchy yoga pants up to my mid-calf. "I'm not sure what to look for," he admitted with a wince.

"It's nothing, just a twist. I hurt it..." I swallowed as the memory seared like a flash. "Before." I peeked up at him, and his attention was no longer on my ankle. He saw right through me.

"The night I jumped from the fire escape," I volunteered in a whisper. Saying it sent a sting through my chest, but also erased the small weight that had settled there in an instant.

His jaw gave a single tick and, with a tight nod, he ran soft fingers over my bare leg.

"Does this hurt?" he asked, pressing his thumb gently into my muscle.

"No," I breathed. "Let me see how it feels to move it." I tested it this way and that, grimacing at the pain when I rotated it to the right.

"What can I do to help?"

"Nothing, I just have to wait. Sorry."

"You don't need to apologize." He plopped down next to me, pulling the stainless-steel water bottle from his pack and holding it against my ankle. I sighed with relief at its chilly touch.

"I could distract you," he offered quietly.

Heat seared through my belly, and I chanced a look in either direction. For the moment, we were the only two here. "Oh really? And what do you imagine would distract me?"

"Hmm...this." With his free hand, he knotted my hair in his fist, kissing the hollow space behind my ear. It was a maddening combination of ticklishness and electricity, the sensation pulsing from the single point of contact like a firework. He let my hair drop, his hand drifting instead down to tease along my ribcage before grasping my hip firmly.

He caught my earlobe between his teeth and gently tugged. "And this," he muttered, not letting go.

I gasped, the ticklishness vaporized, my body a live wire shooting sparks without relief.

His fingers caressed my jaw as he released my ear and turned my face toward his. The brown of his eyes had been swallowed up with darkness as he caught my lower lip between his, so gently, sucking it lightly before pressing his mouth to mine—finally—in full.

He tasted of peppermint, along with an ever-present sweetness that I could now recognize on command, and a slight saltiness of sweat from one or both of us from the hike. I wanted more of him and urged his lips to open with my tongue, and he obliged. I grasped his head between my hands and heard the soft *clink* of the water bottle against the rocks as he let it go. Both his hands worked through my hair, tangling at the base of my neck.

My body sang as I twisted on the ground, pressing my chest against his, searching for that extra inch of contact. His hands drifted down my back once more to stop at its lowest point, pulling me in tighter.

"Ahem...on your right."

We sprang apart, both instantly beet-red as we faced the trio nearing us on the path. The lanky man leading them offered up a knowing grin before diligently looking straight ahead.

When they'd gone, I put a hand over my mouth and giggled. Emil smiled back with a light shake of his head.

"How does it feel?" He jerked his chin toward my ankle.

The pain had been forgotten, and it only twinged a bit when I moved it. "I think...it might be okay now."

"So it worked?" His tone was haughty as he stood and offered me a hand.

"Well," I said as I took it, "I won't be trying that method in the emergency room anytime soon, but...yeah, I think it did."

And then I put my full weight on it and faltered.

"It's not okay," Emil countered, all business.

"It will be." I bit my lip, worrying at the distance we still had to reach the top. "You should keep going. I'll catch up."

The heavy roll of his eyes quickly dismissed my suggestion. "We can just wait here together. It's no rush."

"I have no idea how long it'll take, though. I didn't hurt it badly, but since it already had a sprain, I might be awhile...if at all." The fact that I'd have to find a way down off this mountain eventually was a problem I could solve while he completed the hike.

He bit the inside of his cheek as he thought, then pulled our light day-pack from his shoulders. "Put this on."

I frowned as I took it. "I don't think adding extra weight will help."

"I'm going to carry you."

"What? Oh, hell no."

"Mallory, I told you that I do hikes all the time with my friends back home. I've done much longer and difficult distances than this, all while carrying a full overnight pack that weighs more than you."

"But—"

He took the backpack from my limp fingers and moved behind me. "Arms out."

"Emil—"

"I'm not going to just leave you here. I will put you down when you're ready, but I promised you food—proper food—and I'm not breaking another one of our bargains." My tense shoulders were a dead giveaway that I hadn't given in yet. He knelt as he said, "We made a pact, remember? Don't make a liar out of me."

I knew it was a ploy, but it was a good one. Thanks for the well-intentioned guilt trip, sir. I heaved a sigh. "All right. Load me up."

He snorted, waiting for me to hold my arms out before slipping on the pack. When it was secured, he squatted in front of me. "Climb on."

I hadn't gotten a piggyback ride in...well, ever. My arms circled around his neck uncertainly, and he grasped my forearms to keep them there while he stood. I squealed as my toes skipped through the dirt.

"Hitch your legs up," he instructed. At the same time, he reached down to grab behind my knees. Instinctively, I locked my legs around his waist, still worried I was strangling him.

"Is this okay?" I asked, flexing my arms a little to make a point.

He coughed for effect. "Yeah, it's fine. Just keep them here." He guided them lower so that my forearms rested at the base of his throat and collarbone instead, his fingertips lingering on my skin for a moment longer before setting off.

It was the best hike I had ever gone on, easily, thanks to the now steady press of our bodies together. If I was uncomfortably heavy, Emil didn't complain. Every once in a while, he would stroke his hand in a soothing path along my arms or would reach back to pat my hair, asking if I was still all right. I would sneak in a kiss against his neck or squeeze him a little tighter while smiling like a fool.

I was almost disappointed when we stopped for another break, and I tested my ankle to find that it was much better. Emil traded me for the backpack again, and I gave it a jealous glare as it replaced me, bouncing against his shoulders.

Eventually we made it to the end, and beholding the arch was worth my injury alone. It towered ahead, a beautifully gaping hole cut into the sandstone, creating a stunning picture frame around the panoramic views of the valley and mountains. Nestled between the arch and the neighboring hillside sat the red-roofed restaurant, so perfectly situated between the two, it was as if a sculptor had chiseled through the rock and revealed it. We took our time enjoying a meal there, soaking in as much of the mesmerizing views as we could, before attempting the steep hike down.

My ankle throbbed dully during the descent, and my muscles were screaming before we even made it to the car. The hour-and-a-half drive back to Prague provided them all the opportunity to cool and cramp. I practically hobbled upstairs to the bathroom to wallow under the hot stream of water before I started to feel selfish and gave others a turn.

After our big lunch, Emil and I opted for a light dinner. We went downstairs and put together sandwiches from the hostel's help-your-self-to-odds-and-ends kitchen. Exhausted, we turned in pitifully early and were instantly asleep.

When I awoke, the sunlight blared off the stark white walls.

"Finally."

I didn't move other than to let my eyes drift open and upward. I was in the exact same position I'd fallen asleep, cradled in Emil's arms with my own crisscrossed over my chest.

"Hi," I mumbled.

"Good morning."

When he pulled away, sadness dipped my stomach, but the tingle in my arms as blood returned sent me moving, shaking out my hands.

"What time is it?"

"Probably noon by now," he grumbled.

"Noon?" My heart sank. "But we were going to go on the tour."

"I'm kidding. I don't know. It feels like hours since I woke up."

"I'm sorry it was so horrible for you, lying here."

His lips twitched. "Just terrible."

With a grin, I swung my legs over the bed, grabbing my phone. "It's only nine!"

The whole bed shook with the force of his stretch. "Time passes slowly when you can't move."

"You could have shoved me off." I yanked on my jeans, then pulled my hoodie over my head, the room colder now that we were the only inhabitants.

"Next time I will." He followed suit getting dressed, and we headed down for breakfast.

The tour group met in the town square, beneath what our guide quickly pointed out was the oldest astronomical clock still in operation.

Our little assembly wandered the streets. Around each bend, it was as if we had entered an entirely new city. The square was full of its Gothic spires. The next corner brought us through the Jewish quarter, the street framed by gorgeous synagogues and a historic, cramped graveyard. Cement pillars and boxy buildings took their turn until, eventually, they gave way to the Renaissance of the Charles Bridge and its Baroque statues. The guide spoke of Prague's tumultuous history as we stopped in a clump on the sidewalks in each neighborhood. Various occupations throughout the ages had left their stylistic marks upon the city, still glaringly apparent through the remaining architecture. The resilience of Prague's people marked their own triumphs after repeatedly fighting to reclaim and defend their home, restoring, rebuilding, or preserving those moments from times of great adversity, honoring the good and bad.

At least they got their peace at last. I gazed at the city with heavy admiration.

We crossed the river and made our way through burnt-orange roofed houses to the top of the hill where a castle complex waited, the jet-black points of the vast basilica at its center hovering ominously above it all. It was yet another fascinating conglomeration of different eras. I turned to Emil, my comment stopping as I took him in. His mouth was open with childlike wonder, but it didn't reach his eyes. They were withdrawn, even sad.

"If you'll follow me," the guide continued, leading us to the rear of the cathedral.

When the tour was finally complete, we found ourselves back in the square by the astrological clock. While Emil studied the map we'd each been given, I stepped away with several others in our group to hand the guide a tip.

"Thank you, that was wonderful."

"I'm glad you enjoyed it," he said kindly, pocketing the money. "How long are you here?"

"One more night."

"If you're interested, the theater I mentioned where Mozart held performances of *Figaro* and *Don Giovanni* is around the corner. Right now they are showing his *Magic Flute*. Box seats can be very reasonable compared to America." His expression was playful.

"How did you know?" I asked with a teasing laugh. At this point, I might as well go with the trend and be in on the joke of my obvious foreignness.

"I'm not deaf."

I smiled in concession, then addressed his suggestion. "I've never been to an opera before."

He leaned in with a smile. "Then you must." He waved as he walked toward the square. "Have a good visit."

"Thanks."

Emil joined me. "What was that about?"

I chuckled darkly. "Do you want to go to an opera?"

His look of rebuke was exactly what I'd predicted. "Opera?"

"Have you ever been?"

He snorted. "No."

"Me neither. Want to live on the edge with me?"

"Not really."

"I'll owe you." I added a wink.

His mouth turned up at the corners even as he sighed dramatically. "All right. Why not?"

We purchased the tickets, which were at least as affordable as our guide had promised. In our room, I put on the black wrap dress I'd packed just in case. I slid on shimmering gold ballet flats and twisted my hair up into a knot at the back of my head. Emil was tucking a simple but crisp button-down shirt into black slacks when I came in from the bathroom.

He paused, his eyes widening in a way that was absolutely adorable. "You look beautiful."

I blushed. "You don't look so bad yourself."

His hands slowed as he smoothed his shirt. "Is this okay? I didn't pack anything for a special occasion."

"We're going to be stuffed into a dark corner for three hours. I don't think anyone will really care."

The three hours comment had his nose wrinkling, but then his forehead smoothed. "What will I do if I get bored?"

I bent toward the tiny mirror beside the door to hide my grin, swiping on some lipstick. "I might be able to think of something."

As it turned out, we were both equally enthralled with the beauty of the theater inside. Gorgeous frescoes wrapped the walls along the horseshoe-shaped space and ceiling, decorative carvings twisting elegantly around each theater box. Our seats were situated upon a small platform near the back of our box, but no one ever claimed the chairs in front of us. We were completely alone.

People below chatted as they found their seats, the general buzz of excitement in the room filtering up to us.

Emil's hand rested on my knee. "I'm glad we came."

"Me, too."

"I never pictured this place."

"The theater?"

His head shook. "The city. It's so unapologetic."

"What do you mean?"

"Everything it's been through. No one hid the marks left behind." He paused. "Each attempt to turn it into something else only made it stronger, instead of tearing it down and starting fresh."

I could practically see the wheels turning. Mostar remained very much a town in healing, its wounds still sensitive and open. How would they choose to rebuild? Would they wash the history away completely, fill every bullet hole, repair every window, tear each ruin down section by section? Or would they honor its past, the price of which would be the constant reminders of what it and its people had endured?

"You know you already do that, right?"

"Hmm?"

"Stari Most may have been rebuilt, but you respect it for the symbol it has become. Before, maybe it was just a bridge? Now, it's so much more. And the trench art. You aren't throwing those casings in the trash. You are embracing your past. You can take inspiration from here or not, but there's no shame in rebuilding your own way."

His fingers squeezed my leg.

"My father was an architect." His words were barely a whisper.

A stone settled in my stomach. "He was?"

He gave a curt nod. "I never knew him. I was only a few months old when he died. My mother never talks about him. Mia would sometimes share little snippets of what she remembered, but she was only six when he passed."

I bit my lip, torn on whether or not to ask.

He let out a small breath. "During the war," he said simply, answering my unspoken question. "He was trying to help, handing out food. He was in an apartment building when fighting began and a..." He paused, his jaw tense. "Part of the roof and upper floors collapsed."

Emil's face blurred as tears filled my eyes. "I'm so sorry."

He pulled his hand from my knee, smoothing both his palms down his thighs. "When I was ten, I was going through a chest in our house and found a folder of his designs." He shook his head. "I'd never seen blueprints before. I didn't know they were his. I'd never seen his handwriting. But those drawings, it was as if I was reading a story for the first time, even if I didn't understand the language. I could see them being built in my mind's eye, like magic."

The lights flickered, warning the show was to begin momentarily.

"Keep going," I urged him.

"When I asked my mother about them...it was the only time she spoke about him with me. She told me everything. How they'd met, how he'd lived—and how he'd died. It felt like it was my one chance to learn who he was." He swallowed. "He sounded wonderful. For a while, I used to imagine bringing his visions to life."

"Why didn't you?"

His head gave a slight jerk, stopping it mid-shake. "University wasn't an option. My grades were never good, and without a scholarship..." His tone was clipped when he continued. "Immediate work was more important. I took any odd job. When tourism started picking up in Mostar, Amin needed help at the shop, so I stepped in." His jaw locked. "I grew up."

I could see it so clearly, understood the need to simply get by. My heart clenched. I had been able to realize my dreams, even though it'd taken more time than I'd wanted. But Emil? I cleared my throat softly. "And now?"

"Being here, seeing this city...I haven't thought about any of this in a long time."

"Dreams don't have an expiration date, Emil," I said, my voice firm.

The lights dimmed, throwing the theater into blackness before a spotlight illuminated the actor coming in from the wings. He pandered to the audience, and they laughed at his over-the-top antics. Finally, the curtains drew back. The set pieces were elaborate, painted in rich colors, saturating the magical world and drawing us into its dreamscape.

I was only somewhat paying attention, aware Emil was still absorbed in his thoughts. I reached into his lap, grabbing his hand with a gentle squeeze.

"Come with me," I whispered, tilting my head toward the stage with an inviting smile. "Come dream with the rest of us."

CHAPTER TWENTY-TWO

WHEN THE LIGHTS IN the theater had come up, and the last of the applause following the curtain call had died away, the room filled with a creak and rustle as people filed out of the theater. I sat still in my seat, Emil a mirror at my side.

"Wow."

"That was..." he tried.

"A lot?" I offered.

"Yeah."

"Funny?"

"That, too," he agreed.

"Thanks for coming," I said with a smile.

"Thanks for forcing me to."

It was as though we were rising up for air after a long dive. Reality. But I was still stuck in a strange in-between, the same as when one just finished a great book. With Emil beside me, though, it felt more like I'd stepped from the page of one fairy tale into another...my fairy tale.

I stopped breathing.

"Are you all right?" His hand brushed down my thigh.

"I'm fine," I said, quickly dismissing my errant thought. "Ready?"

He stood, pulling my jacket from my chair and helping me slip it on. His hand eased against my lower back as he guided me out of the box and down through the bustling lobby.

Outside, the brisk night air ruffled my hair, but the goosebumps along my arms beneath my jacket had nothing to do with its cool touch. We walked through the square, somehow both drawn toward the river as though we'd discussed it in advance. Like we were in perfect unison.

We made it to the Charles Bridge. Emil stopped under a flickering lantern, and I followed suit. Together, we leaned against the rail, watching the water billow below, lost in our own musings.

Of course, mine roved across the information he'd shared about his father. Images I'd viewed in the Stari Most museum took on a more personal meaning—the bombings, the subsequent reconstruction, those who had dedicated so much to rebuilding the physical and spiritual ties between the city. As an architect and a seemingly generous human being, Emil's father certainly would have been a part of it if he'd lived.

My mind zeroed in on our conversation at dinner in the pub our first evening here, prior to commencing the Never Have I Ever game. "What did you mean the other night?" I blurted out suddenly. "When you said you'd experienced life as an outsider?"

His fingers twisted. "War makes outsiders of a lot of people," he said carefully, his words stiff. "Even now in Mostar there's some division. I don't know if it will ever go away." He looked into empty space.

"I shouldn't have pried. You don't have to explain, Emil."

He plowed on as if I hadn't spoken. "My mother and Omar are from opposite sides of that divide. When it first came out that they were together, there were some who spoke against it."

I scowled. "It wasn't any of their business."

A hollow smirk crossed his face. "You sound like my mother."

I hoped it was a compliment.

"She said people would always talk. Let them. They are full of hot air and, in the end, they run out of it."

211

"Did they?"

He sighed. "Eventually."

"But in the beginning?"

"I was still in school. It was not fun to hear through whispers. Or to my face, on occasion."

"People can be busybodies."

"Worse things have happened." He cleared his throat, his expression warming for an instant. "And it was worth it."

I tilted my head into his line of sight, and he met my gaze with a small smile to match mine. "What was?"

"Seeing how happy he made her."

I nodded gently and stared out at the flickering city. "I like that."

"Sometimes people work, even through bad times. Sometimes not." His voice was flat.

I wasn't sure what to say. Of course he was right, but was he only talking about the difficulties his mother and stepfather had endured to find love? His tone seemed to imply something more. I mulled over his words, dissecting them piece by piece to see if I could fit them together.

"What are your dreams, Mallory?"

My head snapped toward him. "Huh?"

"At the play, you said to come away and dream. What do you dream of?"

I chewed my lip, looking past him toward the red-topped buildings on the other side of the bridge. "I dream of...making a difference. With my work, but also just a hope of making some kind of impact, you know?" I met his gaze before wrinkling my nose. "I'm not going to make a big dent in the issues of the world, but I like to think every little bit counts, even if it's as simple as giving vaccinations or putting a bandage on."

"It does."

Right, Dr. Tanović. "I suppose you would know, wouldn't you?"

"I have some insight." He turned his back on the river, bending so his elbows rested on the stone edge. "What else?"

"What do you mean?"

"Work isn't everything," he prompted.

"To some people it is."

He picked at a nail, waiting.

"I don't know," I said hesitantly. "I guess the stuff everyone wants."

"Which is?"

"A life well lived."

"I'm not joking."

"Neither am I." I glanced at him, a little frustrated. Where was this going?

His expression was a mask. "When you return home, you will…what?"

I lifted a shoulder, excitement sparking at the thought. And something also twisted inside me. Guilt, I realized. This trip, everything that had happened, had somehow swept the other dreams I'd made real under the rug.

"I have a job waiting for me." The words sounded strange, like I was just discovering this after a long bout of amnesia. "*The* job, actually. I signed up with a company that places traveling nurses all over the country. They had a few postings, one of which wouldn't be available until the fall, and I got it. So I took this trip between graduation and starting. It was…"

Fate.

"Perfect," he finished for me. I couldn't find the air in my lungs, so I simply nodded.

When he spoke, his voice had an edge to it. "That's good."

It didn't sound good.

"Yeah, it is." Why did I sound defensive?

"You fought for it, your future. It's important to you. It should be. You worked hard to achieve it. Whatever it takes to be happy, right?"

I didn't disagree with his words, but his agreeable tone set me on edge. "Yeah, sure. Whatever it takes."

He nodded, looking down at his clasped hands. "So this was a getaway before the start to the next chapter in your life?"

I shrugged. "I always wanted to travel, so it seemed the time before I got settled in."

"You should have what you want."

"Thanks." I twisted to face away from the river, my posture stiff, body on high alert. Something was definitely off. Was it me? He was saying the right things, and yet...

I dodged. "And you? What are your dreams?"

"I already told you."

"Work isn't everything," I mimicked.

"I already have work. That is something else."

"So you're going to pursue it? Architecture?" That was quick, though I wondered if passions ever really faded or just lingered beneath the surface, waiting for you to reach out for them again. My eagerness at the possibility of his happiness mingled with the weird tension that had reared its head out of nowhere.

He shrugged, his brows lifting gently. "Maybe."

"What's there to think about?"

"There are always things to consider," he murmured.

"Such as?"

A puff of wind was the only sound between us as I waited. Slowly, he looked up, staring straight into my eyes, unblinking. I was a captive in his look. There was something desperate, questioning, mixed with a furious kind of fervor. Like he was standing on the ledge of that damn bridge, second-guessing before taking the leap.

My mouth popped open with a tiny intake of breath. My insides tensed, every nerve in my body on edge. I had the sense I was radiating a warning sign, flickering around my entire being with a flashing yellow light.

Whatever battle was being waged inside him, the side urging him to jump lost. The heat left his eyes, a wall shuttering behind them before he broke our gaze. "Nothing. There's nothing."

Even as my body relaxed, it was to a sense of emptiness inside. What had just happened? How had this wonderful, magical evening taken such a cold turn? I couldn't grasp what route we'd taken to get here.

"Are you ready to go back?" he asked gently, already moving.

My heart leapt into my throat. "Back?"

Curiosity pricked behind his blank demeanor. "To the hostel."

Oh. "Sure, I guess so."

As we walked, I waited. Waited for the easy small talk to return, for the brush of his fingers to entwine with mine, to wipe away the strange aloofness that had settled between us. I thought about breaking it myself, the growing barrier. But I hadn't started this. He had with his questions. If someone was to tear it down, it was up to him.

Once more, we prepared for bed in silence, pulling clothes and toiletries from our packs. But whereas last night had included small brushes of clothes and skin in the darkness, tonight was a game of keep-away.

I locked the bathroom door behind me and stared at my reflection in the splotchy mirror. The single bright bulb over the vanity did nothing to help the stark panic building inside me. Instead, it highlighted the worried brightness in my eyes, the paleness of my lips, the sparkle of threatening tears.

It had all been going great, the perfect evening until, suddenly, it wasn't. I wracked my brain for a misplaced word, something that could have been misinterpreted, but came up blank. I quickly finished scrubbing my teeth and rushed into the room.

Emil was in bed, his back to the middle, facing the wall.

Apparently it was my turn to play the big spoon.

I sat on the bed, sliding beneath the covers, my head near his ear.

"Emil?"

"Hmm?"

"Did I do something wrong? I—"

He turned enough for me to see his face in profile. "You didn't do anything wrong."

"But—"

He twisted an inch more, concern etched across his forehead. "You didn't do anything, okay?" he said, his voice tinged with regret. "I'm happy you know what you want."

If that were true, then why did he sound so sad?

I licked my parched lips. "Okay."

He gave a stiff nod. "Goodnight." He settled tighter against the wall.

Hurt punched through my chest. Touching him felt like it was out of bounds, despite the tiny bed. I flipped over to face the room, keeping my hands to myself even as I couldn't help the brush of my back against his. It was cold, so much colder than last night, but it didn't have anything to do with the temperature of the room this time.

The chill followed me into my dreams.

It was bitter sea air.

It was the scratch of gritty, white sand.

It was the whistle of wind through a bus window.

It was the icy fingers down my skin.

It was the deathly grasp of fear, deep, deep down.

"Wake up."

It was ridiculous how easily his voice could pull me from the nightmare now. One second I was in the dream, and the next I knew exactly that I lay beside Emil in this absurdly tiny bed in Prague. The terror faded, but it was replaced by the memory of last night. Or tonight. I had no idea what time it was, other than it was still dark outside.

"Sorry," I whispered, curling up tighter into a ball. I felt him shift behind me and, even though I was convinced it was out of pity rather than want, his arms closed around me. And I pretended it was because he wanted to. Maybe he only wanted to be sure I'd go back into a quiet sleep so he could get some rest. Either way, my heart melted just a little, holding tight to that glimmer of hope with both hands.

CHAPTER TWENTY-THREE

I WAS ALONE. AND what was worse? I wasn't surprised. The lack of it did nothing to quell the panic that had made a home for itself in my chest last night. I wished I could serve it an eviction notice.

I dressed slowly and only noticed a scrawled note on top of my bag when it fluttered to the ground.

I'm downstairs, it read.

I followed the staircase to the bustling breakfast room and had no trouble finding Emil. He sat in a corner, his hands folded beneath his chin as he stared out the window. I watched him for a moment from the doorway, scrutinizing his immutable face. Eventually, whatever was so engrossing outside lost its appeal, and his hand dipped for his coffee. I moved, not wanting to get caught staring. I filled my plate at random from the buffet and grabbed a glass of orange juice before heading toward Emil.

The smile he gave me as I walked up staggered my steps. Had I imagined the coolness between us last night? I returned the smile, hoping this was a sign. Then I noticed up close that his didn't quite match his careful gaze. My hands shook as I put down my breakfast.

"Morning," he said softly.

"Hi."

I picked up my fork and started poking at my eggs, but my stomach was already full of knots. I took a bite anyway and tasted nothing.

"Did you sleep?" There was a note of worry in his question, and I peered up at him. Concern flickered behind his walled gaze, hidden, but still there.

"Yeah, thanks. You?"

He nodded, taking another sip of coffee.

My fork tapped an annoying rhythm against the plastic plate. "Emil."

His Adam's apple bobbed as he swallowed. "I'm sorry."

"For?"

"Making you think I was angry last night."

"But you weren't?" I pushed, my tone skeptical.

"Not with you. I'm sorry I made you feel that way. It won't happen again."

"You're still doing it," I pointed out, done with playing the walking-on-eggshells game.

His mouth gaped as he fought for words, which were colored with shame. "I didn't realize I was. I'm sorry." He cleared his throat, his expression reworking itself into a blank mask striving for lightness. It wasn't working. He drained his coffee, setting it down with a clatter. When he spoke, his tone was friendly. "Did you have anything you wanted to do today? We could go up to the church and look around inside it. I know we weren't able to do that on the tour yesterday."

I waited for him to meet my eyes. Eventually, when he did, there was nothing. Nothing there to hint at our moments together, the heat gone, the humor between us laughed out. Or maybe the joke had just been on me the whole time, but he didn't find it funny anymore.

"Are you ready to move on?" I asked formally. "To the next spot, I mean?" The magic of Prague had turned into a curse. Perhaps a new location might be able to transform whatever had morphed black and dark.

He chewed his bottom lip. "We can leave, if that's what you want. Where did we talk about heading next?"

"Bruges."

Deciding our plans was like organizing a shopping list. Check, check, check. We packed quickly. The desk attendant bade us farewell with a simple kindness that felt far too cheery for the mood at hand. The streets flooded with the sounds of joyful people heading out to explore. Their warmth touched no part of me.

The contrast between arriving and leaving the city was bleak. Even the weather had turned a steely gray, flat clouds hanging overhead, blocking out the sunlight. Lost in my own thoughts as I stared outside, it took me a moment before I realized Emil was speaking.

"Sorry, what?" I asked, turning to him.

He pointed at a sign ahead for a rest area. "Do you mind if we stop?"

"Oh, no. Of course not."

In the bathroom, I fixed my haphazard bun and ran some water over my face. When I went outside, Emil was at the other end of the parking lot, pacing in a loop across the grass. His hands were again stuffed deep in his pockets, and fear spiked in me. I wasn't a gambler, but even I could recognize his tell.

Half of me wanted to go to him, to close my arms around him and feel, as well as give back, the comfort I had found there once. The other half of me was on high alert due to the uneasy distance between us, worried physical touch might do more harm than good at this point. Maybe it was just me who had felt comfort, after all. Smothering someone wouldn't help.

So I stood next to the car, facing away from him. I sensed his approach before I heard his footsteps.

"Ready?" he asked, sliding the keys into the door.

I nodded.

More silence followed us until I couldn't stand it anymore. I switched on the radio, scanning through stations until one came in crystal clear.

My hand hovered over the dial in surprise. "Still Loving You" reached through the static like an old friend.

My favorite song.

Thanks to my rock 'n' roll fan of a mother, I'd run through the apartment more times than I'd admit mimicking the lead singer's impressive range.

"Is this all right?" I asked out of fairness.

"You like the Scorpions?"

"You know this song?"

"Sure. It's a classic."

The spell of the music seemed to soothe the tension in the car while it lasted.

But eventually the song faded away, and loneliness closed in again. I forced myself to focus on the lyrics of an unfamiliar Gothic rock ballad now playing. It wasn't really my thing, but I didn't care. Distraction was the key. It worked. A little.

I lost sense of time as my mind wandered, hypnotized by the endless landscape whizzing by outside my window. But when Emil's phone stuttered to life, buzzing insistently in the cupholder, I looked at the clock and noticed only an hour had passed.

"Zdravo?"

The muddled sound of a woman's voice tittered on the other end. As she spoke, Emil's forehead creased, deep frown lines denting the corners around his mouth.

His answers were short and curt, but his tone wasn't angry. He caught my eye, and I mouthed, "*What's wrong?*" He looked out the window as he wrapped up the conversation.

When he hung up, I waited impatiently. He let his phone drop into the cupholder, then grasped the steering wheel in a death grip.

"There was a break-in at the shop."

"Oh no!" Panic struck my chest.

"Amin was there."

"Is he all right?"

"He got a bit of a beating. They're not sure yet the extent of the damage, but it looks like he'll recover okay."

My mind was racing, running through all the possible outcomes.

"I have to go back," he said quietly.

I didn't think my worry could have stretched further until that stone dropped.

My mouth instantly went dry.

"Oh." Of course he did.

I'd done a pitiful, one word question-and-answer series about the incident, but Emil didn't know much. By the time I'd grown quiet, we were twenty minutes outside of Cologne. The silence was disrupted by static music playing on the radio. I wasn't paying attention to it. Neither, it seemed, was Emil, who stared through the windshield in a trance. Suddenly, he reached down, fiddling with the map directions. He programmed in a new course and began to follow it.

"Where are we going?"

"Cologne."

"Why?"

His throat worked, but he didn't answer.

And it came crashing down.

I'd wanted a sign. Here it was.

Be careful what you wish for.

But this didn't feel right. I *wanted* to go with him. Was it only because I wasn't ready to say goodbye? Or because he was my safe space? Or was it something more? If he asked me to go along, would I?

My stomach twisted.

If I did, then what? I would still have to leave. This—him—it was all an impossible fantasy, one I wasn't even sure I wanted, hadn't had any time to consider it before the decision was being thrust into my lap. My life, reality, was waiting for me back home, everything I'd ever desired. So why did it suddenly feel like there was an empty space inside of me that hadn't been there when I left?

I stiffened, remembering my mother's tearful farewell.

Don't fall in love, Mallory. My poor, prophetic mother.

I winced, fighting tears as I stared out the window. I had fallen into the trap, become the girl with a crush, thinking this could be more. It was a delusion of the grandest kind.

Where before the minutes had dragged along in silence, now they sped up double-time. We were weaving through the city's traffic, my mind a blur. When Emil parked, my eyes searched wildly through the windows.

We were at a train station.

I folded my hands in my lap, holding a breath to suppress the barrage of emotions urgently seeking their release. I wanted to cry, protest, beg—anything to keep him from leaving.

He didn't owe me anything.

The thought hit me with all the tenderness of a truck barreling down a freeway. It had been a fun game between us in the beginning, those little moments of banter back and forth—*I owe you.* Now it was a tough reality pill to swallow. But even as my mind fought against it, I knew he needed to go. And I also knew that, if he did ask, I wouldn't go with him.

"You can get a train from here. It's only a few hours to Bruges, I think." He spoke quietly, his body still except for a finger picking at a seam in his jeans. His voice was dead, his eyes trained down.

"Thank you," I said, my tone detached.

He nodded.

There was nothing else to say. I got out of the car, hearing the driver's side door open and snap shut. He moved to the trunk, pulling Bertha out and helping me to put her on. His hands lingered on my exposed shoulders. His fingertips were cold, and goosebumps broke out across my skin. I turned, and his hands slid from my arms as I took a step back.

"Tell Amin to hang in there," I said. "Let me know if you have any questions. Well, I guess you have Dr. Tanović for that." I twisted my fingers in front of me.

He cleared his throat, looking down again. "I don't have your number."

What? Surely we had—but no. All his scribbled notes. And then we'd never really been far apart, so there'd been no need to...

I shook my head. How on earth had we gotten here? I knew his body and his smell, the way his moods shifted on a dime, his family history, all the little things he'd never done, and the ones he hoped to. Had I only tricked myself into believing I knew him? We hadn't even covered the simple basics. Thank you, life. Once again, the joke was on me.

"Here," I said, reaching for his phone. I entered my information, then gave it back. My hand landed in his, his fingers contracting around it, like he wasn't ready to let go.

Slowly, my eyes raised and locked with his. His gaze was pained, lost even.

He stared at my lips, as if they might hold the key to unlocking this predicament. White-hot heat pooled in my stomach when our eyes met again. Inside, everything was at odds. Desire versus self-preservation, fantasy versus reality. But this was real, it was happening, and we both knew where we needed to be.

"He'll be okay," I whispered. He blinked, the tension in his face easing ever so slightly.

"Yeah," he said, dragging out the vowels into a question.

I bit my lip. I couldn't take a drawn-out goodbye. The bandage needed to be ripped off. A hard shell began to fold around my heart. The softness wouldn't last. I could only fight against it for so long. "You should get going. It's a long drive."

He nodded, the car keys clinking in his hand. He took a step away. "Do you..."

"What?" Traitorous hope jolted through me.

He looked at the pavement. "Do you know where to go?"

The balloon filling me deflated. "I'll figure it out."

He sighed. "I know you will." He opened his door. "Good luck,

Mallory Roth."

I swallowed down a sob, and my defenses held. "Goodbye, Emil."

His jaw locked, and he got into the car.

As he drove away, the hollow space began eating its way bigger inside me. I walked into the station, everything growing a little duller, like my life was fading into a black-and-white silent film. The sound of my feet against the laminate was muted, the shimmer of neon and sunlight subdued. The cacophony of voices and announcements were relegated to the background as I purchased my ticket to Bruges, the next train leaving in minutes. I didn't hurry, barely making it aboard before we were zooming out of the city.

CHAPTER TWENTY-FOUR

IT WAS OVER BEFORE it began.

The adventure.

The train journey.

Me and Emil.

Bruges was a fairy tale kind of place with its gently curving canals, candy stores, horse-drawn carriages, and storybook buildings.

I was done with fairy tales.

I tried to enjoy all this beautiful town had to offer—its quaint shops, walkways lined with old-fashioned windmills, the unhurried bustle of people going about their everyday lives. But instead of each day growing easier, the only thing that grew was that hollow, nagging feeling.

On my third night, I sat swirling my cup of Belgian hot chocolate in a café. The friendly server had presented it with a flourish, a gorgeously carved lump of chocolate transformed into a blooming flower, along with a piping-hot mug of milk. She explained I had to drop the chocolate into the milk, and it would become a thing of childhood dreams.

I thanked her and watched it sink to the bottom like a rock.

When Sydney and I were young, there were two things I could remember making us feel better: a trip to the movies and hot chocolate.

And yet, even stuff as delicious as this couldn't soothe the cold that had settled into my bones and continued burrowing its way in deeper still. Something had broken off inside me and been left behind at that train station in Cologne.

I passed restaurants sporting throngs of happy patrons, turning down narrow streets without purpose, killing time. Eventually, I found myself in the main cobbled square, the giant belfry looming on my right. Cheerful passersby swarmed beneath its shadow, with many stopping to take selfies. I sighed and mimicked them. Proof I was here, nothing else. I sifted through them, each faked smile dull, the third the most convincing out of them all. Swipe, swipe, swipe—stop.

There was a photo of me in profile, taken in the square in Prague. In it, I gazed up at the top of the church, I guessed, based on the angle. My mind raced, remembering Emil had asked to borrow my phone to snap a few pictures. I thumbed backward. Images of the astronomical clock followed, shards of sunlight piercing across its azure face.

I dove down the rabbit hole, moving farther into the earlier days. The grand halls of the palace in Munich. Ones I'd taken during our hike along the Dolomites, Emil leading the path ahead of me. The Venice canals, and the photo of the two of us in Burano...to the very first of him by himself.

The images played out our story in reverse, and the lightness in Emil's face dimmed until he bore that surly expression back in Italy. But even there, a hint of humor was still present. I could recognize it now and could practically hear him laughing at my pushy antics to get him to allow me to take them. I swallowed down the lump in my throat. I knew the rest. Some pictures of Croatia and earlier photos, but no Emil.

Back where I began. Alone.

I tucked my phone into a pocket, doing my best to ignore the confusing waves of emotion fighting for a place in my heart. Anger, grief, love, stubbornness. I battled against the tears prickling in the corners of my eyes. I gave up, letting them spill down my cheeks in silence as I headed to my hotel. By the time I walked through the door, my face was dry.

The hostess smiled as I entered. "Hello, did you have a good evening?"

"Yes."

She perked up at my blasé tone. "Can I help you find anything? We have brochures on activities and sightseeing. Or I could also book you in for a spa. We have some beautiful bathhouses. They're not far from the old town center."

My voice went flat. "No, thank you."

"All right," she said uncertainly. "Let me know if there's anything you need." She returned to rummaging through her papers.

I dejectedly made my way up to the room and face-planted onto the bed. Under other circumstances, I knew I would be in love with this place. It was perfect, quaint, cozy. But my enthusiasm was locked away out of reach, and I wasn't kidding myself as to why. Bruges had been Emil's pick. It was tainted. And wandering down a different alley tomorrow wouldn't help me outrun that fact. Was this how ghosts felt, floating about in limbo, unable to move forward?

I was being dramatic. Of course I was, but it didn't make any difference. I rolled onto my back, staring up at the white ceiling. There were still two more nights before my reservation in London.

I pressed the heels of my hands into my eyes, rubbing hard. "Get it together," I muttered.

And then I froze.

I'd done it once. I could do it again. No one was holding me here against my will or waiting around to judge me. I could leave if I wanted to.

I bounded down the stairs, startling the receptionist.

"What's the easiest way to get from here to London?"

"Um," she mumbled, "you can reach it by train, bus, or plane. Train and bus tend to be cheaper."

"Would you be able to help me book it?"

"Of course. What dates?"

"Now."

It was a testament to my miserable attitude that she didn't question me.

"Absolutely," she said, turning to her computer and clacking away with gusto.

The sun was high in the sky when we pulled into Victoria Station. I hadn't slept on the bus, wedged between two snorers. I knew I must look and smell a fright as I disembarked.

Good, then no one would bother me.

My first order of business should have been to find a hotel. The city was bursting with tourists as I wandered from the station, following directions to the Houses of Parliament. The crowds tuning in for the toll of Big Ben on the hour, ships cruising the Thames, the huge line for the London Eye—it all pointed to a bustling summer season. Instead, my feet dragged me around the city, my eyes itchy and likely a nice shade of red.

When I unexpectedly found myself turning a corner and facing a long, tree-lined stretch of road framing Buckingham Palace, even the bump of locals and tourists couldn't move me forward. I glared at the austere building with malice, Emil's wish list flickering in the back of my mind. It'd been one of his must-sees.

The King's Guard rode by on colossal horses, who stamped along in unison. Black taxis wove through the large roundabout in the distance. All of it, everyone, eagerly made their way toward the historic spot.

Emptiness ate at my insides as I turned to my left and walked through the park, blocking out the sight.

Manicured garden flowers danced in the delicate breeze. Families unfurled picnic blankets beneath the thick canopy of trees. Pigeons took flight, flurrying about for a new place to beg for morsels. Through the park cut a lazy pond, its surface smooth as mirrored glass.

I wandered onto one of the bridges. Long, wispy tendrils of tree branches reached out from the shore, where swans glided through the water. A floral scent danced on the wind, remarkable in a city this size, which by rights should smell of garbage and exhaust.

People snapped selfies with the palace or the top of the London Eye in the background, the golden sun shining like a smile. And yet, I couldn't help frowning as I crossed the footbridge, even while soaking in the fun-loving, beautiful spectacle surrounding me. On the other side, I noticed a smattering of dollhouse-sized buildings lining the pond. It was a magical little village of miniature houses and streets beneath the full-grown plants.

The whimsical sight finally brought a smile to my face. It was infectious. A large tree blocked out what was around the next bend. I hurried forward to see what awaited me and stopped dead. My heart soared from my chest at the familiar curve of broad shoulders and thick hair. His back was to me as my feet flew across the ground.

"Emil!"

He turned, a short young woman revealed beside him as he did. She stared up at him adoringly. Everything inside me dropped like a ball of lead. I was back in the sauna, my breath drawn from my body and completely light-headed, all for an entirely different reason.

No. It couldn't be.

I looked up again, and my shoulders slumped. It was a fair resemblance. Even his face was similar. But it wasn't Emil. Caught somewhere between relief and disappointment, I ducked my head as they walked by, hand in hand.

I was losing my mind now. Fantastic. I held in a sob. This was mortifying, pathetic, and devastating all at once. I dug through my coat pocket for a napkin, anything to wipe away my tears. I came up with a handful, smoothing out a balled-up one to blow my nose. Just as I was raising it to my face, I spotted the writing.

Gail's napkin.

Some deeply ingrained code clicked into place.

Robotically, I pulled out my phone, dialing her number with care.

Ring.

Please don't pick up.

Ring.

Please.

Ring.

Please pick up.

"Hello?"

My mouth opened to respond, but...nothing.

She waited a moment. "Hello? Is anyone there?"

"Hi."

"Hello. Who is this?"

"Um," I muttered, feeling idiotic, "it's Mallory. I don't know if you remember, but, uh, we met on the plane from Arizona and I've written you—"

"Mallory," Gail said warmly. "I'm so glad to hear your voice. Thank you for all your letters. You are such a doll."

My throat tightened. "You're welcome."

"Where are you off to next?"

"Actually, I'm here. I'm in London."

I hoped her sharp intake of breath was followed by a smile.

"Are you?"

"Yep. Hanging out in the park by the palace." I bit my lip. "Do you...only—if you're busy, it's not a problem, but—would you like to meet up?"

"Is now a good time?"

———ꝏꝏ———

It was only twenty minutes later when I turned onto yet another row of cookie-cutter houses. Their white pillars gleamed in the sun, their entrances looking over a small, square park. I found number thirty-seven, taking a deep breath as I shuffled up the stoop.

"Keep it together," I mumbled. I pressed the doorbell, a muffled chime emanating through the house.

The red door swung open, revealing a beaming Gail.

"Hello, dear." She swept me into a hug.

"Are you sure you don't mind?" I asked for the thousandth time. Over the phone, she'd offered for me to stay with her. She hadn't hesitated, but it still felt like I was intruding.

"I'm so happy you're here," she said, ushering me through the foyer, waving for me to follow.

I took the best shower of my life before changing into the only semi-clean clothes I had left, the sweatpants and tank top combo I slept in. Gail let me start a wash as I dragged my brush through wet hair. With the machine whirring in the background, I plunked onto a white chair at the table. My skin was flushed after the steam of the shower, a tired calm taking hold in this welcoming setting.

The kitchen was flooded with soft light as the sun sank below the tops of the buildings. An electric kettle whistled behind two waiting cups. Gail opened a package, spreading chocolate-covered biscuits out for grabs. She filled an old-fashioned ceramic teapot with steaming water, popping in the tea before setting it on the silver tray with the cups and bringing it to the table.

"How do you take it?"

"I don't usually drink tea," I admitted. "However you make it is fine."

I watched her pour the tea, followed by a lump of sugar and a smidge of milk into each teacup, plus a biscuit on the side. I picked up mine, blowing on it lightly, and tried a sip.

It was lovely. "Thank you."

She smiled with anticipation. "So, tell me, was your trip everything you'd dreamed it would be?"

My cup rattled noisily against the delicate saucer. Gail tried to hide a wince.

"Sorry." I set the cup and saucer back on the table, pushing them a safe distance away. My face felt pinched, and I worked it into something I hoped looked mildly normal. "Yes, it was great."

Gail lifted a brow.

I nearly ripped off a nail in my lap, trying to hold in my tears.

Across from me, Gail resigned her own tea to the center of the table. "Mallory, I don't know you. I don't know a thing other than what you've shared. But I am aware you are here in London early. And you were having quite the adventure, based on your correspondence." She sat back in her chair, arms crossed as tightly as the look she shot my way. "And I also know that I am no fool."

I swallowed.

Her fingers rapped across her biceps.

"Well," I hesitated, then overflowed. The whole beautiful, miserable story came out, right up to the bitter end. To her credit, Gail rarely interrupted. Her expression went stony when I reached the news of the break-in, but turned pensive, then amused as I wound to a close.

At one point, we had shifted from the kitchen to her stylish living room. When I told her about Emil leaving, I grew quiet, glancing into the tiny backyard. Night had fallen. Gail's neighbors were framed in mini tableaux as they ate in their kitchens or sat watching TV in their living rooms. So normal.

"Hmm," she hummed thoughtfully.

I drew a stuffy breath through my nose. "That's it."

To my surprise, she chuckled.

"What's funny?"

"You are," she said. The twinkle in her eyes made no sense.

"I don't understand."

"Honey, that's so far from being 'it,' that it's funny."

"I'm glad this is so humorous for you," I said dryly.

"Oh, don't be like that," she said. "I know you're hurting. But where you are right now, how you're feeling, it's your own doing." She shrugged. "And Emil's, too. That boy did neither of you any favors."

"What do you mean?" I was tired. All I really wanted was to crawl into a bed and hide from the world, my patience stretched taut.

Instead of answering, Gail slapped her thighs as she stood. "I don't need to tell you. You're going to do it for me."

And she disappeared around the corner. I gaped at the ceiling as I heard her rummaging upstairs. Soon, she was back, carrying a bundle of papers. She held them out to me and, when I took them, I saw my own handwriting.

"You kept them?"

"Of course. I'm a sucker for a good romance."

I looked at her curiously and was met with that same humorous smirk.

"Read them," she said simply. "*Really* read them. Listen to yourself. You have all the answers. You just can't see it yet." Her flowy skirt billowed as she retreated into the kitchen to clean up.

My mouth turned dry as I flipped over the first postcard, then the next letter, carefully reading every word. My tone shifted dramatically, from bubbly in Paris to cooly flat in Mostar. There was a long gap until Venice, when a lighter, more lively version of me hinted through. And more, more, more. A tiny nucleus of warmth set alight inside me, growing stronger and more defiant. I relived the journey, but the gaps in my words spoke louder than the words themselves, the little pieces I'd omitted and kept only for myself. Even still, my anecdotes progressed from the activities and places, narrowing down to one thing. Emil. At some point, it all became about me and Emil.

I folded the last letter, sent from our first night in Prague, and held it to my chest.

"What did you say?"

I opened my eyes, finding Gail watching me from the doorway.

"I said a lot of things."

Unfazed, Gail leaned against the frame, taking a sip from a fresh cup of tea. She watched me over the brim, waiting.

"I fell for him," I said reluctantly. Why did it feel humiliating to admit? It was all so new, so confusing. I'd never been in love before. And I didn't like it, not like this. "That's why it's my fault I'm a mess," I continued. "I let him get to me."

Her lips twitched. "Okay. That's part of it, so you can blame yourself there. But how you're feeling...is that a bad thing?"

"It is, since we can't be together."

Gail grunted, raising her eyes to the heavens. "And he left because?"

That was easy. "Because he had to go back to help Amin."

"No," she said, wagging a finger. "I mean, yes, but that wasn't *why* he left. Think about your last night in Prague. What was he *really* asking you?"

The last thing I wanted was to revisit that night. "I don't know," I said like a stubborn teenager.

"Yes, you do." She wasn't going to let me off so easily.

"What does it matter?" I countered. "He's there. I'm here. I'm leaving. That's it!"

"It doesn't have to be."

"He left me!" I said, my voice rising with a crack. "It was his choice."

Her tone was soft. "And yet, here you are, crying over a boy."

I scowled, which only made her grin wider.

"Those letters," she said, redirecting the conversation, "what do they tell you?"

I shrugged.

"What do you see there?"

"Something I want, but can't happen."

"Why not?"

"I already told you why."

"No, that's an excuse."

"You're acting like I'm the one who chose this," I snapped.

"You're angry. That's good."

"Because?"

She sighed. "Because angry, sad, heartbroken? They're all feelings showing you still care. You are still fighting, even if it's with yourself." She sat and nestled my hand in hers. "What are you fighting so hard against?"

My words were faint. "That I love him."

"Good girl."

"But—"

"That's not necessary," she cut me off. "Don't talk yourself out of this with all the problems. Solve it."

"I don't think I can," I admitted.

She released my hand, folding hers in her lap.

"I've been truly in love once in my life, Mallory. I was with her for over forty years and they weren't nearly enough. There's time to figure out all the details, but don't you dare wait to start. Not if it's real."

"What about home? My work—"

"Keeping those things doesn't mean giving it all up. Relationships require compromise, yes. Compromise, not sacrificing one person for the other. When two people care for each other, as equals, they champion the others' dreams. They fight for them, maybe more than that person does for themselves. No, that's not the issue at hand here. The real question now is, how far are you willing to go to fight for one another in the long run? How much is it worth to each of you?" She lifted a shoulder, her brow arching as she took a sip of tea.

My lower lip trembled. "What if he doesn't feel the same?"

She leaned forward, holding my gaze. "How would you feel if you never found out?"

I gave a weepy laugh. "Miserable."

"Then what do you have to lose?"

If I didn't act, then everything. Everything a future with him might entail. But was that future even possible?

In my mind, I searched through another of my check-lists, flitting between each true thing, forcing myself to focus on one at a time. I loved him. On some level, I was pretty sure he cared about me. He was afraid. I was afraid. Fear had driven the divide between us, not love. Maybe it could be mended, but it had to be done soon. Otherwise, we'd be on opposite sides of the world, adrift, alone, searching for something we had and lost—something that wasn't easy to find once in a lifetime, never mind twice.

Suddenly, I was laser-focused. I still had time before my trip home...

"I need to book a flight to Sarajevo."

Gail grinned.

CHAPTER TWENTY-FIVE

Even the forlorn bus stop was a sight for sore eyes as we wheezed to a standstill in Mostar. I burst from the van, following the same path from the station I knew so well. My steps faltered outside the supermarket where we first met, picturing him in line with his warm grin. I smiled at the empty store, my feet propelling me forward once more.

The once dark and scary courtyard beyond it pooled with light, sunlight flickering off the broad leaves of the tree at its center. Chiaroscuro shadows painted the narrow alley he'd led me through, until I arrived in the blazing path following the water's edge. The bridge was more majestic than my memory had served, though the flock of people at its apex was just as familiar.

I was hyperaware of the shop on my left. I stared at the entrance for a long while and drew a few stares myself as I stood there, completely immobile. When I at last moved forward, evidence from where the thieves had broken their way in caught my eye.

The beautiful, old, ornate door was now fitted with an ugly steel padlock, while new wood patched the doorframe. As I crossed the threshold, the smell of iron and leather hit my nose. Dust swirled around me in the air. My dark outline sprawled in a lanky block across the space, slicing the light from Amin seated in the back. His head remained bowed as his eyes snapped up to me, one of them bloodshot and severely blackened. I hesitated under his inspection. Without so much as a word, his focus returned to his work.

I did a quick scan of the shop. It was empty except for the two of us. The floor appeared recently swept, the shelves fewer and sparser, and my stomach clenched as I wondered how extensive the damage had been. I roamed through the rows of wares as I worked up some courage, my gaze continuing to find Amin as he ignored me completely. Finally, I ended up at the cash register, waiting.

He selected a different tool, then pattered an imprint against the metal.

I cleared my throat.

"Can I help you?" His voice was coarse and wispy at the same time, like sawdust floating above discarded sandpaper.

"Is Emil here?"

"No."

"Do you have any idea when he'll be back?"

"No."

I bit my lip, turning on the spot to look toward the door. But I couldn't leave.

"Do you know who I am?" I pressed.

"Yes."

"How are you feeling?" I asked. His body was stooped. In addition to the black eye, there were tiny cuts along one cheekbone and a slice in his lower lip. I winced.

"I'm fine."

"I'm sorry about what happened."

"Did you do it?"

I frowned. "No."

"Then there's no need to apologize."

All righty, then.

I itched to ask him more. How much did he know? Had Emil told him anything at all about the trip or its end? The idea of that being their discussion after everything that'd happened with the shop seemed improbable, but he had admitted to knowing who I was. Was it only because he knew Emil had gone with me on the trip, or had there been more?

My fingers were cold as I crossed my arms. "Do you know about us?" I fished.

His head dipped deeper into his work. I took that as a yes.

My foot tapped a staccato rhythm against the stone floor. It didn't appear I was getting anything more out of him. I wasn't in the honorary inner circle like when Emil was with me, very much feeling the outsider once again. I turned for the door, defeated.

"Why did you come back?"

I whipped around. "What?"

He sighed, looking up, but not at me. "Why did you come back now?"

I swallowed. "Because I never wanted to let him go."

"What changed?"

I lifted a shoulder. "I just—reconsidered."

He situated a pair of extremely magnified glasses low on his nose with a grunt.

"Do you...do you think he did, too?" I pushed.

His eyes were piercing as they flashed to me. "I couldn't say."

"When he spoke about us, did you get the impression that he might?" Amin had made the mistake of opening the door to conversation again, and I wasn't going to stop it until he did.

"Anyone can change their minds."

I heard the "but" coming.

"But," he said, "I can't say if he has. He has to be willing to look harder."

I hesitated before asking the one question I wasn't sure I wanted answered. "What if he's never ready?"

He coughed dryly, like there was a pebble stuck in his throat. "Then you need to leave and live your life."

"You make it sound so simple."

He gave a short nod. "Yes. It's that simple."

I watched his careful movements. I knew Emil admired him. I could understand why, after everything he'd lived through, but I wasn't so Zen.

"How?"

Finally, his eyes met mine. The bags beneath them pulled at his skin, drooping and making him appear a bit like a basset hound. His mouth was slack, but the burn in his gaze set his otherwise blank face alight.

"You just do it. Life is for living, not waiting." He thumbed the tiny hammer in his hand absentmindedly.

So basic, but reality was so much more complex. Or was it? I supposed it was straightforward, if you let it simmer, reducing it down to its very core. Which begged to question...what was at the nucleus of my life? What drove it forward?

I sifted through the obvious of family, work, passions, hopes, and dreams, expecting it all to settle into a wide picture of clarity. But of course it wouldn't, each dashing after the other, battling one another for a place in the hierarchy. How could I choose a path if I couldn't force it to make sense? How could it all be so murky, so undefined, so stagnated?

And then I realized it.

Since Emil and I had gone our separate ways, I had been numb, unfeeling, stuck in this limbo, looking for something outside myself to jolt me out of it.

I couldn't stand by hoping for the pieces to fall into place anymore, even the things I felt sure of, the things I knew gave my existence meaning. It required action on my part, real action, not just running, not just searching. Doing. Feeling. Taking it in. All of it, the good and the bad. And suddenly I was full circle.

When dreaming of this trip, that was I'd wanted, to experience everything life could throw at me. And I'd done it, for a while, been open to it all. Then I'd shut down, closed the door, until Emil had come along and cracked it open again. When he'd left, that inch had slammed shut. It wasn't up to him to unlock it this time. I had to wrench it wide all by myself.

Well, it was a place to start, at least. And I had chosen real action back on Gail's couch when I'd decided to return to Mostar. Perhaps it meant something. Whatever it might, I wasn't about to figure it out standing here.

I nodded to Amin. "Thank you."

He returned to his tapping, the spell broken. "No need to thank me."

Noted.

"Are you going to tell Emil I was here?"

"Do you want me to?"

I considered it for a moment. "No."

"Then he won't hear it from me."

Which implied he'd hear it from someone at some point. I let out a dark chuckle. Small-town life. My being here wouldn't likely stay a secret for long.

"What's funny?"

"I was just thinking about home. It's the same, where everyone knows everything eventually."

Amin shrugged. "So he'll know you're here. So what? Then he'll find you when he's ready," he said with the cock of an eyebrow, sounding like some morose fortune cookie. He bent his head back to his work, his jaw set.

It was clearly a dismissal. I spun on my heel and exited the shop, automatically checking each direction for a familiar face. People bustled about the market, but none of them were whom I sought.

I wandered to the right and over a modern bridge to the other side of town. I moved with the crowd, swallowed up in the ebb and swell as they explored. Eventually, I found myself in a narrow nook where a creek made its way toward the river. A mini version of Stari Most spanned the gap between streets. I stopped at its pinnacle, staring down at the trickle of water, taking in a deep breath as the wind ruffled my hair. It carried voices from downstream, one which I instantly recognized as Dani's. The sound set a smile upon my face. I closed my eyes as I pictured him gathering the unsuspecting tourists with his magnetic presentation. I didn't imagine their shouts and cheers that came next in response.

My eyes snapped open as I sucked in a breath.

And then I was moving.

No more numb.

No more limbo.

Release. That was what I'd yearned for when I last stood atop Stari Most. Hoping to not feel, to forget, to escape what had happened to me.

Not now. This time, I wanted it all. The fear, the exhilaration, the release, but of a different kind. No more holding the door closed with both hands. This time, I was blowing it off its hinges. Old Mallory had wanted this, even in her naivety. Now, so did new, wiser Mallory.

These tiny streets were barely more than narrow paths, twisting in mazelike patterns. I took my best guess at each fork, turning up and to the left every chance I could. Finally, the diving club tower loomed ahead. As I slipped up the bridge's incline, I tossed Bertha to the ground, tripping as I kicked off my shoes.

"Excuse me," I muttered, pushing past the crowd. "Please let me through."

The wave as people parted lulled a hush even from Dani. His attention locked on to me, first in confusion, then in delight.

"Ljepotice!" he cheered, but I wasn't stopping for a chat. He helped me uncertainly as I climbed up next to him, concern transforming his normally carefree expression. "Are you all right?"

"I'm great." Butterflies danced inside me as I twisted toward the river. The railing blazed beneath my fingertips as I started to climb over it.

Dani's hand grasped my wrist. "What are you doing?" he whispered.

"Jumping."

He shook his head. "No."

I looked for Luka and finally found him. His face was stony.

"Tell him," I said quietly.

At first, I thought he wouldn't. But his expression softened as he stared at me, seeing my resolve and the smile playing around my lips. I was calm enough, centered.

"I taught her," he said at last. "She can do it."

I whipped toward Dani, an eyebrow raised in a dare.

After a moment, he huffed, his gaze shooting past my head. There was no doubt what—or rather who—he was looking for. The shop was in a direct line of sight to where we stood. I didn't look back, waiting impatiently. Then his fingers left my skin.

"All right," he said. "But be careful."

"Naturally."

He returned to the waiting crowd. "A rare treat for you all! It is not only myself who can get all the glory from a jump off of the beautiful Stari Most. So can you! And here we have our lovely visitor from California to demonstrate." He gestured at me with a flourish. "Take a bow."

With a roll of my eyes, I bent theatrically into a curtsy. "You know I'm not from California, right?" I said through clenched teeth as they clapped.

He grinned. "Take one for your old friend, won't you? The people love a good show."

I snorted.

Dani eased onto the other side of the barrier, offering his hand to help me over. I took it. The butterflies had begun a conga line, their tiny little legs pounding a rhythmic heartbeat into my ears, their powdery wings threatening to take flight in my belly.

"You sure?" Dani asked.

I nodded. The uncertainty I'd fought against the last time I stood on this precipice was gone. "Absolutely."

He turned back to his audience. "Give it up for Mallory!"

The applause swelled. As it began to die, I flexed my toes against the edge and heard my name once more. But it wasn't a cheer. It wasn't just another voice. And it was getting closer.

"Mallory?"

Deep breath.

"Mallory!" Emil shouted.

My life, my choice.

And I let go.

I flung myself into the open void, leaving behind the crowd, the past, and the future. Now. This was all that was real. Fear, joy, abandon—they jostled for place inside me, but I allowed them to swell through me in a symphony, feeling each in turn. As I fell, my spirit soared, exhilaration propelling me upward even as my body sank toward the earth. This was the world at work as it was meant to be, with our circumstances constantly in flux around a strange sort of tug-of-war. All I could do was pick a direction...and give in to it. My own choices. They were what I could really depend on in life. And I had *lived* over these last few weeks. I would continue to live.

With that thought, my toes pierced the icy water, plunging straight and clean through the depths. The dull roar of water filled my ears as I floated beneath the surface. It was tranquil down here, the thump of blood pumping vigor through me, singing a message through my veins.

I'm alive.

I'm alive.

I'm alive.

With a single, unified thrust of my arms, I broke the surface. Air whooshed into my lungs. I gulped it in, eyes closed against the burning sun. It was like a movie, the slow crescendo of sound returning from nothingness, the churn of the river, the cheers from above. Opening my eyes, I paddled to shore.

My legs shook as I scrambled up rocks slick with algae. Laughter bubbled from my chest, a giddy high making me feel lighter than air. The few people standing on the rocky beach called out their awe or congratulations, but I turned, looking up to the bridge, raising my hands over my head with a wave. Dani whooped while Luka grinned proudly by his side. I scanned the other faces.

I hoped.

Hope was dangerous.

My stomach twisted.

No, hope was beautiful. Hope had delivered me here.

Stranger's faces looked back at me.

He will find you when he's ready, Amin's voice echoed in my head.

I did one final pass, the smile fading from my lips.

I had heard Emil. I knew I had. But then where was he?

My heart clenched painfully, dismay, desire, and triumph all taking their toll. The chill of the water dripping from my hair began to penetrate my skin, starting as a trickle from the nape of my neck, down my insides, coiling through my muscles, working all the way to the tips of my toes, dulling everything. I watched the people begin to disperse, but it didn't register as I remained rooted to the spot.

I raised my hand, inspecting it. It didn't seem to belong to me. I couldn't feel the tremors shaking my fingers. My arm dropped to my side, lifeless.

This was wrong.

I focused, forcing myself to permit each pang of emotion take hold for an instant before letting it go. When they had all faded into something manageable, I could feel myself again, my hands once more mine, the numbness gone. I looked at the steps leading to the beach, but they were empty. That jolt of hurt seeped in before it, too, washed away. When there was nothing more to sift, in the end, sadness lingered, but so did a little of the euphoria from the jump, now joined with a strange sense of calm.

He will find you when he's ready.

I held Amin's words inside, close to my heart, but not quite touching it.

Not yet.

CHAPTER TWENTY-SIX

"I'm so glad you had a room available," I said to Ivan. "Thank you for taking me in so late."

"Of course," he said. "What brings you here again so soon?"

My smile flickered. "I missed it."

His words were warm. "Welcome back."

Waiting inside was another slice of cake. I couldn't help but laugh. "You spoil me."

"I'm happy to." He smiled as he began to close the door for me. "Have a good night."

This room was a floor lower than the last, but it faced toward Stari Most. I waited as dusk fell and the lights illuminated the bridge before finally leaving the terrace and falling into bed.

A beautiful call to prayer woke me every morning.

The first day, annoyance battled my newfound, work-in-progress Zen approach. I picked up my phone to call or text Emil, to demand we talk. However, considering talking was something Emil had consistently chosen not to do, would forcing it cause more harm than good? My resolve to act contradicted my decision to let life take the reins. But surely there had to be a balance, right? The result was me whipping out my phone throughout the afternoon and writing up long-winded texts, then deleting them with a sigh.

On the second day, I reminded myself that Emil knew I was here, so I repeated Amin's words in my head as a mantra. So I went out into the city and genuinely enjoyed exploring beyond the boundaries of the old town. I saw new sights, tried new foods, and, when I crashed onto my bed at the end, I wrote about it all in a letter to Gail, my dry-humored fairy godmother, as I'd come to think of her.

Around noon on the third day, I was in the middle of lunch at one of the many cafés along the river when I realized two things.

First, it was my birthday. I ordered an extra portion of baklava to celebrate and to help soothe the second thing.

Which was that, today, I hadn't once looked for Emil. Until now, I'd secretly been expecting to see him lingering around every corner—by the gate of the apartment, the bridge, any random alley. I'd been conscious of each gaze. But today I'd merely gone about my morning and afternoon, dropped here out of a void, no history, no ties, nothing.

It scared the hell out of me.

We were each living our lives, one without the other. Did that mean this was truly it, that I'd grow tired of simply standing by and leave with my tail between my legs? That had been Amin's sage advice. Perhaps I was meant to follow it.

I paid and left silently, gazing around at the buildings, soaking it all in, along with the immense sense of complete rightness being here. I couldn't explain it. I'd only spent a few days total in this place, but it I felt like I fit here, too, like I was home. But I would have to find my own Mostar. He was where he belonged—here. This was his home. We couldn't share it. It could only be one of ours, and it had to be his. If he hadn't sought me out yet, then he'd made his decision. And here I was, waiting.

My jaw clenched, and I drew a shallow breath through my nose.

It was time to start saying goodbye.

I did so by walking through every street I could, twisting and turning, whispering silent farewells to the people, the houses, the trees, the river. The scents of freshly ground coffee, blooming petunias hanging from baskets overhead, and toasted earth waved goodbye back.

When I turned the next corner, I found myself in the street between a row of beautiful restaurants on my right and a small square on my left. Even in the daylight, the place was unmistakable, its arbored entrance still cascading with vibrant ivy.

The restaurant Emil had taken me to on our first date.

I licked my lips, my mouth gone dry. The square was empty, but I spotted a water fountain in the shade and shuffled to it. I drank deeply until I couldn't stop the sob searing in my throat any longer. My back flattened against the wall, and I sank down to the warm stones, pressing my hands to my face as my knees curled up toward my chest.

So this was how grief felt.

A clenched, aching burn deep inside.

The tears you can't suppress.

Breathing too fast.

I took my pulse, focusing on the task, trying to ground myself. I'd never had a panic attack before, if this even was one. Maybe those feelings weren't grief after all. Or maybe they were the same thing.

My eyes slid shut as I counted the feather-light thumps at my jugular.

"Mallory?"

I jumped at the sound of my name, then squinted up into the brightness.

"Dr. Tanović?"

Emil's stepfather stared down at me, concern creasing his forehead.

My body jerked as I tried to stand, but he rested a hand on my shoulder.

"Stay there," he said softly as he crouched in front of me. His attention zeroed in on my fingers, which were still pressed to my neck. "How fast?"

"Um, I didn't finish."

He reached out, gently pulling my hand away and letting it rest against my thighs. He replaced it with his own, his fingers a comfort against my skin.

I worked on not passing out as he counted silently.

The seconds dragged until he finally let go. "One-twenty," he said, "but dropping quickly." He sank down next to me, his head resting against the rough stone at our backs.

"Thank you," I breathed out, the lightheadedness beginning to ease.

We were quiet for a time before I began to feel somewhat normal again. I twisted without getting up, drinking a few more swallows of water.

"Can you walk?" he asked when I was done.

"I think so. Why?"

"I'd like to check you out at the clinic, just to be sure."

"It's okay," I said. "I'll be fine."

"That was a polite way of saying you're coming with me," he said. I quickly assessed how I might get out of it as he stood, then reached his hand toward me. I frowned, but took it.

I hadn't realized how close we were to the clinic. We walked through the doors minutes later, and he led me past his surprised receptionist. He did a basic checkup, finally confirming what I already knew. I'd live.

"Thank you," I said, biting my lip as I hopped down from the examination table.

"Do you have a moment?" he asked.

"Um, sure?"

He didn't wait, and I followed him into his office.

"I'm glad you're here," he murmured as I stood awkwardly inside the doorway. He took the seat behind his desk and gestured toward the two others across from him.

I sat down in the chair nearest the door, not sure where to look, and watched my hands strangle each other in my lap. "Why?"

"Because I love Emil. In every way it matters, he is my son. And I don't need words to sense he's going through something." His head tilted to the side. "That you both are."

I couldn't help asking. "How is he?"

"How do you think?"

I lifted a shoulder. "I wouldn't know."

Omar shook his head. "He's heartbroken, draga."

"But we barely know one another," I countered, trying to be realistic. "Barely spent any time together."

"Mallory," he sighed, "time doesn't matter. Love can happen in a moment or decades. It doesn't mind."

I sucked in a shuddering breath. "What do you know? About what happened, I mean?"

Omar spoke carefully. "He didn't say much."

Shocker.

"But from what I can tell," he continued, "leaving...it was what he needed to do." His eyes slid expectantly to the door for a second. I took the opportunity to duck my head and wipe away threatening tears. The squeak of a floorboard sounded behind me. I should let him go, but I wasn't ready.

"Was it a mistake coming back?" The words slipped out. It was what had been twisting inside of me since the moment I looked up at the bridge after I jumped, and he hadn't been there.

He pondered my question. "If your roles were reversed, what would you think?"

I tried to imagine it—Emil standing in Blackthorn, out of place, uncertain. Yet he was there, for what else but me, so we could be together. A flicker lit inside me, sputtering to become a flame.

"I want him," I admitted, sounding pitiful. "I want him so badly, but—"

"No." His voice was sharp for the first time. "Love doesn't work in buts. It's a choice. It doesn't care if you live in the same town, if your families get along, if you listen to the same kind of music, if you fight and get under one another's skin at times. Each moment, you choose that person above all of it. And do you know what happens?"

I shook my head cautiously.

Omar smiled, leaning forward. "It all works out. Being with someone, it's imperfect. Some days you'll get what you want, then it's the other person's turn. Sometimes neither of you will, because that's what it takes to make it through that day. It's work to be with the one you love, but those things are what make it worth it. No matter what barriers stand in your way, together you tear them down and say—not today." Omar rapped his fingers against the table with those last words, sitting back again in his chair. "If you fight together to stay together, nothing can keep you apart."

I knew how deep that truth ran for Emil. "I think he's already made his choice."

"What do you mean?"

"I saw him a few days ago, at the bridge. Did you know that?"

Omar frowned. "No."

"He didn't come to me. I decided not to force it, so I waited, but he never came."

He looked past me, his eyes focused somewhere over my head. To my surprise, he seemed to be holding back a smile as he said, "Did he tell you why you scare him?"

"I don't scare him."

"Oh yes you do," he chuckled, meeting my gaze again with a twinkle. The light in them dimmed a little as his fingers fumbled in his lap. He appeared to be making up his mind about a difficult choice, his face set with determined creases. "When Emil was, oh, twenty or so, there was a woman. Red hair, blue eyes, pretty—fiery. From America as well." He watched me closely. I tried not to squirm. "She spent a while here as part of some international volunteer organization. Once they met, one wasn't without the other. Emil was captivated by her, even loved her. Maybe," he added with a half-shrug.

"Anyway," he continued, "when her group was set to leave here, he was ready to go with her, abandon everything he'd known, his family, all of it. He's always been a dreamer. I believe, with her, he thought he'd found everything he wanted. The girl, a way out into the world, something worth risking it all for." He paused with a little shake of his head. "He went so far as to tell us he was going, that he would follow her. It broke his mother. Mia hated the girl, for good reason, as it turned out."

"What did she do?" I whispered.

His mouth pressed into a thin line. "She left with nothing but a note. He didn't show it to me. To my knowledge, he never heard from her again." He was silent for a beat. "I don't believe she had any real intentions with him, other than a good time." He sighed. "It broke his belief in people, in love, I think. Too young."

"I'm not her," I said, my voice fierce. "I didn't come here looking for anything. Not from anyone else, at any rate."

"But you found it," he said, studying my reaction. "Trust—it's a precious thing. And it's difficult to have faith in again if you've been stung by it before." He raised an eyebrow at me pointedly, and fear squeezed my insides. He couldn't know my story. At the very least, I trusted Emil wouldn't have told anyone my secrets. But perhaps Omar perceived as much about people as he professed, and he could see glimpses through the cracks in their armor, mine included.

I sniffed quietly, dropping my gaze to my lap. "I get it."

"I thought you might."

I managed a sad smile, wiping my hand roughly across my face.

Omar grabbed a box of tissues and passed it to me.

"Thanks," I snuffled, taking one as I stood.

He rose as well, stepping around the table to stop beside me. "All I want for him is happiness. He tends to stand in his own way when it comes to that. I wish I could get him to see he can have it, but he's...stubborn."

I let out a wet laugh. "I've noticed." I tossed the tissue into the waste-basket near his feet, then grabbed my purse from the floor.

"Will you be all right?" he asked.

I took a steady breath. The tightness had eased, the panic gone.

"Yeah," I nodded. "Thanks for your help. For all of it." The corner of my mouth hitched up in an attempt at a smile.

"You deserve happiness, too," he said, not letting me go so easily. "I don't know if you share in Emil's stubbornness in seeing that, but you do."

This time, I really did smile. "Thank you." I bit my lip, feeling silly as I asked, "Can I hug you?"

"Of course," he said, but when I barely pressed against him, he snorted. "I'm not as old and fragile as I look. Give me a real one." I obliged, needing to give as badly as I needed it back, sinking into his embrace.

"Thank you, Doctor."

"Call me Omar."

"Okay," I murmured shyly before releasing him with reluctance. "Goodbye Omar."

He paused, thoughtful. "I'll see you later," he countered. I quirked my head in question, but he only offered a quick wink.

CHAPTER TWENTY-SEVEN

After I left Omar at the clinic, I took my time walking to my apartment. The golden light of magic hour cascaded across the rooftops as I passed through the old bazaar. Along a narrow walkway, swirling mosaic lamps dangled from shop entrances, their rainbow of colors flickering in the polished cobblestones. When I reached my building, I kept going, forking onto a path I'd never ventured down before.

I strolled through yet more side streets and stopped when I came upon a charming courtyard. I scanned the empty space for signs I'd entered a private home, but there were no markers indicating that it was a restricted area. Hesitantly, I wandered in.

Lush flora and fauna poured across a rickety gazebo in the center, which nestled around a well that could've been pulled straight from a Grimm's story. The well's wooden frame was rough and threatened to crumble beneath my hands as I stood on tiptoe to peer down into the pit. The twinkle of water looked back at me.

Along the riverside edge sat a trellis spilling over with bright pink flowers, the little vine tendrils climbing the foliage all the way to the top. Windows had been cut into the dense leaves, and I squinted through the nearest down to the river pooling below. Behind the hills, the horizon's peach hues hinted that I was in for another spectacular sunset this evening.

"Why did you come?"

I stilled, then turned.

Emil stood at the entrance, just inside the courtyard. His hands were buried deep in his pockets. Tense lines scored his face, his eyes dark and distrustful.

The hope I'd been clinging on to so tightly dissolved. "If you don't know why, then I can't tell you."

"I'm not playing a game."

"And you think I am?"

He licked his lips, doubt flickering behind his stony expression.

I sighed, now knowing what fueled it. "It was never a game for me." I paused before asking, "Why didn't you find me after I jumped?"

His stare bored into me. "I wanted to. It took...too much not to."

Annoyance flared through me. "I don't know what that means. Why couldn't you?"

"Because nothing had changed."

Threatening tears burned in my eyes, and I blinked stubbornly to keep them at bay. I glanced around the patio for a distraction, and then it dawned on me. This little, out-of-the-way oasis. It couldn't have been a coincidence. "And now? What's changed since then? Why did you follow me here?"

His face softened a fraction, his look pointed. "A choice."

My mouth popped open. "You talked to Omar?"

The corners of his lips drew down as he stepped further into the courtyard, shaking his head. "No. I heard you."

A flash through my mind—*Omar's eyes skimming over my head. His watchful gaze.*

"You were at the clinic," I breathed. "You heard the whole thing?"

Wordlessly, he moved to the well, leaning against its rough top. The wood cut into his hands, his elbows locked in place. Looking down into its depths, he gave a nod.

I pushed away from the trellis, my arms tightly clamped over my chest. "Do you really believe it was all some trick?"

The muscles in his neck stood at attention. "I don't know."

"Why do you think I'm back here?"

"I don't know."

Anger pulled taut inside me, his canned responses ringing hollow. I scanned around my feet, finding a smooth, round stone. I burst forward with a feral growl of frustration, throwing it down into the well with all my might.

The water wasn't as far down as I'd thought.

The rock ricocheted off the walls, finally landing with a cartoonish *ploink.* Water spattered the mouth of the well, speckling Emil's hands before he pulled them away with a startled noise.

"Mallory!"

My sudden, albeit tame, act of violence had shaken him awake.

"What?" I spat. My arms rose, as though challenging him to a fight. In a way, I supposed I was. "I can't do this anymore, the nonanswer thing. It's not my job to guess. If you want this—us—then you have to *talk* to me, Emil!"

When our eyes locked, his flashed with a mix of fear and fierce hope. The force of it sent sparks flying through my veins, like he was feeding his determination directly into my soul.

"Why did you leave me there? In Cologne." The words were simple, deadly, but I needed to know that I wasn't fighting for a one-sided wisp of a dream.

"Amin—"

"I could've helped with Amin. He's not why you left *me* behind."

His nostrils flared. "The choice was coming anyway. So when the break-in happened..." His expression implored me to fill in the rest.

"What? You thought it was some kind of divine intervention?" I scoffed.

He scowled, scrubbing his shoe across the cobblestones.

"Why did you think the universe was sending you a sign?" I pushed.

"You know why."

"Is that it? The only reason? Because some girl broke your heart years ago?"

His mouth twitched in indignation or pain, I wasn't sure. He turned away, gutting himself silently in front of me while fighting to hold everything in.

"Just tell me. If you really don't want me here, I'll go." My matter-of-fact tone jerked his head back toward me.

"No, that's not...I don't...And that wasn't the only reason."

I waited, barely breathing.

His mouth worked soundlessly before he managed, "Because you saw my dreams...you saw *me*. You saw it all better than anyone, especially me. That I've been fooling myself. It was a smack in the face. It stung. It's as if...when I'm with you, you just—" He faltered, and Omar's words floated back to me.

Did he tell you why you scare him?

My heart clenched, but my focus snapped to attention as he continued.

"I never stopped wanting them. You gave me permission to want them again, that they weren't some silly fantasy." He paused. "I want them as much as you do yours." His lips thinned into a tense line. "Back in America."

The last piece of the puzzle clicked into place. Finally, confirmation. That night in Prague on the bridge, he'd asked me about my life, my future. He saw what I wanted. I told him my ambitions. And he saw how he didn't fit into my life, just as I had eventually seen it myself when I chose not to follow him. And now, with his past laid bare for me, it all made sense. He knew what it was to be abandoned by someone, to be dropped like a gem into a heap of unpolished stones, and forgotten. But he also knew what it meant to abandon himself, to have his hopes and dreams pushed to "someday" which turned into "never."

And then there was the part of him, I hoped, that meant it when he'd said I deserved everything I wanted. I'd clung to those things for myself, but his desires had only suddenly become real again. Dreams that had been shut into an old, dusty trunk long ago now peeked back into the light.

He was as lost as I was in all this. How could we rectify our opposite lives? His vision of the future only showed division, loss, and hardship if we fought to be together. So, by following what he had sensed was fate interceding, he'd freed me of him. Freed us both.

And with it, had condemned us.

Our eyes met, and the tension in the space made me want to scream.

I shook my head as the silence stretched. Was this it?

He looked away. "I couldn't ask you to give everything up for me, the life you'd worked so hard to build before we ever even met. One part of me was afraid that, if I asked, you would come and regret it. You deserve so much more than living some half-life, never seeing through your potential. I wouldn't take that from you."

"And the other part?" I waited with bated breath.

A cringe wrinkled his nose. "And the other was terrified you wouldn't come if I did ask. So I just...left."

It was so simple. Fear, not want. Desperation, not a need to escape. With the latter, there would be no going back, no reconciliation, but with the former?

Hope.

A new sensation began to build inside me, something unstoppable. I couldn't help it, a smile breaking out across my face, followed by a giddy cackle. He watched me carefully, perhaps wondering if I'd gone completely mad. But as I stood there, laughing my stupid head off, my growing joy seemed to be feeding into him. We were a perfect circle, each of our separate, contrasting emotions coursing through and sustaining the other in a silent dance.

Eventually, the giggles faded. In their place was a simple, divine, completely inexplicable sense of peace. Neither of us had moved an inch. He'd watched me, his face slowly lightening, his gaze growing hungrier, his body more relaxed. His mouth hung open a fraction as he finally began to breathe more steadily after this marathon race. Tears pricked in my eyes once more, but they weren't sad or angry this time. He followed them as they slid leisurely down my cheeks.

"So...do you want a penthouse in New York?" he said, as if he was offering to pick up something from the store.

I grinned, playing along. "Hmm, actually, I heard there's a vacant house down there." I pointed vaguely over the steep cliff behind me. "Just a few blocks up, I think?"

"Oh, so the fancy part of town?" He rolled his eyes. "Typical woman."

"You did say you didn't want me to give up my dreams."

"True."

"I'll owe you."

His jaw ticked. "No more transactions."

I stepped closer to him, running a trembling hand down his chest. "Not all transactions are bad. One could even call ours a gift of compromise."

"Compromise" drew a frown to his lips.

"That's not a dirty word," I said, skating my thumb along the bottom of his mouth, pushing up the corner into a forced smile.

"It depends on the situation," he countered.

"Yes," I agreed. "It does."

I waited, but he seemed to be curling into himself again.

"Hey," I said, "we can play a different game instead."

"Games with you are dangerous."

I pouted, and he couldn't help his small flicker of a smile.

"I don't want to play a game," he said, his voice still heavy. "Maybe later." He pulled me closer, his hand roving to my lower back, drawing me against him while the fingers of his other threaded through mine. He swayed, guiding me into a dance, his heart pounding against my chest. It didn't feel odd that there was no music. We were creating a rhythm all our own. The melody of the song we had first danced to wafted through my memory, and I hummed it. That the lyrics were about lost love fueled the emotion in my voice, along with the meaning our present situation now ascribed to the theme.

With our foreheads together, his eyelashes brushed my skin, and I tilted to meet his gaze. We stayed like that, swaying lightly, eyes locked, staring into one another's souls.

When enough unspoken words had passed, I gave a slight nod. *I'm in*, it said. *Whatever it takes.*

He slowed us to a stop before pulling away, stepping fully back from me. I didn't approve, but his words soothed the space. "Whatever it takes." His fingertips trailed a soft line down my jaw, eyes following the path until they at last flicked again to mine. I drew in a breath as he let his hand fall open, palm up.

An invitation.

I bypassed it, closing my arms tightly around the back of his neck and pulling him in.

The instant our lips met, every inch of tension, each worried knot, and all the gutting apprehension evaporated. It didn't matter that we were surrounded by homes—heck, an entire town. We were the only two people on earth at this moment. His hands tangled in my hair at the base of my neck, a small, wordless plea uttered through a break in the kiss coming from one or both of us. More, *more*.

The only thing I wanted was every inch of him, all at once, for forever. The way his free hand combed up and down my body told me he felt the same.

When we came up for air, I let out a single, elated laugh.

Emil smiled. "I have missed that sound."

I brushed my thumb across his cheekbone. "I've missed your touch."

His voice heated. "What else have you missed?"

My throat constricted, telling me it was impossible to pick just one. "Everything," I managed. "All of it."

He pressed his forehead to mine before he moved down to leave a soft kiss in the hollow of my throat. "Me, too."

"What do we do now?"

We'd made the most difficult decision, but a series of new ones spread out in a trail of breadcrumbs.

"What do you mean?"

"I'm not her," I said firmly. "You know that, right?"

A muscle in his jaw pulsed. "Yes."

"So what do we do? I'm not going to take you away from your family, but I need to go back. How *do* we solve this?"

As he thought about it, he seemed as overwhelmed at the prospect as I was. But then he relaxed. "One day at a time, we make our choices."

"That's not helpful."

"But it's the truth."

I sighed, not feeling any better except for the fact we were together.

"What do you hope for?" he asked quietly. Which reminded me.

"Will you grant me a wish?"

His head cocked to the side at my playful tone. "Wishes are for kids."

"Or birthday girls," I retorted.

He stilled, putting two and two together. "Today is your birthday?"

I nodded.

"Happy Birthday, Mallory Roth." His words were painful, an apology patched with a promise. "What can I give you to celebrate such a special day?"

"You've already given me what I wanted."

"Hardly worth the trouble," he said flatly.

I shook my head, running gentle fingers across his jaw. "No. Priceless."

He kissed me, maybe to stall, maybe just because we both wanted to make up for lost time. I didn't care, except for when he broke it. The worry in his eyes made my heart skip.

"What's wrong?"

He swallowed, then made a decision. His hand dove into his pocket, but he paused before pulling it out again.

"I should have given this to you earlier," he said. "I meant it as a thank you for bringing me along, but I waited too long. Then..." He drifted off, and I was more than okay with him not rehashing the day we parted ways.

"What is it?"

"Fate, I guess, is finally on my side," he joked halfheartedly. Slowly, he opened his hand, palm down. Silver dangled from his fingers, the light setting fire to the crystal gems and iridescent pearl at the center.

The necklace, the one from Split.

"But..." I stammered. "But how? When?"

"When you looked in another section in the tunnels, I went back."

"You had it this whole time?" And here in his pocket? Was it just coincidence he had it on him at this moment or...?

He cleared his throat, bringing the chain between his fingers and fiddling with the clasp. "It was a little piece of you." His gaze came back up as he reached around, his hands working at the nape of my neck. "Of course I kept it with me." He let go, the metal cool against my skin as he freed my hair, letting it drape across my shoulders. He stepped away, admiring the necklace and me.

I smiled shyly at his expression, then held the pendant between my fingers as I lifted it for a closer look. It was as pretty as the day I'd first seen it. Maybe even more now.

"Thank you." It was the most perfect present I'd ever received. Then again, no. The necklace was a close second-best. I let it go, looking up at my first choice—Emil. "It's beautiful."

"You make it beautiful." His voice was quiet, bashful. It melted my heart.

"I think this is the best birthday ever."

"Really?" Why did he sound surprised?

"Really," I said firmly.

His eyes lit up, and he closed the distance between us again. "Can you handle more?"

More? If he was by my side, I would always want more. More of him. More of us. More of this feeling.

"If you insist," I said, my tone teasingly flippant.

He grinned that devilish grin I loved. "One last surprise, then. I still owe you."

"You do?" I asked, genuinely curious. I'd lost track of our tally a long time ago. "What?"

"Fulfilling the promise I broke." He held out his hand. I took it instantly, and he pulled me through the streets.

"Which?" I called as I practically ran to keep up.

"To eat at my favorite place."

"You're hungry?" I said, amazed. My stomach was still untying its knots.

"I will be. And so should you. There's no stopping her once she gets going."

We had crossed the river, working our way farther from it than I'd ever ventured.

"Stopping who?"

He sped around a bend and halted abruptly. Houses surrounded us, none of the picture-perfect cafés or restaurants in sight. He led me to a door identical to all its neighbors and gave a knock.

"Emil, where are we?"

His smile was huge when he looked at me.

"My mother's house."

CHAPTER TWENTY-EIGHT

FIVE MONTHS AND NINETEEN days later...

"Mom! I'm leaving!" I shoved my wallet into the top pocket of Bertha, shaking her wildly so all my stuff sank down far enough to close.

"Hold on, I'm coming!"

I gritted my teeth, listening to her footsteps patter overhead as she ran around her bedroom. I followed the sound to the stairs as she scurried down them. In her arms were two small, badly wrapped Christmas gifts.

I sighed. "I don't really have room."

"They squish," she said. "Here, give me your bag."

I cringed as I watched her smash them in. Thankfully, almost everything inside was clothes, so she couldn't do too much harm.

"There, see? Have a great trip." She grinned as she pulled me in for a hug. "And give my love to Emil."

Upon discovering his existence—which had been met with a betrayed, "But you *promised*!"—my mother's attitude had flipped during our first video chat with him. Her eyebrows waggled at me when she was out of frame, adding in a mouthed, "*He's so cute!*" and "*HOT.*" I fought back fits of laughter. Emil was confused, wondering why everything he said was suddenly so funny.

"I will," I said, throwing Bertha over my shoulder, smacking a kiss on her cheek, and running for the door.

The five months apart had felt like eons. Our phones were our lifelines, speaking every day, planning the next possible getaway where we could be together. Even so, life kept up its invisible pace. I updated him on my first official position in Houston for the last four months, which had been a whirlwind of emotions. Balancing between patients, colleagues, and the politics no school could prepare you for was overwhelming, but I couldn't deny I loved it. I told him all the details, from workplace drama, to showing off my apartment, to giving him a tour through my neighborhood.

He gladly returned the favor, speaking passionately about his apprenticeship with Marko, a local architect, telling me about Asja applying to art schools far and wide, how Amin had caved and hired on a second sales assistant to fill in Emil's new part-time schedule, and that Dani sent kisses. He grumbled through the last bit.

We were both living the versions of our lives we'd always dreamed of, but the pictures were incomplete. When I wasn't working, I daydreamed about him and relived our adventures with something akin to reverence. Time hadn't faded the magic, but imaginary Emil wasn't nearly enough. I wanted to touch him, feel his heat, lose myself in him in every sense.

So the first thing I did when I bolted through the arrival gate at Heathrow Airport was to run and jump into his waiting arms.

"Oof," he grunted, but he was holding me just as tightly.

"Hey," I whispered in his ear.

"Hello," he muttered into my neck. He shifted to let me down, but I moaned in protest.

He chuckled. "Do you want a kiss or not?"

Those were the only words that could peel me away from his embrace.

My toes touched back to earth, but I was lost again as I gazed into the galaxy of his eyes. The warm brown at the center, green tinting the edges. I'd tried to replicate the details of them in my memory, but had fallen utterly short of their intricacies. They drifted down to look at my lips, and I smiled.

"Well, what are you waiting for?"

It was the first kiss of many during our trip from the airport through the city. I stole one while we waited for the underground. He stole one back as the car filled, and we were forced tightly into a corner. Neither of us minded. Discreetly, his hand moved up as he shifted us into a different position. Comfortable it was not, but with the extra inch of closeness, it was certainly preferable. His fingers grazed the skin beneath my jacket, and I sucked in a breath.

He murmured something in Bosnian, his voice husky. I didn't have to know what it meant, only how it felt. His hands paused at my waist, and I looked up at him heatedly.

"Don't stop," I whispered.

The trip between the station and our hotel was a jumbled blur of want and need, building into a cacophony of anticipation. When he finally kissed me properly, with no audience to hold back for, I melted into it. The press of his touch invited me home. My hands worked at his clothes, aching for the feel of his skin, beginning a dance that lasted the rest of the night until we ordered room service and lay in each other's arms before drifting to sleep.

The morning dawned with birdsong and the glow of a promising new day.

I stretched with a groan. My arm flopped to the side and hit something solid and warm.

I flipped over. Emil glared at me through sleepy eyes.

"You're here!" I practically tackled him in a hug. He circled his arms around me and rolled so I sat on top of him.

"Where else do you think I'd be?"

"I thought I'd dreamt it." I ran my fingers through his tousled hair, down along his jaw. This was the Emil I'd been waiting for, flesh and bone and *all* mine.

"A common mistake of yours, I remember." He squinted. "Your dreams must be much better than mine."

"Why? Do you not dream of me?"

"I do. But it's not enough. If yours are as good as the last twelve hours, did you really need to come all this way?"

I lowered myself slowly so my chest brushed against his before we pressed together. My hands folded beneath my chin as I stared up at him innocently. "Would you like me to demonstrate how in-person outweighs the cons?" My lashes batted flirtatiously.

Please, please take the bait.

"Tempting," he said, his fingers stroking lazy circles across my back. "But I have other plans for today."

I rolled off him. "Where are we going?"

His firm hand gripped my hip, pulling me flush against his torso. "It's a surprise."

Excitement lurched through my stomach. "Really? Where to?"

"By definition, a surprise would mean I can't tell you." He nuzzled my hair, pressing a kiss at the base of my ear. "What do you think?"

My voice shook when I spoke. "I think I would be happy to stay just like this for eternity."

"But?"

I pulled away. "No buts, remember."

"I remember."

"So," I tried instead, "I trust you. Lead away."

It wasn't until the afternoon that I realized what was happening. Following a stroll through the Portobello Road market, we passed Buckingham Palace to gawk before continuing to the Houses of Parliament. From there, we wandered past shops and beneath theater marquees as Emil led me to the huge roundabout of Trafalgar Square. The impressive lion statue-guarded fountains framing the path up to the National Gallery stared out at us, and it hit me.

"This is our list," I breathed. The things his grandfather had seen, the exact places I'd mentioned to encourage Emil to come with me on the trip in the first place, all so he could see London. And, here and there, were also the ones we'd added ourselves when we had imagined visiting together, before being torn apart.

Emil's grin as we passed through security said it had taken me long enough, but he raised my hand to his lips. He guided me to the right while my neck craned to stare at the gorgeous vaulted ceilings, which were surrounded by rich, deep-hued walls of burgundy and forest green. We went straight into the Van Gogh room, where we circled the space until landing in front of his beloved sunflowers.

"You got me flowers," I teased.

His smile dimmed. "I should have."

I punched his arm lightly. "These ones last longer."

"Is that so?" He seemed appeased.

"And they're *pretty*." I couldn't help but marvel at the fact I was seeing this in person, the brush strokes somehow tactile even without touching them. It was truly a humbling experience, and it continued as we explored other marvelous rooms: Monet, Vermeer, Rembrandt, Michelangelo, Turner. In spite of my nonexistent art history knowledge, the names were astounding, the works bewitching. We could have easily spent the whole day there, but eventually we had to move on.

Tit for tat, we alternated checking off our bucket list items. At least, as many as we could fit in until our stomachs were grumbling, and our feet were too sore to carry on. We stopped for takeout, pausing to eat along the Thames, before wandering to our hotel in no particular hurry.

After we had showered and changed into our pajamas, I grabbed my jumble of presents from Bertha and dumped them onto the bed. A cascade of green-and-red paper topped with smooshed bows littered the fluffy comforter. Emil laughed, then mockingly checked his phone.

"Santa Claus came late," he teased, flashing the screen with the date in my face. It was true we'd spent Christmas at home, but that didn't make our holiday now any less special. We were making our own traditions—time zones and calendar dates be damned.

I shook my head stubbornly. "No, he made accommodations just for us."

He humored me with a indulgent sigh and then stood, grabbing his own packages from the dresser we shared. When he turned around, my attention latched on to the perfectly wrapped gifts in his hands.

"What. The. Heck?" I sputtered, playing with a bow as big as my face. "How are these so nice?"

"Magic," he whispered as he slid onto the bed and pressed a kiss to my cheek. "Santa had a special helper named Asja."

"That explains it." I grabbed the closest and was about to rip into its gold-and-green paper when I hesitated, biting my lip. "How do you guys do Christmas at home? Do you take turns?" Or demolish them simultaneously as fast as humanly possible, which was how the Roth house operated.

"Hmm," he murmured, turning a present my mother had wrapped over in his hands. Then he considered me. "What was the phrase you used once? Last one is a moldy egg?"

My snort was like a shot at the start of a horse race. We flew through the packages, taking breathers to *ooh* and *aah* and chuckle over our haul.

He burst out laughing at the hat my mother had horribly knitted for him, all lumpy and uneven, but he still popped it on his head. I'd gotten him two things. The first he opened was a box of Cards Against Humanity to torture him with. He read the back of the box, then his eyes grew wide with fear. Mission. Accomplished.

I saved the best for last, pushing the skinny gift toward him across the bed. He seemed a little apprehensive after the card game, but he relaxed when the top of the supple leather blueprint tube appeared beneath the ripped paper. He ran slow fingers over the spot where I'd had his name embossed.

"There's this great leather worker downtown," I explained, "and he made it by hand. I wasn't sure if you already had one, but I passed his shop on the way to work, and I just thought of you."

He rested the tube beside him gently. "It's perfect," he said as he leaned forward and cupped my cheek. His lips pressed against mine, and I could sense the gratitude transferring like energy passing between us. "Thank you."

Asja had sent me a small painting of Stari Most, an original showcasing her talents, Emil explained. His mother and Omar gave me a box of goodies, including baklava. My mouth instantly watered. With it was a card from his whole family. Even Mia had scratched her name at the bottom.

The last two left for me were from Emil, and I stared into the first box for a moment before pulling out a pair of earrings. They were the kind you threaded through your ears, and they had a single elegant, teardrop-shaped bead at one end.

"Do you like them? I wasn't sure they would be your style, but after the necklace in Split, they seemed similar." The lift of his shoulder said women's jewelry was beyond him, but I couldn't love them more.

"They're gorgeous." I tipped them out of the box and went to the mirror to put them on. I looked at him through the reflection. "What do you think?" I shook my head and the silver tendrils danced.

His expression warmed. "Beautiful, as always."

Even now, the compliment made me flush. I skipped to the bed where I opened the second gift, which was a mosaic, spiral lamp I'd seen dangling outside so many shops in Mostar.

"Oh, I loved these!" I gushed.

"I know," he chuckled. His gaze flashed to my trusty companion near the door. "But it's a little oversized for Bertha."

I waved a dismissive hand. "I packed light, and I'll have more room now with your gifts out." He lifted a brow, but let it go.

"You did pack something for going out, though, yes?" he asked instead.

He had pressed the point so hard once during a call while I was packing, I'd rolled my eyes.

"Yes," I said, playing it straight. "I put my lacy negligee in. That works, right?"

His Adam's apple bobbed, alarm flashing across his face before the fear froze, and his eyebrows dropped. "Ha ha," he mocked.

He was getting faster.

With a roll of his eyes at my devilish smile, he suddenly turned serious. He leaned back, reaching for the drawer in the nightstand, and pulled out an official-looking blue file folder. I frowned. Paperwork and Christmas glee didn't align in my book.

"One more gift, though this one comes with a warning," he said, shoving the drawer closed as he straightened.

Definitely not Christmassy words.

"Okay." At my core, worry formed with the sudden change in mood, like a slowly expanding bubble.

His mouth quirked into a small smile. "It's not bad."

"Okay," I said again, my tone still wary.

He held out the folder. I gripped the bottom, but he didn't let go.

"The warning is that nothing's confirmed," he explained, his expression pointed, attempting to temper my expectations. "It's out of my control still, but I'm trying."

The conviction in his voice finally did the trick. My anxiety bubble popped and vanished.

"Okay," I said tenderly, and he released the folder.

In it sat an application. And behind it, another. And another. I checked the information in the headers and a pattern grew.

"You're applying to architecture programs in the US?" I breathed.

He swallowed. "And scholarships," he clarified. "Marko is writing up a recommendation, along with a few others for character references. It's a long shot—a very long shot—but..."

"But it's possible." Warmth trickled along my skin, excitement tittering through my veins. "Are you sure? Mostar, your family..."

"Will still be there when school ends," he said. "And with a degree, we could go pretty much anywhere, wherever we decided to be."

And with that, he gave me the best Christmas gift of all. A future with him, no more questions, no more maybes, a solid foundation. It didn't matter that it wasn't set in stone yet. I could feel it in my gut. This was it, where our diverged paths met at last.

"Unless you think it's a bad idea..." he started, but I cut him off as I dropped the folder to the side and stopped his words with a kiss.

"I knew you were Santa," I whispered when we broke apart. "You got my letter."

He stared at me, confused.

"You're what I wanted," I said, cupping his face between my hands, "this year and every year."

His lips parted, and I kissed away his surprise until he truly believed it.

CHAPTER TWENTY-NINE

THE NEXT MORNING, WE continued the list, visiting Soho, China Town, and the various markets nearby. The dreary history of the Tower of London was lit by a glimpse of the crown jewels. We indulged in an afternoon tea inside a posh hotel before taking the underground to Hyde Park.

Once we were sure we'd hit everything possible for the day, we returned once more to our hotel to prepare for our evening out. Emil's covert planning was once again in play, so I had no idea where we were headed.

Hogging the bathroom, I finished my makeup as my curls set, an emerald-green cocktail dress hanging from the doorframe behind me. I smacked my lips together with a plum-colored lipstick as the butterflies began to stir in my stomach.

When I stepped into the bedroom, fully prepped and preened, Emil turned from the window, and his jaw went slack. I'm pretty sure mine did, too, but my face was numb. He was gorgeous in a simple, elegant, coal-black suit. His polished shoes winked as he moved around the bed to stop next to me and smoothed down his tie.

I chuckled, and it sounded breathy.

"What's funny?" he asked.

"Your tie," I admitted. "It's the same color as my lipstick."

His gaze snapped to my mouth before traveling down and raking across my dress before he looked back up. "The colors suit you," he said, his eyes playfully dark. "Though the lipstick means I can't kiss you. I like that less."

I went to bite my lip and remembered I shouldn't for the same reason. "I could wipe it off." *On your mouth*, my salacious mind suggested. *On your skin. On your...*

"Later," he whispered, taking my hand.

I was too busy calming my racing heart to notice exactly where he was leading me until I spotted signs for the underground. I smoothed my evening dress down nervously as we swayed onboard, but we didn't stand out as much as I'd thought we would. Half of London was calling it a day in their workwear, while others joined the car in more formal attire for a night out on the town.

Once above ground, I'd watched the sun dip as we walked. It now gleamed from between the high-rise buildings raised into giant fortresses that comprised London's financial district.

"Where are we going?" I asked for probably the millionth time. My heels clacked along the slick pavement, which glistened from the early morning rain.

"You'll see."

I huffed, but Emil offered me his arm, slowing his pace to match my careful strides. Gently, he guided me up a short set of stairs toward a huge building. Tilting my head skyward, I noticed its profile curved near the top, as though it was beginning to take a bow.

The lobby was all sleek lines and strip lights. Our footsteps echoed in a chorus off the white marble. After passing through security, we joined a group funneling into the elevator. We steadily climbed higher and higher to the thirty-fifth floor, which was labeled Sky Garden.

My jaw dropped as the elevator doors slid open, revealing a 180-degree view of the London skyline. The Shard stood straight ahead like a spike as we walked out, groups and couples surrounding us with cocktails and chatting happily. We neared the vast window overlooking where the Tower Bridge stretched over the Thames, all aglow with the rosy light of the impending sunset.

"This wasn't on our list," I said with awe.

The corner of his mouth quirked up. "I improvised."

Groups huddled on sofas and around tables. A bar and café combined into one served a long line of guests. Foliage filled enclosed curved benches and bordered the stairs, which surged upward on either side of the wide-open space. It was noisy with all the chatter and background music. People sat enjoying drinks and food, while others meandered, taking in the stunning view.

I stopped in front of the windows, staring down at the tiny insect people and toy cars far below. Water taxis cut rifts into the murky waters of the River Thames, while birds swerved by at eye level. The last rays of sunlight breached the fluffy clouds on an otherwise clear day.

"Want to go higher?" Emil offered.

I tore my eyes away from the mesmerizing scene, eyeing the stairs. "What's up there?"

"More views, from what I read."

"Lead the way."

We climbed the polished staircase through London's indoor jungle, the next level giving us a 360-degree overlook of the city. The other famous high-rise buildings nodded the tops of their heads in our direction, so close it seemed you could reach out and touch them. Inside, people lounged along the windows in a mix of formal and casual wear. We blended right in with them.

"Wine?" Emil offered, gesturing toward the slick bar.

"Please," I agreed distantly, still dumbfounded by the view. He returned in short order, handing me a glass of chardonnay before extending his. I met it with a soft clink.

"How did you know about this place?"

"The internet," he said simply.

I snorted. "Well, that's too easy."

"It looked like a cool spot."

"I think that's an understatement."

We people-watched and took turns circling the gardens before Emil checked his watch for a third time.

"Got a hot date?" I teased.

"Yes, actually." I lifted my brow in a challenge, and he added, "Our table is ready."

"Table?"

"For dinner."

"But we just got here," I protested.

"We're not going far." His hands spun me away from the views, and he pointed toward the structure at the center of the garden room, which dangled above the café below. It was the same as the rest of the building, ultra-modern, though the tinted windows refused to give a hint of what waited inside the spaceship-esque form.

"We're eating inside a box?"

He chuckled, but didn't respond, instead leading me to the entrance. He held the door open, guiding me forward with a gentle pass of his hand along my back. Beyond the waiting staff, the muted glow of candle-lit tables instantly bathed us in the restaurant's romantic ambiance, the warm, moody interior not reflecting the cool exterior.

It was easily the fanciest restaurant I'd ever been to. As we were guided to our table, waiters passed by carrying huge platters with intricate, bite-sized morsels. I couldn't begin to guess what they were. It was the stuff you saw on highbrow travel shows or between the pages of a Michelin-starred chef's cookbook.

We were seated near the railing on the upper level, giving us a prime view over the people below in the café, as well as the rafter-framed skyline. Across the river, the Shard continued to be a marker of both space and time as the sun slowly set. Fiery light flashed across its windows before the reflections grew dim.

"Wow," I murmured when, eventually, darkness finally took hold. London was a glimmer of earthbound stars, the night sky flipped on its head.

The pop of a cork made me spin. Our waiter poured champagne into delicate flutes, resting the bottle in a silver bucket of ice before leaving. Emil raised his once more as I reached for my glass.

"Wow," he agreed, his eyes glittering. Bubbles burst and simmered in our glasses as they met.

Course after course graced our table, each plate prettier than the next. At first, it was intimidating to the unrefined foodie in me, never having given the haute cuisine world much attention. I got over it pretty quickly, savoring each delectable bite.

"Well, are you a fancy food convert?" I asked Emil after a mouthful of the most delicious seared salmon I'd ever tasted. So far, fine dining was a strange mix of opulence I was enjoying, accompanied with the feeling of being a kid who had to remain on their best behavior.

He laughed, the only response I needed to know he felt the same. I chuckled with him, turning to stare out once again at the city at night.

"This is amazing," I breathed.

His thumb brushed against my knuckles and squeezed. "I'm glad you like it."

"It's perfect. All of it."

"Present company included?" he teased.

"It wouldn't be perfect otherwise." The words came without thinking, without worry, without hesitation. Because it was true. I'd experienced other wonderful things in everyday life since returning home, but they paled in comparison to the times we'd spent together. Everything was more alive, more real, when shared with Emil.

His gaze didn't falter, and both of us became easily enraptured in our own little corner of heaven.

"Your dessert," the waiter interrupted, dropping a plate of family-style assorted delicacies. He reeled off what they were, a bunch of fancy ingredients paired with desserts I knew by name, but I just smiled up at him politely and thanked him before he retreated into the shadows.

"What did you think?" Emil asked after the server returned to clear the empty plates and drained glasses.

"You didn't let me lick the plate clean," I grumbled, gathering my purse as he stood.

"Do you want me to have them bring it back?" he said dryly. He swept my jacket off the back of my chair, holding it out for me to put on. I stared at it for half a second too long. No one had ever done that for me before.

"No," I said, my voice small as I slid my arms into the holes.

We thanked the passing waiters as we departed. While waiting for the elevator to arrive, I stared longingly out at the view. It was picture-perfect. The soft ding and slide of the elevator opening left a lingering sense of nostalgia for the place even before the doors closed.

CHAPTER THIRTY

WHEN WE FINALLY DESCENDED from the Sky Garden and walked out of the lobby, the bustle of London nightlife met us at street level. I moved to my right, expecting to return to the hotel, but Emil's hand in mine jerked me to a standstill.

"Not quite yet," he smiled. "Follow me."

"Where are you taking me?" I checked my phone. It was already past ten o'clock. I knew well enough that he would normally be getting ready for bed right about now.

"Where's your sense of adventure?"

I stuck my nose in the air at the challenge and followed him without any more questions.

He bit back a laugh.

The maze of streets didn't faze him. He zigzagged confidently until I was thoroughly turned around, and the noise of heavy traffic had faded into the background. Small pubs and quaint restaurants took over from the financial district's modern vibe. When the deep thrum of bass echoed in my bones, I hazarded a guess.

"Are we going clubbing?"

As if on cue, Emil brought me to a gentle stop with a nod. During the day, the club could have been a coffee shop. Flashes of colorful laser lights danced through the heavy, old-fashioned door onto the sidewalk. Inside, a small but enthusiastic crowd filled the space, occupying every nook and cranny from the bar to the dance floor to the bay windows up front.

I looked at Emil. "I'm not really dressed for clubbing."

"Neither am I," he said, leading me in anyway.

It was a themed night, and music from the eighties punched my eardrums. Emil grabbed drinks as I scouted a place to sit or stand, ending up at a narrow table near the edge of the bar. Eventually he found me, sitting in the dark, my foot tapping against my will to the sounds of my childhood.

"Do you know this?" he asked, nearly spilling his overflowing glass as he gestured at the DJ.

"Yeah, my mom loved the eighties. She controlled the music in our house until Sydney and I went out into the real world."

"Do you like it?" His skepticism was showing.

I laughed. "Some of it."

He held out his glass for a quick cheers. We were silent for a while, observing the scene. It was a mixed crowd. About half were our age, while the other seemed as though the eighties might have been the peak of their heyday. I couldn't help but smile as I witnessed a couple from the latter group belting out lyrics straight into each other's faces.

"Relationship goals!" I shouted over the song at Emil.

He followed my eyeline and frowned. "Really? You want to scream in my face?"

"Only if you really, really want me to."

He shook his head, taking another sip.

"I meant they're so obviously comfortable together. It doesn't matter that they're surrounded by people. They're just doing...them."

He eyed them before nodding softly.

We stayed longer than I thought, carried away by dancing, more delicious cocktails, and then more dancing. When the crowd thinned, we found a hidden corner nook all to ourselves near the back. His arm wound around me, my head resting on his shoulder.

At one point, I felt his fingers run a soft trail along the inside of my arm, between my shoulder and elbow and back. Shivers radiated through me at the simple touch as I looked up at him. He was doing it absentmindedly as he stared at pictures adorning the walls, as though there was nothing more natural in the world. I watched him before I leaned in, catching his face as he turned toward me, and pecked a single kiss upon his cheek.

A lazy smile spread across his face. "Thank you." He returned one to my forehead. I sighed, resting my head on his shoulder again and snuggling in close. "Are you tired?"

"A little," I admitted, but in no hurry to leave. My eyes were struggling to stay open. "What time is it?"

He shifted, checking his watch. "Nearly midnight."

I pouted.

"What's wrong?" he laughed.

"The most perfect day. I don't want it to end."

"It hasn't. Not yet." His hand rubbed against my shoulder. "Come on," he said, standing and gathering our glasses. "Let's head out."

I let Emil guide me once more. Traffic picked up as we neared the Tower of London, where we merged with large, boisterous crowds heading toward the river.

"Is it all right if we make two stops before going to the hotel?" Emil asked. I mumbled a yes.

As Tower Bridge lit up the night, I woke up to the beauty of this glimmering gemstone spanning the Thames. Even amid the honk of taxis and the ever-persistent wail of ambulances, it was an oddly calm setting. We paused at the outcroppings, staring down at the water as it was churned by the odd boat passing by beneath us. We took our time, eventually walking along the South Bank. Museums, shops, and cafés dotted the curved bank, while the riverside trail flickered with elegant lampposts every few yards. Past the famous Globe Theatre, my feet felt like blocks of lead, and I leaned more heavily against Emil.

"Are we there yet?" I grumbled.

"Almost." His voice shook slightly.

I shifted against his shoulder, peering at his face in the semi-darkness. "Are you okay?"

"Yes, why?"

"Dunno. You just sounded funny."

"I'm glad you find me hilarious." He angled left toward a short crop of stairs.

"No, no more stairs," I groaned.

"Only a few."

I sighed and pushed away from him a little so I didn't trip over my own feet. A wide, switchback ramp awaited at the top, which merged onto the glowing blue pathway of Millennium Bridge. St. Paul's Cathedral was a beacon at the other end, its golden radiance a contrast to the bridge's cool light. Except for the occasional screech of the train on the next bridge down, it was eerily quiet. We were the only ones here, save for a street busker and the lone silhouette of a woman farther down, leaning on the rail and staring off into the distance.

"Wow," I whispered. "How lucky are we?"

Emil swallowed. "Very." His hand clasped mine tightly, his fingers gone cold.

"It's well worth being up past death to see."

"I'm glad you think so."

As we approached the busker, his plucky melody grew sweet, a drawn-out affair that tugged at my heartstrings even without the lyrics. Despite the fact he was playing it in a romantic Latin style, the tune was unmistakable. It was "Still Loving You." Shocked, I pointed at the guitarist, who sneaked a look up at me with a smile.

Like he knew it was my favorite. Like he knew *me*.

Confused, I looked at Emil. He watched me apprehensively, though a corner of his mouth lifted a fraction. His eyes, however, were steely.

"What's wrong?" I asked, sucking in a breath. Something was off. Was it excitement coursing through my veins? Fear? Both? Why was I panicking?

My attention flashed to the busker before returning to Emil. "How did he know about this song? *Did* he know?"

Emil's fingers brushed across my lips, silencing the beginning of my blabbering. "It's okay."

My racing heart calmed, and I nodded beneath his hand. But he stepped closer, pulling me to his chest, swaying to the music. And, next to my ear, he began to sing.

My body froze with shock as he continued to move gently.

Never have I ever sung in front of anyone before.

His voice trembled, breathy and uncertain. I listened to quite possibly the most exquisite thing I'd ever heard in all its perfect imperfections. More spoken than sung as those insanely high notes sprung out of reach, each word sent a drip, drip, drip of love through to my heart.

He continued turning me in a slow circle, and it was as if I could see us from the outside, panning around the scene of our own little movie. As I faced St. Paul's, I detected that the woman in the distance had moved closer, her hood drawn up against the chill, her phone out snapping pictures. I tucked my head into Emil's shoulder shyly, not wanting to share this with a random stranger.

The song drifted to a close, and I drew Emil tighter against me, willing the moment to last forever. His shaky chuckle was far more at ease than his singing, but he gently pulled out of the cage of my arms after a few seconds.

"Why did you stop?"

"Because the song was over."

"It was beautiful." I ran a hand along the side of his face. "You're beautiful."

His jaw ticked, his gaze dropping to our clasped hands, my left in his right.

"Mallory?"

"Yes?"

Suddenly, like a giant weight had collapsed onto his shoulders, he bent to the ground.

"Are you okay?" I worried.

He fumbled in his coat pocket before his eyes met mine, heavy in a way that made my stomach coil. "That depends."

"On?"

"Your answer."

"You haven't asked me anything," I said stupidly before zeroing in on the tiny box in his other hand. And I stopped breathing altogether.

He noticed and ran a gentle thumb across the flat of my palm to try to bring me back to life. "Mallory Roth."

Oh my god.

"I have been a fool. But I think we are all fools in love. Or so they say."

My hands turned to ice. My brain quit working completely.

"So I must really love you for the time I wasted being one. I will happily spend the rest of my life making up for those lost moments. If you'll let me." The top of the box popped open. Something shiny glimmered in the dim light, but the sparkles became orbs as my eyes filled with tears. "I'm not good with words, so I'll keep it simple. I love you. Will you marry me?"

I crumpled, kneeling in front of him, the chilled concrete seeping through my tights in an instant. The sensation woke me up, and the tears fell as I tugged him into a rough hug. I bawled into his shoulder.

"Are you all right?" he asked after a minute, rubbing soft circles into my back.

"No," I sobbed idiotically.

"Okay."

"No!" I hiccuped. "I mean, yes! Yes, I'll marry you."

His hand hesitated a moment before moving up to my jaw to pull me back. His look searched my face, first tight with concern before growing lighter, a sheen of his own brimming at the corners of his eyes.

"Really?" Beneath the happiness, there still—somehow—lurked uncertainty in his voice.

Salt filled my mouth as I smiled through my tears, laughing. "Of course, you fool."

When he kissed me, it was as if every warm, lovely thing that had ever happened to me throughout my life was reborn. Every embrace, success, friendship, discovery, and show of love seeped through my body from this one point of contact, filling me with an indescribable lightness. When I eventually floated up from the kiss, our eyes met, and I saw the same relief looking back at me.

He brought the box back up, prying the delicate ring from its velvet pillow inside. A laugh landing somewhere between a giggle and a sob escaped me as he slid it on. It shimmered even in the half light.

"It's perfect," I breathed, looking up at him. "It's all perfect."

He swallowed, cupping my cheek during another too-brief kiss. Then he stood, pulling me up with him into a tight embrace.

And there we stayed, crying, laughing, just holding on to the blissful moment for as long as we could. When I realized this, having him, would last for a lifetime, I started giggling all over again. He squeezed me tighter, like he couldn't get enough of the sound.

Eventually, I remembered we had an audience. I sent the guitarist a bashful smile over Emil's shoulder before we finally broke apart.

"Congratulations," he said in a thick Cockney accent.

"Thank you," I said. "Really, thank you. It was wonderful." I dug into my purse and retrieved the measly amount cash I had, but he refused the tip.

"Your fiancé was generous," he said. My heart stuttered at the word fiancé in a way I rather liked.

"He better have been," I teased.

"Well, I had help," Emil admitted.

"Help?"

He jutted his chin past me, and I looked behind to see the woman drawing closer. She slipped off her hood and pinned us with a Cheshire cat kind of grin. My jaw dropped.

"Gail?" I ran to her, pulling her into a hug. My joy knew no bounds tonight.

"Congratulations, dear," she said.

"How are you here?"

Emil stopped beside me. "She helped me coordinate everything. I couldn't have done it without her." He gave her a hug once I'd gotten my fill.

"And I am a sleuth photographer." She winked. "I think I earned my deerstalker and pipe." At the questioning tilt of my head, she sighed. "Sherlock Holmes." She waved her camera in my face. "You two are too cute not to capture the occasion."

Sneaky, sneaky lady.

"I want to see!" I reached for the camera, but she yanked it out of reach.

"Later," she said, then cocked an eyebrow. "You need to finish your evening."

"There's more?" I gaped.

"That's up to you," Emil said, his blush visible in the dead of night. "Are you ready to go back to the hotel?"

"Strangely, I'm not tired anymore," I said with a thick hint.

Emil's eyes went slate-black.

"Have a good night," Gail said, innuendo dripping from each word as she walked away.

Emil's fingers laced through mine, and I shook my head, trying to wrap my mind around what had just happened. The bow of the bridge sloped gently toward the bank as we walked, and I glanced left and right before chuckling.

"What's so funny?" Emil asked.

"What is it with us and bridges?"

He mirrored my gaze and grinned. "Seems appropriate enough," was all he said before pulling my hand up and grazing my knuckles with his lips.

And through the streets of London we wandered, reveling in every moment, every sight, every kiss—no longer stolen, but freely given. Each touch was a reminder that nothing would take him from my arms, or me from his.

Not our pasts.

Not our fears.

Not our dreams.

Not even oceans could keep us apart now.

Next In Series

Thank you for reading Two Worlds Apart! I'd love to hear your thoughts shared in a review, which help authors immensely.

This is just the beginning of the Concrete Hearts series...

———ele———

*Sydney, Mallory's reclusive older sister, is done with the corporate grind—and people in general. Hot-headed and driven with determined self-reliance, only one person had ever **really** managed to get under her skin. Luckily, she's moved on from that old life, left her career aspirations behind, and spends her days out in the woods with her trusty cat, Nova.*

But even here, after all this time, she can't escape Lee Howell.

———ele———

Receive exclusive sneak peeks, book updates, and more when you join my newsletter at www.lenoracade.com.

ACKNOWLEDGEMENTS

Thank you to all those who supported me along the way, from my early critique partners, beta readers, writer groups whose members shared their wealth of knowledge, and all the ARC readers for giving me a leg up as I began my author journey. For those close to me, like my family and friends, to those I've never met in person, but who championed my little story all the same: you are all rock stars and I couldn't have made it this far without you.

I am eternally grateful.

About the Author

Lenora Cade is a contemporary romance author who seamlessly blends heartfelt love stories with the complexities of real life—because even the most captivating romances require characters to earn their happily ever afters.

Her storytelling journey began at the age of twelve with a manuscript now safely tucked away in storage where it belongs, though it ignited a lifelong passion for crafting compelling narratives. Since then, and complemented with a background in film and photography, Lenora has spent her life chasing stories in every form. Whether nestled in the quiet countryside or exploring new destinations, she always keeps a notebook nearby, ready to capture the next spark of inspiration.

You can find out more about her upcoming projects through her website, www.lenoracade.com, or the social media platforms Facebook, Instagram, Threads, Bluesky, TikTok, and Goodreads.

MALLORY & EMIL'S PLAYLIST

Available online at spoti.fi/3DMosSu

1. "Angela" The Lumineers

2. "Sous le ciel de Paris" Cover by Pomplamoose

3. "Yamaha" Delta Spirit

4. "Fix You" Coldplay

5. "Riverside" Agnes Obel

6. "Wonderwall" Cover by Ryan Adams

7. "Stay" Cover by Lavrans Svendsen

8. "Every Breaking Wave" U2

9. "How Gorgeous You Are" Dominik Gerda

10. "Shell Suite" Chad Valley

11. "Show Me What I'm Looking For" Carolina Liar

12. "Drive" The Well Pennies

13. "Be the Song" Foy Vance

14. "Island in the Sun" Weezer

15. "Shelter from the Storm" Bob Dylan

16. "Anywhere" Passenger

17. "The Way We Move" Langhorne Slim & the Law

18. "High Hopes" Kodaline

19. "Always Remember Us This Way" Noelle Johnson

20. "Personal Sky" Lina Mayor

21. "Comes and Goes" Greg Laswell

22. "Believe" Mumford and Sons

23. "Breathe Me" Sia

24. "Home" Foo Fighters

25. "Wake Me Up" Avicii

26. "A Beginning Song" The Decemberists

27. "I'll Keep You Safe" Sleeping At Last

28. "Coming Home" Skylar Grey

29. "The One" Kodaline

30. "The Story" Brandi Carlile

31. "Still Loving You" The Scorpions

www.ingramcontent.com/pod-product-compliance
Lightning Source LLC
Chambersburg PA
CBHW020354110726
47899CB00006B/1724

* 9 7 9 8 9 9 2 8 7 1 5 0 0 *